I0768127
TO KEEP HER SOUL, SHE'LL HAVE TO MAKE A DEAL WITH THE DEVIL.
When Flowers Wilt
G. E. MASTERS

Content and Trigger Warnings

Some content may be disturbing and/or triggering to some readers. Please read responsibly.

This book includes:

-Sexually explicit scenes

-Verbal and emotional child abuse (discussed)

-Mental health issues, specifically anxiety and depression

-Loss of a significant other (discussed)

-Death of a family member

-Mention of murders

-Sexual assault (not between main characters)

-Torture

-Dubious consent

-Blood play

-Wing play

-Shadow play

-Bondage

-Use of sex toys

-Scissoring

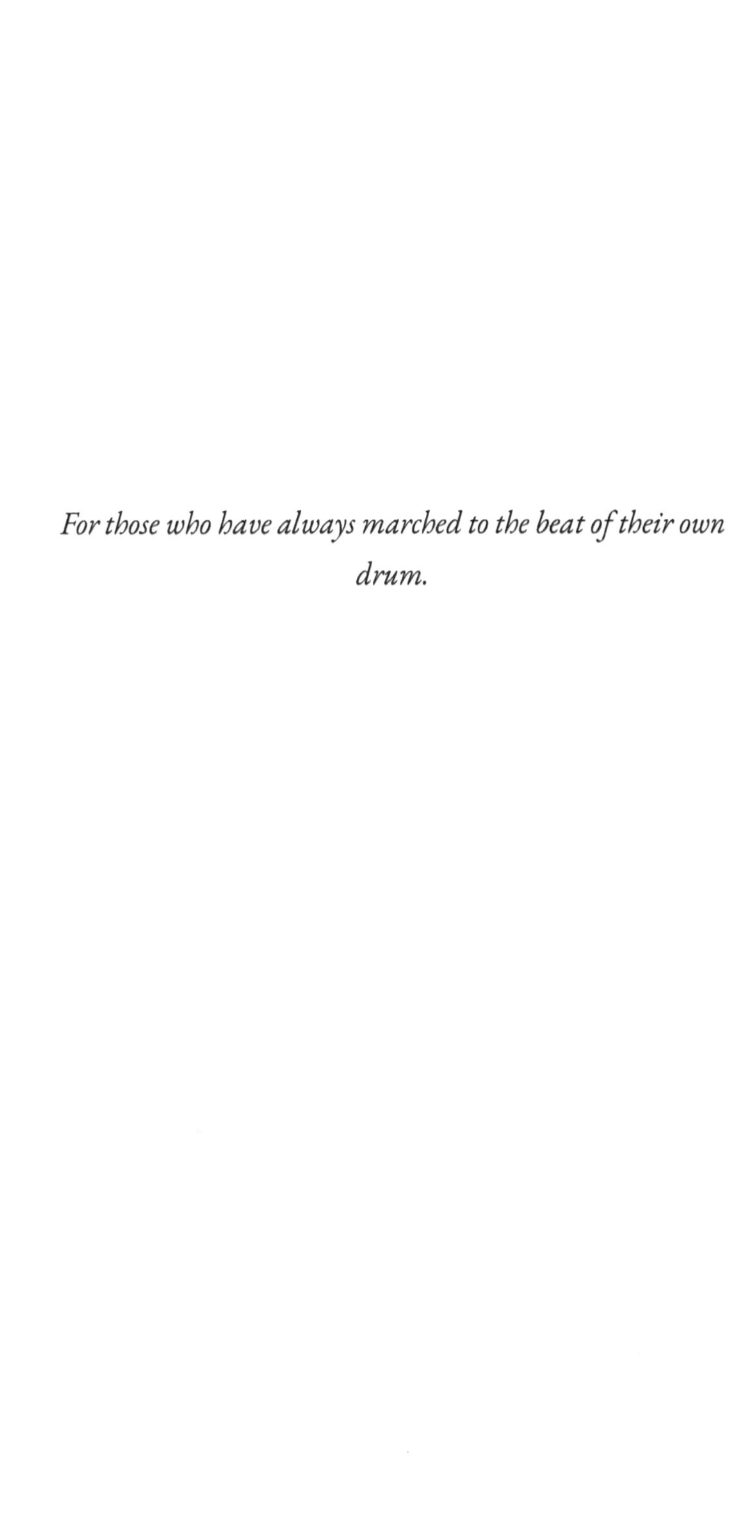

For those who have always marched to the beat of their own drum.

Prologue

Vivian

I'm standing in front of a floor-length mirror, looking at myself in the reflection. I'm wearing a wedding dress, but I'm not getting married.

At least, not in the legal sense.

Not in the romantic sense either.

I run my trembling hands down the front of my gown. Upon first glance, the gown is modest, covered in black lace with a high neckline and long sleeves, but it's tight, hugging every curve of my body, and the back is completely open.

It's beautiful, but I don't want to be wearing it.

Upon their eighteenth birthday, every witch must sign over their soul to the Devil herself—our Dark Lady. The fallen angel, the shepherd of the damned. All witches must sign over their souls to her in exchange for a long life and a VIP spot in Hell. As if Hell is simply an exclusive nightclub.

The door to my room opens, and my mother and my aunt shuffle into the space. They both smile at me, their identical faces making it difficult to tell them apart, but I always know which is which—my aunt is always nicer to me.

It's my mother who steps up behind me and places her hands on my shoulders, smoothing them down my arms as we both look in the mirror. I assume this is her attempt at motherly affection, but it feels wooden coming from her.

"Today is the day," she sighs happily.

I worry my nerves will make my voice tremble, so I say nothing.

This is an exciting moment for my mother. She became the matron of our coven right before my birth, and it is a title she holds dear. She acts as the leader of our coven, ensuring we all fall into line, following whatever orders we are given from Hell.

She is ecstatic to finally present her daughter to the Dark Lady.

My aunt comes to my side, placing her head on my shoulder. With both women standing behind me, they're like what you see on TV: an angel on one shoulder, a devil on the other.

"It's normal to be nervous, dear," Aunt Judith says.

My mother tuts. "The day she signs her soul over to our Dark Lady is the greatest day for a witch. There's nothing to be nervous about."

Aunt Judith straightens the amulet around my neck. It's a simple design, an oval with a circle in the middle. She gave it to me on my sixteenth birthday, and when I asked what it symbolized, she had merely said, "*It will protect you.*"

"Come, child," my mother says. "It's time."

We make our way from our Victorian home towards the woods that border our land. The entire coven, made up of seven families, lives on this land nestled in the northern Pennsylvania forests, and each lives in their own Victorian home on the property. We aren't completely cut off from society, although we mostly keep to ourselves, growing our own food and homeschooling the witchlings. Rarely does anyone venture into town, which is about thirty minutes by car.

It's only about twenty on a broom, though not many witches use brooms anymore.

A lush forest surrounds the property, constantly teeming with wildlife and other creatures that go bump in the night. The wilderness was always my favorite place to go when I was a child. I would spend hours among the trees and the small animals that would be brave enough to approach me. When I turned twelve, my mother forbade me from going into the woods again—she was worried I would be attacked or killed by whatever lurks in the darkness. Then her only child wouldn't be presented to the Dark Lady, and that would be a disgrace.

Luckily, Aunt Judith let me slip out now and then so I could have a bit of peace.

Judith has already gained the reputation of a rebel in the coven. She never married and hasn't had children of her own. Every witch is meant to have at least one child, but Judith never did. For some reason, the Dark Lady made an exception for her—but the rest of the coven did not take kindly to this. They still look at her with disdain whenever she's out around the commune.

The train of my dress trails behind me, snagging on twigs and pebbles as I follow my mother and aunt into the woods. The entire coven will already be at the summoning spot to receive us and to witness the Dark Lady taking my soul. My nerves are fraying out of control now, winding through me like a hoard of snakes has replaced my organs.

I want to fiddle with my hair or bite my nails, but my hair is all pinned back, and I don't want my mother snapping at me if I can help it. So, I ball my hands into fists at my sides.

We enter the wilderness and walk along the small path towards the summoning place.

The woods seem to be as on edge as I do—the air is charged in a way I've never experienced before.

"Do you feel that?" I ask quietly.

"What do you feel?" my aunt asks curiously as she peeks over her shoulder at me.

My mother shushes us both before I can respond, and I snap my mouth shut. Judith throws me a sympathetic glance before turning back around.

The sun has set, and it's growing dark in the woods as we continue down the path.

I've only been to the summoning place once when another young witch had signed over her soul. It was terrifying. I didn't see the Dark Lady then; only the witch handing over her soul and her guardian get to see her during this ritual.

I had felt her, though. Her oppressing dark magic had swirled around us as if she was testing us, looking to see who would cower. A dark cloud of shadows had wrapped around the young witch for what felt like an eternity, the dark magic continuing to press down on us, making me feel like my bones were going to break under the pressure. Then the shadows were gone and all that remained on the forest floor was the young witch, unconscious. Her skin had a sickly pallor to it, her hair limp. She had to be carried home and hadn't gotten out of bed until the following week.

There is a break in the trees, and we are standing in an open field. The coven is in a wide circle around the clearing, their heads down. In the middle of the clearing is a monolith, a pillar of black stone, standing high above the tree line. According to legend, ancient magic allows it to be hidden from the sight of non-magic wielders. There are several across the planet, all used as an easy way to summon the Dark Lady and her minions. She might not answer, depending on what she is being summoned for—usually, naïve magic wielders will call upon her for some inane reason, and instead of her appearing, one of her demons will appear instead. And you do not want a demon to answer your call.

My mother and aunt slow their pace so they are walking on either side of me. They each take a hand and guide me toward the monolith. The ground under my feet feels rotted, dead. It feels wrong. My stomach constricts. Something isn't right. The air gets thicker the closer we get to the monstrosity before me. I'm trying to suck down air, but my lungs can't get their fill. My mother and aunt's grip on my hands tightens, whether in comfort or warning, I'm not sure.

We stop a few feet from the monolith, and my mother and aunt bow at the waist. I take a second too long to realize I should be doing the same.

It's silent in the clearing—no sound of wildlife, not even a breeze.

I'm about to ask why when I feel it. That dark overpowering feeling.

She's here.

My mother and aunt stay bowing, though, so I do too. I hear the beating of mighty wings and the air around us being interrupted. Everything around us goes dark—I know if I look up, I won't be able to see the coven. We're trapped in the shadows. I try to stop my body from shaking.

"You may rise," a powerful voice says to us.

All three of us straighten and my eyes land on the being in front of us.

She's tall, maybe a head taller than me, and her eyes seem to twinkle in the dark, even though they're pitch black. Her matching hair cascades down over her left shoulder until it reaches her chest—her hair on the other side is shaved to the scalp—and she has a serpent tattoo on the side of her neck that winds its way under the collar of her dark clothes.

What catches my breath are her wings. She has huge, black-feathered wings that flare out to the sides.

Our eyes lock, and all I see is Death.

Death made flesh.

"My lady," my mother speaks before I can throw up all over myself. "My sister and I present to you my child, Vivian."

My mother and aunt let go of my hands and my mother shoves me forward. I stumble, nearly tripping over the dress I've been forced to wear. I manage to right myself and my gaze locks again with hers. She tilts her head as if she's curious, and I quickly look down at my feet.

"Jessica and Judith," she says in that foreboding voice, "I accept your offering. You may stand amongst the others."

I don't even hear them leave, but suddenly I know we're alone.

I try to swallow the lump in my throat, but my mouth is too dry. I knew this was how it worked, but—they left me. Abandoned me to be taken.

"Come closer, little one."

I will my feet to move, one in front of the other, until I can see her black boots in my line of vision. When her golden hand grips my chin and forces my head up, the curiosity in her dangerous eyes terrifies me.

"Are you frightened?" she asks.

I shake my head slightly.

She grips my chin harder, her nails lightly digging into my skin. I imagine to show me that she could easily hurt me and I would be helpless against her.

"You lie. I can smell it on you," she purrs before letting go of my chin. She smirks at me. "It is time for you to give over your soul. You will reap the generous rewards I bestow upon all witches who do so. You will have a long life here on Earth, and upon your death, you will have the infinite luxuries that Hell has to offer. You will become my loyal and willing servant. I may call on you at any time, for anything I wish."

I know she didn't ask me anything, but I nod my understanding.

She produces a dagger from thin air and holds it out to me. "Take this and mark your flesh." She nods at my balled fists.

I shakily reach out and grab the hilt of the dagger, its dark blade sucking what little light is in the clearing straight into it. I feel its energy, its dark heart—as if it wants me to know what horrors it has committed against her enemies. I open my free hand, and with a deep breath,

I press the blade into my clammy palm. There is a prick of pain and blood immediately begins to well. I shove the dagger back at the Dark Lady, not wanting to hold it for another second.

Her chuckle skitters over my bones. "Now press your blood into the monolith. It will take what is rightfully owed to me."

She steps off to the side, allowing me to approach the obelisk. The closer I get, the more energy I feel around me. It feels like it's warning me, screaming at me—I raise my bleeding hand in front of me and place it on the black stone.

Pain and screaming and decay and death—

It feels like my insides are being turned inside out, like I'm being sucked into the stone.

No no no.

Rot and festering wounds and death and death and death—

You are mine mine mine—

No!

I rip my hand from the stone and stumble back, landing on my ass. I'm covered in sweat and my breath is sawing in and out of me. I look at her in complete bewilderment. "What—what is that?" I gasp, cradling my stinging hand to my chest.

Her wings stretch out, making her look larger than life. "Get up," she commands, her voice booming. Shadows start to coil around her like snakes.

"What *is* that?" I repeat, screaming this time and shuffling further away from her.

"You dare question me?" she growls, the shadows seeming to writhe all around us now. The ground underneath me starts to vibrate. "Get up and give me what is mine."

I can't, I think to myself. *I can't and I won't.*

Without thinking, I scramble up and break into a sprint. There's nowhere to go except through the writhing shadows, and I brace myself for impact, but the shadows don't lunge for me, as if I've surprised them so much by running that they're frozen.

I don't have time to ponder that. I keep going, breaking through the barrier she put around us and running past the coven still standing in a wide circle.

"Vivian?" my aunt calls out, but I don't stop. I can't stop. I grip the edge of the dress in one hand and haul ass down the small, dark pathway I walked down lifetimes ago.

"You will give me what I am owed!" I hear the Dark Lady shriek, and it shakes the entire forest. I feel her dark magic spearing towards me—whether to kill me or drag me back to her, I don't know.

I kick my shoes off and run barefoot, my feet most likely bleeding from the rocks and sticks I'm stepping on, but I can't feel it. My lungs are screaming for air. When something barrels into me from behind, I face plant, and her magic wraps itself around my ankle, dragging me along the forest floor. Sobs wrack my chest as I claw at the dirt to slow myself from being taken back there.

"Please!" I cry out. "Please, please—" I don't know who I'm begging. No one is going to save me. Not from this.

"Please," I gasp out again.

The magic around my ankle releases, and I stop moving. I blink a few times, disoriented, and look behind me. The path is gone. It's now just a mess of trees. I furrow my brows. I was running straight down the path—why would her magic take me in a different direction? I sit up and look around, trying to get my bearings.

Something wraps around my ankle again, and I scream, but it's not her magic. Looking down, I see a tree root wrapping itself around my ankle, and then another wraps around my other ankle. Then another around my waist. Two around my wrists. Before I have time to consider how the Dark Lady managed to manipulate the wilderness to do her bidding this way, the roots gently lift me and carry me.

This feels different from her magic. It feels...loving.

Soft.

Safe.

I'm crying in earnest now, the tears spilling down my cheeks as the trees shift and sway, carrying me, passing me from one root to the next until I'm on the outskirts of the forest, my house in the near distance. Tenderly, the roots lower me to the ground until I'm standing. I turn around just as the trees reposition themselves into their original places.

I walk up to the closest tree, lean my brow against the bark of its trunk, and whisper, "Thank you."

Witches have never been known to have earth magic, and many witches don't experience their magical abilities until after they sign away their souls, so I have no explanation for what happened.

But I don't have time to think about it.

I turn and run, and I don't look back.

Chapter One
Vivian

Ten Years Later

"Mrs. Lehigh, we can't approve your order without the appropriate form being filled out. You sent us form nine when we really need form eleven—"

"This is ridiculous! I completed form eleven," the elderly woman on the phone complains.

"No, Mrs. Lehigh," I rein in my annoyance. "You completed form nine, and we need—"

She interrupts me. "I just don't understand why the forms look identical..."

I stop paying attention to her complaints. We do this nearly every week. It's not her fault she's nearly eighty years old and regularly gets confused. But it isn't my fault either, is it?

I examine my nails—pink and red heart French tips—letting it give me a bit of a mood boost.

"Oh, I'm so sorry, Mrs. Lehigh, but someone just came to my desk and needs my help immediately. Be sure to submit form eleven!" I say cheerily before hanging up.

I sigh and rub my temples.

"She's an old bat. You should just screen her calls," my coworker, Michael, says to me over the cubicle divider.

I snort. "I bet that'll go over well in my performance review. They'll say, *Vivian does not respond to customer complaints in a timely and professional manner.*"

He laughs. "Haven't you heard? No one gets fired around here."

I roll my shoulders and fiddle with my amulet. It's the one thing I kept from my old life—for some reason, I just can't bear to part with it.

But everything else? I happily got rid of. Including all the black I had to wear.

When I started working for the local hospital's accounting department, I wasted no time decorating my sad, gray space. It looks as if Barbie and Legally Blonde threw up in here—it's so pink, you can immediately spot which is mine from down the hall.

Pink decorations, pink computer accessories, a pink chair cover, pink everything.

I also did it because I knew it would confuse my aggressively male co-workers.

Michael is the only one who doesn't seem off-put by my style. He even bought me a tiny, pink disco ball keychain for my birthday last year, which is still connected to my keys.

He peeks his head over the divider to look at me. "I mean it. They rarely fire anyone here. You'd have to do something really fucked up to get fired from this place."

I'm not sure if that's a good thing or a bad thing, so I simply smile at him before throwing my blonde hair over my shoulder.

"They'd also never fire me because they need me as eye candy," I joke.

Michael rolls his eyes but doesn't deny it. "Any plans this weekend?" he asks.

I swivel in my chair a bit. "Nope. Just going to go home, get into my comfy pajamas, and watch whatever love competition reality show is currently on TV. What about you?"

He runs a hand through his hair nervously. "I don't have much going on either. If you'd like—"

The universe decides to spare me from another awkward moment where Michael asks me out and I must politely decline because my phone starts to ring.

"Accounting, this is Vivian."

"I swear I filled out form eleven!"

Two hours later, I've kicked off my kitten heels, stripped out of my work clothes, and am pouring myself some wine, buck naked. My one-bedroom apartment would be what many might consider maximalist. A bright purple sofa, a tie-dye rug, side tables shaped like strawberries, and a pink disco ball hung from the ceiling, throwing a kaleidoscope of colors throughout the space.

I walk over to the apartment's floor-to-ceiling windows that overlook the Chicago skyline, surveying the bustling city below. It probably isn't wise to stand here in all my naked glory, but I don't have any neighboring buildings to peek into, so hopefully no one can peek into mine. And even if someone did see me, I guess I don't really care.

I've been in Chicago for two years now, and I'm enjoying it enough. The people are friendlier than the people in New York, and they're better drivers than people in Boston but have a bigger sense of urgency than people on the West Coast.

I picked Chicago because it's known as a concrete jungle. Its towering skyline and busy streets don't provide much in the way of nature. I try to avoid nature at all costs. I refuse to have any plants in my home, just in case.

It's too much of a risk.

I walk over to my sofa, setting my wine down on the coffee table before plunking down on the cushions. I nestle in and turn on the TV. Flipping through the channels, I settle on a new reality show where singles live on a remote island and try to find the person—determined by matchmakers—who will be their perfect match, but if they choose to couple up with the wrong person, they get sent home. It's garbage TV, and I love every moment of it.

A girl is crying in her confessional interview about being confused about which mediocre man is her perfect match when my mind starts to wander. Michael has been trying to ask me out for months now. I always manage to politely skirt around his advances, but...should I consider saying yes? There's nothing really wrong with him—at least from what I can tell. He's nice, he's attractive, and he's definitely interested in me. I chew on my bottom lip. He isn't really a good candidate for what I'm looking for, which is just sex. I can't sleep with a coworker—it'll just make things awkward—and he seems like he's looking for more commitment than I am.

I can't let others get close to me. I make friends in every place I move to, but I don't keep them. I never let them get too close. It's a cycle. I get lonely, I make friends or even find myself having a crush on someone, then I get overwhelmed and scared that I'm damning them and dragging them down to Hell with me. Literally.

So I keep everyone at arm's length.

But a girl does have needs. Itches that need to be scratched.

I sigh, burrowing into the assortment of brightly-colored cushions. Maybe he wouldn't make it weird. Maybe I could say yes, and we could hook up once—or a few times—and let it be that.

I feel something slithering up my leg. It's light as a feather, traveling up my calf gently, as if it's exploring my skin. Another one slides up my other leg, slithering across the inside of my knee to my thigh. I squirm a bit, wondering if they'll move up even further. My eyes are closed. I try to open them, but my body won't obey me. I must be dreaming, teetering on the edge between being asleep and awake.

The touches continue, slowly gliding up the inside of my thighs. I'm not sure why, but I'm certain they must be shadows.

I've only seen sentient shadows once before—

Panic doesn't have time to grip me because the shadows have reached the top of my thighs. They skirt around the skin delicately as if they're trying to tease me. I feel my body try to press into them without me thinking about it. The shadows slither along my skin, barely there, testing how much I want them to touch me.

A whimper escapes my lips. Apparently, I really want them to touch me.

They seem to sense it too because they finally make their way to my center.

I gasp at the sensation. They feel like the gentlest fingers, just barely touching me.

One of the shadows swirls around my lips while the other darts around my clit, not quite giving me the pressure I need. I tilt my hips into them, seeking more.

They seem to like that because one starts to enter me as the other presses against my clit.

I cry out, my hips bucking. The shadow inside of me is slowly pumping in and out of me, going deeper each time, as if trying to see how much of it I can take. The other is circling my clit gently, applying just enough pressure to drive me wild but not enough to finish me off.

I start gyrating, trying to get them to go faster, harder. The shadow inside of me presses to the hilt and I let out a ragged moan.

It's too much and yet not enough, I need more—

"Please," I whisper.

Something snaps in my brain.

Flashes of a forest, a torn black wedding dress, dirt under my fingernails, crying for someone, anyone to save me—

My eyes fly open, and I look around, frantic and panicking.

My empty wineglass is still on the table in front of me, and behind it, the TV is playing the stupid reality show. Everything looks exactly the same. No shadows to be seen. No sign of her at all.

The only difference is that there's a blanket draped over my naked body.

I rub my trembling hands over my face, trying to get my bearings. I'm in my apartment. I am alone and safe, and I am not stuck in the woods.

It was just a dream.

I loose a breath and throw the blanket off of me. I must've pulled it over myself when I fell asleep. I shuffle off the couch, turn off the TV, and pad over to my bedroom. I take one look over my shoulder, to tell myself once more it was just a dream.

Chapter Two

Vivian

My heels click-clack against the tiled floor of the copy room as I make my way over to the industrial printer. I have about thirty contracts to review before the end of the week. It's made my week so hectic that I haven't even had time to think about the semi-wet dream I had a few nights ago—is that what it was? Do women even have those?

I stand over the printer as it spits out my documents, fiddling absentmindedly with my orchid earrings, when something small and green enters the corner of my vision.

I look over at the small windows and notice someone has put a plant on the windowsill.

I frown at it. I'm not sure how long it's been in here, although I rarely need to come into the copy room.

With the printer still buzzing next to me, I slowly approach the little plant. It's a succulent that has seen better days—some leaves have dried and fallen off; the soil is bone dry.

A pang of sadness hits me out of nowhere. Whoever brought it in here has clearly abandoned it, leaving it in this sad room to die a slow death. This plant doesn't deserve to die in here. Tentatively, I raise my hand towards it, lightly stroking the few leaves that are still intact.

"I'm sorry someone dumped you here," I tell it softly, as if it can hear and understand me.

Suddenly, the plant under my hand starts to transform. Its leaves perk up, growing greener and larger, and the soil begins to churn, transporting newly found nutrients throughout the pot.

I gasp and recoil, snapping my hand to my chest.

The plant looks like the picture of health. New leaves have even sprouted on the stem.

I slowly back away, horror sluicing through me.

I didn't mean to do that. I hadn't tried to channel magic or even think—

Can the Dark Lady sense when I use magic? I've always assumed she could. It's what keeps me moving from place to place, refusing to use any magic, not even looking at greenery if I can help it.

"Looks like someone has a green thumb."

I gasp and whirl at the sound of Michael's voice. He stands in the doorway, rubbing his thumb over his lower lip in contemplation.

"I think Nate's wife made him give it to Lawrence as a gift for his retirement," he comments before sauntering into the room.

My heart is beating wildly in my chest. I'm still clutching my hand to myself, as if I've hurt it and it needs protection. I swallow and say a bit breathlessly, "Oh," because it's all I can think to say.

He continues to approach me, not stopping until he's in my personal bubble. He looks down at me, his blue eyes sparkling, and reaches out to grab the hand I'm still cradling to myself. He looks down at our hands, his thumb drawing circles on my skin. I'm trying to calm my breathing, but I'm failing miserably.

I need to get out of here, in case—

He can't be here. No one can be around me right now. If she shows up, she'll kill everyone and drag me down to Hell. I can't be responsible for that.

"Viv, we've been dancing around each other for months now," he drawls.

My mind is struggling to understand what he's saying. I'm too caught up in my panic.

"What?" I gasp out.

He chuckles and brings our hands to his face, placing a gentle kiss on the back of mine.

"You know I want you." He looks at me from under his dark lashes.

My anxiety feels like a hand is wrapped around my throat, choking me out, depriving me of oxygen. I can't breathe. I try sucking in a breath, but it doesn't feel like enough.

"I think we'd have fun together," he continues, either ignoring or completely oblivious to the crushing panic I'm experiencing. "Go out with me. Just once. I'll make it worth your while." He skates his lips against my hand again.

I swear I'm trying to answer him, but I can't seem to form words—

The lights go out and we're plunged into darkness.

"What the fuck?" Michael exclaims.

The printer completely stops working. The room is eerily quiet, too quiet. The hallway lights are out too. The darkness isn't normal—it's a darkness where you can't even see your hand in front of your face.

Oh god. She's here.

I rip my hand from his.

"I'm sorry," I squeak out before stumbling out of the room, my arms out in front of me, feeling for the door.

"Viv!" he calls after me, and I hear him trying to follow me out, but I don't turn around. I keep feeling with my hands, trying to find my way.

My hands touch the wall, and I nearly sob with relief. I run my hands over it, navigating myself out of the room and into the dark hallway. Down the hall, I hear people talking, trying to figure out what happened and how to get the lights back on, but I know what they don't.

The lights won't go back on unless she wants them to.

I've managed to evade her for ten years. Ever since I ran away from home after refusing to give her my soul, I've been obsessive about staying out of her grasp. The first thing I did once I got away from the coven's commune was go to a church and have them baptize me, hoping a connection to a religion that hates her would help keep her away from me. I stuff my magic down, even when it begs to be let out. I've had a few close calls over the years, but she's never managed to catch me.

Until now.

I figured I would have to answer for what I did all those years ago upon my death, but my life is supposed to be for *me*.

I make my way down the hall, trying to find the exit. I need to get out of this building, out of this city. Maybe going abroad would help. I know where every one of her summoning monoliths is—I'll find a place far away from any of them.

I feel something behind me. A presence. It feels angry.

A sob tries to claw its way out of my throat as I stumble into a blind run, skimming my hand over the wall. The presence slithers along the floor, keeping pace with me. Letting me think I can get away before they pounce. I find the door and shove my entire body against it. It opens without issue. The lights nearly blind me as I stumble towards the stairwell. It looks like she didn't cut the power everywhere then. I break into a sprint, ripping the door to the stairs open, and fly down the two flights before bursting into the lobby.

A few people startle when they see me. Nothing seems awry down here—it looks like business as usual.

I self-consciously clear my throat and smooth down my hair, my floral blouse, and my bright pink skirt. I left my bag upstairs, but there's no way I'm going back up there. She can have all my shit if she really wants it.

I nod at the security officer at the front desk, who eyes me suspiciously.

"Not feeling well, I'm just heading home," I tell him, trying to sound like my normal self, but my voice sounds too high, too breathy.

His brows narrow, but he goes back to looking at his phone.

No one else seems to know what just happened. Outside the hospital, the world is a flurry of its regular activity. Ambulances come and go, people walk in to get to their appointments, and loved ones pick up discharged patients from procedures.

I swiftly begin my trip home. Luckily, I have, like, five bus passes in my skirt pocket because I always seem to misplace them—even though they're always in my pockets.

I walk down the block to my bus station just as the bus is pulling up. I take a seat behind the driver and study the hospital as we pass it. Everything still seems normal out there.

I let out a sigh of relief as I lean my head against the window behind me, closing my eyes for a moment.

That was close—too close. The closest she's ever gotten.

I stifle a groan. I can't believe I'm going to have to start all over again. I was just getting used to the brutal Chicago winters.

That fucking bitch, I think as the bus begins to weave through the city traffic. She's the reason my life is like this. She's the reason I've moved to eight different cities in ten years. She's the reason I can't have friends or lovers or pets or even a fucking succulent.

By the time the bus stops outside my building an hour later, I'm brimming with barely suppressed rage. I know I'm working myself up, but I don't care. My life is like this because of her and it isn't fair.

I stomp into my building's lobby. The front desk manager, Pascal, blanches when he sees me. Usually I'm incredibly friendly, bubbly to him and everyone who works here, but today the fury on my face is impossible to conceal.

"Miss Winters," he greets me nervously. I bristle at the fake name.

I kept my first name when I left, figuring my name isn't unique enough to raise any alarms, but I've changed my last name with every move—it's cost me an arm and a leg to forge all my government documents. Even my diplomas have been forged, although I did actually receive my degrees. I was running out of names, so when I moved to Chicago, I figured the last name Winters would be funny—considering how cold it gets here.

Now, it just reminds me of the absolutely fucked up situation I'm in.

"Lost my key," I manage to bark out. "Need a copy."

Pascal audibly swallows. "Yes, of course. Give me one moment." He rushes into the back.

I close my eyes for a few moments, trying to calm myself. I can't barge in and just act like an asshole because I'm angry. It isn't Pascal's fault I'm in this position.

I breathe in through my nose and out through my mouth, trying to let go of the anger that's rising within me.

I've taken five deep breaths by the time Pascal is back.

"Here you are!" His tone is a bit too chipper. He places the silver key on the desk. "It'll cost two hundred and fifty dollars for the replacement, but I'm sure we could make an exception—"

"It's fine," I say, trying to smile brightly at him, but it must come out more like a grimace because Pascal's eyes get wide. I swallow. "It's fine," I try again. "Just add it to my bill for the first of the month. I'll pay it when rent is due if that's alright."

He nods. "Of course, Miss Winters."

Before I make him piss himself from fear, I march over to the elevators and stab the button up to my floor. I take my heels off in the elevator, not even caring anymore. I can't let my anger get the best of me. It serves me no purpose—it's not like my anger will solve any of my problems or make the Dark Lady stop hunting for me. I focus on deciding where I'll have to go next. Maybe I can manage to just disappear for a few months and then come back here.

If I hop around a lot, maybe she'll get confused and lose my trail.

I'm considering this plan as I step off the elevator, unlock my door, and take a step in, the door closing behind me.

I freeze in the entranceway.

The hall stretching out into my apartment is dark and silent in an unnatural way. The alarm bells start going off in my head.

She's finally caught me.

Chapter Three

Vivian

I spin around, reaching for the door handle, but it doesn't open, as if it's locked from the outside. I claw at it, throwing my body weight into it, but it doesn't budge.

"Don't bother."

Horror floods my system. I slowly turn around to face the open hallway and the dark, foreboding voice beyond. "Come. I'm sure you had a long day at work," she snickers, causing the hairs on my arms to stand.

I creep down the hallway, transitioning a shoe into each hand.

Just in case I need to bash her face in with the heel.

I slowly enter the open space.

She's sitting on my sofa, precisely in the spot I was last night. She looks nearly identical to when I saw her ten years ago. Hair and eyes as black as a starless night, golden skin, all black ensemble, and ass-kicking boots. Her hair is no longer shaved on one side—braids now line her scalp and fall down her back. Her serpent tattoo seems to suck the life out of the room. She's without her wings tonight, for whatever reason. No sign of her shadows, either.

Her black eyes drink me in, slowly moving from my toes, snagging on the heels in my hands before traveling up to my face. She tilts her head, her dark hair shifting with the movement.

"Time has been good to you," she states casually, as if we're simply old friends. "Although, last time I saw you, your hair was brown."

"I colored it." My answer burns my dry throat.

She nods as if this information is necessary and important. Her gaze moves from me and takes in my apartment. "Your interior decorating skills are...interesting." She frowns in disdain. "It's like a bubblegum princess lives here."

I don't answer.

She leans back on my sofa and crosses her ankle over her knee. "Come, Vivian; sit with me."

"I'm fine standing."

She fixes her dark gaze on me, and I grip my heels tighter. She seems to notice, her gaze dipping to my hands and then back up to my face. She grins. "Are we going to brawl?" she chuckles. "I'd like to see it. Although, you don't use your magic, so it wouldn't last very long."

She reaches out and pats the cushion next to her. "Sit," she demands.

I slowly move to the sofa and lower myself into the seat. We both shift to angle our bodies towards one another. Something within me seems to stir at the proximity. I haven't felt this in years. I try to push it down, shove it into a small box, and ignore it, but it feels like it's right at the surface, pressing into my skin.

She sniffs and then sighs. "Your magic is happy to see me, at least."

I work harder to tamp it down.

The snake tattoo on her neck seems to blink lazily at me as she looks at the heels still gripped tightly in my fists. "I'm not here to argue," she states after a beat of silence. "I'm here because I need your help."

Chapter Four
The Dark Lady

Vivian looks at me with this mixture of anger, confusion, and outright fear. Her fear is the tangiest scent in my nose, but her emotions keep warring with each other, causing her scent to change rapidly.

And yet her emotions cannot hide her intoxicating cherry blossom and pomegranate scent.

She looks like an actual Barbie, her bright pink outfit, her bright blonde hair curled lightly at the ends, her make-up impeccably applied. I want to laugh at how opposite we look right now, the princess and the Angel of Death, sitting next to each other. We might look like opposites, but she still belongs to me. Her magic is trying desperately to get free, to alert me to its presence.

My Vivian has used her magic sparingly over the past ten years. I struggled to keep tabs on her all that time—that is, until her magic would decide it was time to play. Whenever she used it, it was like a beacon of light, giving away her location.

She has evaded me each time I've gotten close. It would be impressive if it wasn't so incredibly irritating that she managed to get away from me every single time.

An alarm from her magic sounded two years ago, letting me know where she was. I've been a hound on a scent ever since, desperate and feral about finally finding her. Her magic seemed to feel the same—it sent me right to her.

Clearly without her knowledge.

She hates that she belongs to me. I can see it all over her face, the bald hatred that flits across it every few moments. She can hate me all she wants. It doesn't change her circumstances.

She is mine—in body and in soul.

"What could you possibly need my help with?" she asks sharply.

I quirk an eyebrow at her tone. "When was the last time you went home?"

She blinks at my question, not expecting it. "I—I haven't been home since..." She trails off, pure fury filling her expression.

Her magic flares inside of her, and her expression changes again, but this time she looks almost like she's in pain. I'm sure she is. It's detrimental for witches to bury their magic, to not let it out every once in a while. I would imagine she's uncomfortable quite often. I swallow the emotions that brings to the surface for me. I don't care how she feels—she's a tool, a means to an end, that's it.

"I figured," I murmur. "And I know you've had no contact with any of them. Your mother would have told me the moment she heard from you." Some emotion flashes across her face before I can catch it, but she's back to looking frightened. "The problem," I sigh, "is that witches have been disappearing at alarming rates. A few here and there aren't usually a cause for concern—you witches tend to get yourself into interesting predicaments."

Her nostrils flare when I call her a witch, but she doesn't say anything.

I continue, "But whole covens are going missing. It's mostly covens furthest from the summoning places, so it takes me and my intelligence too long to realize there's something amiss. By the time we arrive, there's no trace of them. And no trace of where they went."

"Maybe they got tired of serving a tyrant and went into hiding," she bites out before she can think better of it. She clamps her lips shut and her eyes widen slightly at her little outburst.

It makes me want to laugh, but I bury that feeling. Instead, I scowl at her. "Fealty to me does not allow entire covens to simply get up and leave."

She clenches her jaw but doesn't respond. I know I'm goading her, but I can't help it. She doesn't seem to realize she is incredibly easy to read, even if I didn't have the ability to sniff out her changing scent.

"At every coven, there's a sign of a struggle," I admit. "I have no reason to believe they went willingly."

"Who would want witches?" she asks, her brows furrowing slightly. The grip on her heels relaxes.

"That list," I say, waving my hand dismissively, "is very long. The better question is, who would be stupid enough to take witches from *me*?"

"Well, they can't be dead," she muses aloud. "If they're dead, then they'd already be in Hell, and you would've asked them what happened."

I nod. "Their souls never made it to Hell. Which means they're either alive—which isn't likely, or their souls were destroyed."

"Souls can be destroyed?" she squeaks, her nervousness tainting her scent. I want it out of my nostrils immediately.

"Yes," I grit out. I don't want to have this conversation.

Surprisingly, she drops it. Her gaze flits around for a moment, snagging on her purse on the coffee table. When she fled, I took the liberty of collecting her belongings for her—just to see how she'd react, to flex my power over her that I can simply waltz into her life and disrupt it however I please.

From the expression on her face, it's safe to say she's confused by the gesture. Her hazel eyes rove over me, as if she's trying to understand me. Trying to understand why I'm sitting here, in her home, and not spiriting her away to my realm. Trying to understand why my wings and my shadows aren't present for our little catch-up.

"I decided a tamper on my magic would make this conversation more...comfortable for you," I admit begrudgingly.

She swallows and nods. "That was wise of you."

"Even though you are the only witch that did not hand over your soul," I try to keep the irritation out of my tone, "I'm here for your help."

"So let me get this straight," she says, dropping the shoes and flipping her blonde hair over a shoulder. "You want me, the girl who defied you, kept her soul from you, and who has denounced all witchcraft, to help you find these missing covens."

I simply nod at her.

She stares at me for a moment before bursting into a fit of giggles. She barrels over, her arms clutching her stomach, as her giggles become hysterical. Her eyes begin to water, and her laughs are broken up by random hiccups.

I sit back, waiting patiently for her little breakdown to end.

Once she's pulled herself together, she wipes her eyes, careful not to smudge her pristine makeup. "That's hilarious," she giggles softly. "Thank you, really—I haven't laughed that hard in a long time."

I raise my eyebrows at her but don't respond.

A few moments of silence pass before the realization that I'm not joking sinks in, and her eyes widen as her mouth goes slack. "You *are* joking, aren't you? I don't have any way to help you."

"You do, actually," I counter. "You have the rare ability of earth magic. You can do so much with your magic if you simply let it out."

Her magic seems to jump up like an excited puppy at the mere mention that it exists. Her face contorts in discomfort. "I don't understand."

"I'll explain it all to you," I reply. "After you agree to help." She furrows her brow again, seeming to hesitate. "We have work to do," I say slowly, as if I'm speaking to a child. "There's no time to waste. I suggest packing a bag of comfortable clothing that is also inconspicuous." I take a look around the room to emphasize my point.

Her eyes narrow as she spits, "I'm not going anywhere with you. You'll have to drag me, kicking and screaming."

"If I remember correctly, I did exactly that," I remind her impatiently.

Her fear coats my tongue, but her face is surprisingly blank. "But what about my job? My life?" she asks me.

I tilt my head at her. "You've disappeared from your fake lives before. I don't see how this will be any different."

She chews on her lip for a moment. I stifle my irritation at why she might be hesitating to pick up and leave like she has multiple times before. Is it because of that human male she was with when I arrived today?

If it is, I'll have to kill him and make sure his soul never finds a resting place.

I sigh. "I'll give you the day to figure out whatever mortal things you must figure out. We're going to where the covens most recently disappeared. One is a few hours from here, and another is a few hours from there, and the third is not too far from the second. Seeing as you take public transit, I'm assuming you don't have a car."

She nods.

I slide a hand into my pocket and pull out a black credit card and a small piece of folded paper. I hold it out for her to take. "Here. Go get a rental car tomorrow and get to the address on this piece of paper."

She quickly reaches up and snatches the items from my fingers as if worried any physical contact between us will burn her. She seems to be done battling whatever she was thinking because she squares her shoulders. "If I help you, I want to be free."

It's my turn to look at her with confusion.

"I want to be free—no more running, no more being chased. I'm tired of living like this." Her voice trembles, but she continues. "If I help you, I want you to stop looking for me. To leave me *and* my soul alone to live a normal life."

I want to laugh. A normal life? She doesn't even understand that a normal life would bore her and that not getting her soul is non-negotiable. Her soul has always belonged to me. I'm not giving it up now, not when I'm so close to finally having it.

But if this is what she needs to agree, then I'll play along.

So I look her in the eye and confidently lie. "If you help me discover who—or what—is taking my witches from me, I will no longer chase after you or your soul. You will be free of me."

She seems to believe me because she holds out her hand to me. "It's a deal."

I grin at her. "It's a deal," I parrot, sliding my hand into hers.

Chapter Five
Vivian

I had a few blissful moments this morning where I didn't remember the night before happened, and then it all came crashing back into me. The Dark Lady finding me, showing up in my apartment, telling me entire covens have gone missing, and needing my help to find them. What gives me a feeling of hope is that she agreed to finally let me go if I helped. I'm absolutely terrified. I've been running from her for so long. This has been my life, my sole purpose. What do I do now that she's found me?

I spent all morning getting everything in order. I called work in tears, babbling out how my imaginary uncle suddenly died and I needed to go out of town to attend the funeral. They were incredibly sympathetic, telling me to take however long I need—although I only had about a week of leave I could use.

In the past, I used to just skip town without even quitting. I used to rent short-term in case she showed up and

I needed to bolt. This is the first time I have anything somewhat permanent.

And, of course, she found me here.

I shove some clothes into a bag, unsure of how long I'll be gone. The address on the little piece of paper is near Alton, a town that's a little over four hours away. I walk over to my coffee table, where I put the paper and the black credit card after she handed them over, and pick up the card to inspect it. It looks real, although it doesn't have a name on it. Why would she need a credit card? I hope it's actually hers and that she hadn't simply stolen it off someone.

Guess I'm about to find out.

About five hours later, I'm pulling up to the little bed-and-breakfast outside of Alton, a small town known for being just a wee bit haunted. Alton is a small town north of St. Louis that borders the Mississippi River. According to witch history, covens used to convene close to one of the many summoning places on the globe to allow for easy access to the Dark Lady—and she to them. As the world industrialized, witches started to branch out and move to new lands. The Dark Lady was resistant to this at first. She only agreed when witches managed to prove to her that they would still serve her as readily as they did when they lived on the land of the summoning stones.

Pulling into the parking lot of the B&B, I switch off the car and drag my bags to check-in.

The Dark Lady made sure to throw a snide comment about my clothes last night, which I took great offense to. So I made sure to bring many brightly colored ensembles.

Walking into the B&B, I greet the front desk person, telling her my name, and she gives me a big smile, welcoming me, and hands over my room key. After a few huffs and puffs up the stairs with all my shit, I throw my door open to find the room empty.

No Dark Lady—no signs of anyone being in here at all. She didn't specifically say she would be joining me here, but I figured she wouldn't want me out of her sight. Not since she finally found me.

Brows furrowed, I peek around the room and notice a note on the small desk.

Vivian,
I have something to attend to, so I will not be joining you this
	evening.

I know you're gutted to hear this.
I will see you bright and early tomorrow morning at the
  address below.
DL

I roll my eyes so hard at the note before crumpling it up and tossing it into the little garbage bin. I should be happy I won't see her—the less time with her, the better—but I find myself feeling a bit irritated, a bit off-kilter.

Is this some kind of test, to see what I'll do when she's not around? What if she's secretly watching me from the rooftop across the street, just waiting to see if I'll bail?

Which would be ridiculous, I think to myself. I'm finally in a bargaining position to be free of her. Why would I leave now?

The thought of running makes my heart skip a beat, though. I've been doing it for so long, I barely know anything else anymore. I want to have a life like everyone else, a life where I can put down roots and make friends and keep a job even if that job is shitty.

My life in Chicago had started to feel permanent.

Yet here I am, uprooted again. All because of the same woman. Or being. Or whatever she is.

My emotions are warring inside of me, too quickly for me to process what to do. So I stand, frozen, in the middle of my temporary room.

My magic nudges me, making me jump.

"What?" I snap aloud. It flares a bit at my tone but seems to settle back into me.

Dormant once more.

As if to remind me that it, too, has a say in this and to not forget what it wants. Which is to do the Dark Lady's bidding.

I let out a little screech of frustration, throwing myself onto the bed with a huff. I flip over and stare at the ceiling, still wondering if she's perched on the building across the street like some massive, deranged pigeon, watching me have my meltdown.

I don't care, I think to myself. Let her see what she's done to me. Maybe then she'll think twice about picking a fight with me.

As an idea forms in my head, I sit up, suddenly full of giddy energy.

She said she needed my help—said it was because of the magic I possess.

Which means...just as I'm stuck with her, she's stuck with me.

I don't need to be afraid of her anymore, I realize. For whatever reason, I'm the key to figuring all this weird shit out. She might still think my soul belongs to her, but she was desperate enough to bargain that away, all so I could help.

Meaning we are equals here.

An evil smile spreads across my face. I can't wait to make her life a living Hell.

Chapter Six
The Dark Lady

I needed to get away from her.

It's ironic—I spent a decade obsessively searching for her, just to find her and immediately need to get away from her. The little witch has managed to worm into my brain, making me unable to think of anything else but her. For the past ten years, I have focused solely on finding her, but I was unprepared for what it would be like when I finally succeeded.

Her scent immediately assaulted my senses, rewiring my mind. Cherry blossoms and pomegranates. It took everything in me not to grab her and spirit her away to Hell immediately. I need to play this right. I can't let her get away again. If I crowd her, she'll most likely run. I need her to think I'm serious about her silly bargain. I can't leave her alone either—at least, not completely.

I fly above her rental car, zigzagging through city traffic. She's a terrifying driver. It aggravates me. What if she gets into an accident before I get her soul?

At least she's actually on the move.

I continue to tail her from the skies, not quite able to remove her scent from my nose.

I already have a good idea who took my witches from me, but I need Vivian's magic to confirm it before I act. And there's much more I need from her than what she suspects.

She finally arrives at the bed and breakfast, lugging three bright pink suitcases into the building. I groan in disgust at the mental images of what brightly colored ensembles are stored away in those bags.

Swooping lower, my magic swirls around me to keep me hidden from detection. I position myself on the building across the street from the B&B, giving me an unobstructed view of Vivian's room.

I watch her read the note I left early this morning, crumple it up, and then just...stand there. She doesn't move for a few moments, as if she's frozen. It's peculiar behavior. I wish I could scent her to tell me what she's feeling, to give me any insight into her mind.

Then she starts talking to herself and throwing her body onto the mattress like some insolent child. I roll my eyes—I forget how erratic and difficult the living can be.

She's a strange, little creature. I've obsessed over her for a decade, shirking all responsibility to find her. I must know how someone so loud and impertinent managed to hide from me for so long. There must be a reason for it—some form of magic at play that kept her from being detected.

Just as I'm pondering this, she sits up, a grin spreading across her face.

What does that mean? Why the sudden change in demeanor?

She must have figured something out or has decided on something.

A smile matching her own slithers across my own mouth. I think the little witch is ready to play.

Chapter Seven

Vivian

T he Dark Lady told me to meet her today, but she never specified what time. Technically, she did say morning, but I've never been known to be timely. I'm pulling up to the address on the piece of paper mid-afternoon—after I spent the morning pampering myself on her dime. I went to a spa down the street, trying to decompress and mentally prepare for what might happen. I peek down at my newly painted nails—letters on each finger that spell out FUCK YOU!—as I follow the cobblestone road the GPS is leading me down.

When I was young, I asked my aunt why witches tend to congregate near haunted towns. She told me places still blessed by spirits allow for a closer connection to Hell—little cracks in the borders, she told me, but that didn't mean the Dark Lady would damn your doorstep any time soon. Only the most powerful of witch covens are allowed to reside closest to the summoning places. That decision goes back to the first witches, although most of that information has been lost to time, and the Dark Lady tends to utilize the most powerful covens for any witchcraft needed on earth.

While all witches are her loyal servants, it was made clear to me that she relies heavily on our coven for 'favors'. Whether that be from actual magical ability we possess or just pure laziness on her part, I'm not sure.

All witches are taught that the common understanding of Hell has been completely altered in modern times. Hell has always been the realm for the dead, no matter the soul's journey when they were alive—you ended up in Hell, whether you were a good person or not. Witches and demons run the realm, for the most part. The witches reside over all departed witches, and the demons reside over the departed human and animal souls. Most souls are left to exist in peace—they move about in a ghost-like form, spending their eternities doing whatever is interesting to ghosts, I guess, while witches can switch between their corporeal form and their spirit form.

But some of the worst souls? Those get sent to the levels below Hell.

The levels below are usually referred to as the dungeons. Not much is known about the dungeons or what happens to a soul once it enters, but we do know a soul can never leave once it is locked away down there.

I drive past McPike Mansion and get a general sense of unease.

Yep, definitely haunted, which means witches definitely live here.

The GPS guides me past the town limits toward an uninhabited forest. I look around, expecting to see a commune similar to the one I grew up in, but I don't see much of anything other than trees. There's nothing around—no sign of anyone living around here.

Furrowing my brows, I check the navigation again. It says I've arrived, but...

I'm about to reverse when the Dark Lady suddenly appears in front of my car.

I shriek, my stomach flying into my throat.

She has her wings out and they're stretched wide, blocking my vision of anything behind her. She's smiling widely at me, obviously finding my terror hilarious. Grumbling nasty names under my breath, I shut the car off and exit, slamming the door behind me.

I make my way over to her and cross my arms. "Are you trying to kill me?" I ask.

She rolls her eyes. "Why would you think that?"

I make a show of looking all around. "You send me to the middle of nowhere, with no sign of human life, and then jump out in front of my car. Is this where you murder me and harvest my body for meat?"

She wrinkles her nose. "I doubt you would taste very good."

I scoff. "I know a few people who would disagree with you."

Her eyebrows shoot up. "I wasn't aware you were into vore."

"I'm not," I groan. "Just forget it." I wave my hand dismissively. "So, what are we doing here?"

"This," she says, gesturing to the wilderness, "is where the coven commune was."

"I'm not sure who is responsible for your intel, but they must be smoking something because there's clearly nothing here."

She clenches her jaw. "You'll do well to not insult my team. Just because you're feeling bold after our little deal doesn't mean you can be disrespectful."

"Um, excuse me, I can be however I want," I snap.

She sighs, exasperated. Then she extends her arm, palm up. Black shadows shoot down her arms, skittering around, flying in every direction.

I yelp and drop to avoid them, but they ignore me, flying past me into the tree line.

It looks like they flew into a force field. The air crackles and then a gust of wind blows past us. Where the shadows disappeared is an open field. Various homes are lined around the clearing, looking nearly identical to coven's land I grew up on.

"Magical wards," I breathe, looking around the field I couldn't see just a moment ago.

She nods. "I'm not surprised you couldn't feel them. They're keyed to this specific coven." She jerks her chin to the clearing. "Get to work."

I blink at her. "What?"

She glances sidelong at me. "We're here to figure out how the coven was taken."

"I'm aware." I roll my eyes. "You do know I'm not a detective, right? Like I'm not trained in solving mysteries. I don't even like watching mysteries on TV."

She gives me a bemused look. "When you walk into the commune grounds, your magic might react. Let it guide you through."

Panic suddenly grips my heart. I don't let my magic out. Ever. It isn't a dangerous magic, but I've shoved it down for so long that I'm not sure how it'll try to manifest if I let it loose. Still, the reason I always kept it locked away was because I was afraid of her finding me, and that's already happened.

I steel my shoulders, trying to not let her see the emotions warring inside of me. I flip my freshly highlighted hair back—the highlights were on her dime too—and stride confidently into the clearing, even though I feel anything but.

I can do this, I tell myself.

There are five Victorian-style homes lined up in the clearing, all equidistant from one another. A smaller coven, then. There are a couple of barns further back, although they look derelict. As if they haven't been used in quite some time. I stand in the middle of the field, trying to figure out how to best do this. I've never used my magic before—at least, not on purpose. It would sometimes sneak out on me whenever I'd get a bit too close to any greenery, but that was the only time the leash slipped.

My magic starts roiling inside of me, pressing up against my skin to the point it's almost painful.

"Okay," I say, trying to keep myself calm. "Do your thing, I guess."

It leaps out of me, causing me to double over from the force. Images and feelings are racing through me, showing me images of wildlife passing through this land, humans growing up here, seasons passing—life, growth, death.

I'm on my hands and knees, trying to bring my magic back into me, but it's burrowing down further and further, deeper and deeper into the earth.

My mind feels like it's going to split in half. I might be screaming, or crying, or maybe I'm being sucked into the ground, I'm not sure. Suddenly I'm yanked backwards and I'm staring up at the clear sky above me. My magic races back into me, snapping like a rubber band. A whimper escapes my lips as the pain recedes.

The Dark Lady comes into view then, looking down at me.

She crosses her arms and exudes an *I'm pissed off* energy.

"What was the point of that?" she growls.

"You mean the point of using my magic, which is exactly why we're even here together?" I groan, my voice sounding breathy.

She scoffs, a look of disgust now transforming her face. "You destroyed the site and any evidence with it."

I roll onto my stomach and look around the clearing. It appears that the space around here was abandoned many, many years ago. Vines have enveloped the homes and the grass around us grows as tall as my waist. The rundown barns are completely leveled, grasses completely covering what was left of their destroyed forms.

"I…" I'm at a loss for words. "I didn't…it wasn't…"

"Save it," she snarls at me before she stomps away, the grass hissing as her boots destroy it.

I hear her wings beating in the distance, and I realize I'm all alone.

Chapter Eight

Vivian

I'm not sure how long I lie on the ground in the clearing, but it's dark when I finally pull myself together to leave. I know I fucked up—I get it. My magic and I aren't exactly friends and I have no idea how to manage it. The guilt keeps building inside me without a way out. How am I going to figure out what happened if I can't even get my magic to cooperate?

Dragging myself back to the B&B, I spot the Dark Lady at the front desk.

"Name?" the woman behind the counter asks.

"Venus," she replies.

The sound of her name catches me so off-guard that I stumble and bump into a table, the vintage lamp atop it toppling over. I manage to grab it and place it back on the table, but not without receiving glares from both women in front of me.

None of the witches ever speak her true name. I don't think any of the witches even know what her name is—she's always just been known as the Dark Lady.

The Dark Lady—Venus—narrows her eyes at me before turning around. Once she's done checking in, she barks that she will see me tomorrow morning, and that's that.

The guilt in my stomach feels like stones dragging me down by the time I get back into my room. I don't stop the tears that prick my eyes and roll down my cheeks. This is why letting my magic out is a terrible idea. I have no idea how to control it—it always fights me.

I get myself into the bathroom and crawl into the tub, turning the nozzle and letting the warm water wash over me. Leaning against the back of the tub, I stare up at the ceiling, my tears continuing their descent down my face.

Tomorrow, I decide, I'll do better. I have to do better. I'm not going to jeopardize my freedom just because my magic wants to ruin everything.

I stay in the tub until the water gets cold, and when I pull the plug, I watch my tears swirl down the drain with the bathwater.

My room is an absolute disaster.

Clothes are strewn across every surface—the bed, the desk, the tiny TV—so I can figure out what to wear today. I'm between a simple pair of black leggings and an oversized band t-shirt or a pair of wide-legged jeans with a crop top. Both options go well with my pink Doc Martens, so I'm struggling to pick.

Venus isn't the only one who can wear ass-kicking boots.

I hear a knock on my door and nearly jump out of my skin.

"Just a minute!" I say, frantically shoving my rejected outfit ideas into a pile.

I jolt in surprise when I hear a click of my door and heavy footsteps enter the room. My magic reacts with me, ready to attack.

Venus stomps into view and surveys my space with disdain before turning her attention to me. "It's time to move on to the next coven."

I blink in surprise.

"Seeing as you destroyed the last one, we'll have to move on," she informs me, crossing her arms over her chest. She's dressed in all black again—shocker. Her shadows dance around her shoulders menacingly. I try not to cringe.

"I didn't mean to ruin the site," I tell her, trying not to let my guilt overwhelm me. "You know I don't use my magic."

She glares at me. "Pack up all your frilly shit and I'll meet you at the next location tomorrow." She reaches into her pocket and drops a piece of paper on the desk. "Don't spend all my money."

"Look, I'm sorry," I say, my tone pleading, "my magic just took advantage of being let out. I'm trying—really, I am."

Venus simply shakes her head before exiting the room, the door slamming shut behind her.

Chapter Nine
The Dark Lady

I'm in a horrible mood.

A few hours have passed since I told Vivian we were leaving Alton and heading to the next coven site. I decided to fly, letting my wings soar with the winds.

Flying usually relaxes me—it's one of the few things I have that brings me comfort—but it doesn't seem to work today. A sick feeling has crept over me since I left her in her room, Vivian close to tears, apologizing for what happened.

I wish it was as simple as her making a mistake, but it isn't. She has no control over her magic. I didn't understand the gravity of this--not until I saw the coven site completely overrun by the earth in just a few seconds. I'm kicking myself for not realizing this. I was so desperate to get close to her that I got tunnel vision.

Ultimately, it's her own fault. If she hadn't run from me, from her destined path in life and in death, then she wouldn't be in this position. All she cares about is getting her freedom from me. Freedom that I said I would grant her, even though I have no intention of doing so.

The winds shift, pushing me from behind. My wings expand further to coast along this current. I stop flapping and let my body glide through the mid-afternoon air. The sun is still shining, which is at complete odds with how I feel. I don't come to the realm of the living unless I have to. I hate it up here—all the sunlight, the colors, the people who are very much alive.

Maybe that's why I feel like I want to rip someone's head from their shoulders. I've been around the living for too long.

Especially around someone like Vivian, who is just so...alive. She's bouncy, frilly. So at odds with everything I—and witches—enjoy. I puzzle over this as I follow the current, the feathers on my wings rustling as I fly. Was Vivian always this lively or did this develop after she escaped me? Knowing how witches operate, I doubt they would take kindly to a pink fairy prancing around.

She would've been a pariah in the coven.

And what would I have done, if she had shown who she was when we first met? Truthfully, I don't know, but I doubt I would have accepted it.

A pang in my chest startles me. I look down at myself, expecting to see I've been struck in the heart, but there's no wound, no weapon sticking out of my skin.

It takes me a few moments to realize the sensation I feel is...shame. Deep, ugly shame. If I'm the ruler of witches, how can I not accept one of my own—even if they act or dress a bit differently than the rest?

I try to shake this feeling out of me. It doesn't matter, I remind myself. There's no point asking myself 'what-ifs.'

But the feeling nags at me the rest of the flight to the next town.

Chapter Ten

Vivian

After loading up my bags and driving for a few hours, I reach the address on the slip of paper—a bed-and-breakfast in the middle of Missouri. Pulling into the parking lot, I look down at my nails for a bit of a mood boost. I'm determined to not let Venus's shit mood get in the way.

Growing up, my mother always told me I was a pushover—whenever another kid was mean to me and I quickly forgave them instead of retaliating, it was seen as weakness. Even when she was nasty to me, I'd always forgive her shortly after. She seemed to find this confusing and off-putting and would ignore me for days afterward.

I'm not sure why I've always been quick to forgive others. It's clearly not something I learned from her, but I did learn that not everyone is like that.

Venus is definitely a grudge-holder.

I'm determined to not let that rain on my parade though, even if my parade is currently the worst in history.

Sighing, I straighten my shoulders and step out of the car. I grab my bags from the trunk and make my way into the B&B.

The Dark Lady is already standing at the counter, speaking to the front desk person.

"What's the name under, dear?" the woman asks.

She's stowed away her wings and shadows, but it doesn't make her feel any less intense. Her presence is overwhelming and my magic leaps in my stomach at the sight of her.

"Venus," she answers the elderly woman.

"Ah, yes, I see it. The Honeymoon Suite." The old woman eyes us both. "You two together?"

"Yes," Venus grits out, clearly upset by that fact.

The woman hums, "No one rents that space out. You two some kind of adrenaline junkies?"

"Why?" I ask, walking up to the counter.

"Because it's haunted," the woman responds. "A couple died in that very room fifty years ago. Murder-suicide. People only stay in that room if they're ghost hunters or a bit kooky."

Well.

"We're neither," Venus sighs. I try not to shoot her an irritated look—I'm trying to be very zen right now, and she's making it difficult.

"Well, it's just up the stairs at the end of the hall. I live in the building, so if you need me, just holler. Breakfast is at six a.m." The caretaker hands over the keys to the suite and shuffles off to the office behind the desk.

I nearly groan at how early that is.

Venus stalks to the stairs without a glance back at me, and I have to run a bit to keep up with her.

"So, the honeymoon suite, huh?" I probe. She grunts at me as we ascend the stairs.

"Interesting, interesting," I sing-song at her back. We reach the top of the stairs and start walking down the long hallway. "I didn't know that it was this type of trip. I would've brought some lingerie."

She throws me a look over her shoulder, eyebrow quirked. "Is that right?"

I chuckle, curious to see if she'll cut off this banter or if she'll play with me. "Of course, I have one set that's reserved for my future spouse."

"Spouse? Not husband?" she asks.

She slows her pace so I can walk beside her. Interesting.

"I like both men and women," I offer, my hair sashaying behind me as I prance next to her. "I can see a fulfilling life with either." She's eyeing me curiously. "What about you?" I ask.

"What about me, what?"

"What do you...like? Men? Women? Both?"

She seems to consider her answer. "I have no preference. I've taken lovers of many different forms."

I hum. "That's called being pansexual."

"I have no such use for your mortal labels. Looks like this is our room," she says as we stop in front of a door at the end of the hallway. Inside the suite, it looks like the owners attempted to update the space with renovations, but then gave up halfway. The shag carpet is a deep green and yellow floral wallpaper is splashed across every wall. The small hallway opens into a large bedroom with the bathroom tucked into the side of the space. A four-poster bed sits against one wall, flanked by two light wood night-stands that are adorned with large vintage lamps. There's a white dresser across from the bed with a large TV on it, with a small writer's desk pressed against the window. On the other side sits a plaid loveseat that has seen better days—and likely many fucks.

It would look like any other suite, except for the large porcelain bathtub in the middle of the room

We both stop at the threshold, confused by the setup.

"Did she tell you the tub was in the middle of the room?" I ask, trying to clamp down on the laughter trying to bubble up.

"No," she responds, a bewildered expression on her face.

I can't help it—I burst out laughing. Like hands-on-my-knees, can't-breathe-properly laughing. She's looking at me like I've grown two extra heads, and it makes me break into another fit of giggles.

"What's so funny?" she asks, clearly annoyed and confused by my weird outburst.

"I just," I gasp, trying to wipe my tears, "You...you just look so...confused."

She presses her lips together, but her obsidian eyes seem to dance in the light.

I manage to pull myself together enough to straighten and walk over to the bed. I drop my bag on the floor and flop onto the mattress. "I can't wait to get to bed," I sigh. "So, where are you going to sleep?"

She's still standing in the hallway, simply looking at me strangely.

"What?" I ask, suddenly feeling self-conscious.

"I swear I asked for two beds," she mumbles, looking away from me, appearing to find the wallpaper *very* interesting.

Horror washes over me.

"No," I breathe. "No. Absolutely no way."

She reaches out and runs her fingertips against the wallpaper. For some reason, that makes my blood heat. Which makes me panic even more.

"There are no other rooms available," she informs me, dropping her hand and looking back at me.

"I can't sleep in here with you," I gasp out. Panic begins to overwhelm me. I know we have a deal, and working together is one thing, but sleeping in the same bed? I can't, I just can't.

My vision starts going dark around the edges, my body trembling from fear.

"Hey," she says softly, walking towards me with her arms outstretched, as if she might reach for me.

Terror and pain and death and—

I recoil from her as memories from that night ten years ago flood my senses.

She immediately drops her hands and stops her approach.

"I just—" I try to control my breathing, to get myself together. "I just...can't."

Some emotion flits across her face, but it's gone before I can name it and her face goes carefully blank. "Of course," she responds. "I'll sleep on the couch. It's alright."

The lump in my throat is making it difficult to speak properly, so I don't say anything. I just stare at her, wide-eyed, fear clouding my senses.

"I'll use the bathroom first," she offers, clearly trying to give me some privacy to either pull myself together or to have even more of a breakdown. With that, she leaves the room and clicks the bathroom door closed behind her.

I put my head in my hands, trying to calm my breathing and my racing heart. I breathe in for four beats, out for four beats. I do this seven times until I feel my heart rate slow. I'm not sure why I didn't put two and two together when we walked in here. I should have known when the old woman told us we were getting the Honeymoon Suite.

I sit up straight and stare at the floral wallpaper.

Part of me feels like I shouldn't care if she's sleeping on the couch. She's the reason I've been on the run for the last decade. She's the reason I can't get close to anyone or stay anywhere for long. If anything, I should be making her life way more difficult.

The other part of me feels like she's trying to act in good faith with me. She entered into that bargain with me to leave me and my soul in peace when we're done figuring out what happened to the missing covens. So there's no harm in us simply sharing a bed.

Is there?

I toss my head back and groan at the ceiling.

A few minutes later, she exits the bathroom and I've made up my mind.

Until I see what she's wearing.

She didn't bring a bag with her, so I'm unsure if she was hiding this under her clothes or if she conjured this out of thin air. She's dressed in a black spaghetti strap tank top that hangs low around her chest and hugs her stomach. The matching black shorts are basically booty shorts, hugging her generous curves. Her snake tattoo travels down her neck, over her shoulder, until the tip of the tail reaches her wrist. My mind short circuits as I look at her.

The Dark Lady has always been striking, but her beauty has never really affected me before. Not like this.

She's walking towards the couch when I realize I'm supposed to tell her I've changed my mind. "Wait!" I shout, then clap my hand over my mouth. She startles at my loud voice. "Sorry," I try again, clearing my throat. "I wanted to say that it's...okay if you want to, you know, share a bed. It's fine."

She cocks her head, scrutinizing me. I fight the urge to shrink under her intense gaze.

"It's okay if you don't," she finally responds after a few beats of awkward silence.

I shake my head. "Seriously, it's fine. I was just caught unaware, but I'm good now." I smile awkwardly at her. "You done in the bathroom?"

She nods and I hop off the bed. "Great! Well, guess it's my turn!" I grab my bag and scamper into the bathroom before I can think better of my decision.

❧❧❧❧❧ ❧❧❧❧❧

After I've gone through my skincare and hair care routine, I pad out of the bathroom into the bedroom. Venus is already in bed, propped up by some pillows and tucked under the comforter. I try to push my nerves aside and stride towards the bed. She looks at me and presses her lips together like she's trying not to laugh. I don't need to look down at myself to know I look ridiculous. I'm wearing a pink pajama set with cartoon poodles, I've got heat-less curlers in my hair, a few pimple stickers in the shape of stars on my blemishes, and my mouth guard in.

I shuffle over to the bed, eye mask and miniature noise machine in hand, and climb in. After awkwardly nestling in, we're both propped up against the headboard, avoiding eye contact.

"Um, wanna watch TV or something?" I ask, unable to handle the charged silence.

"I'm okay just how I am," she replies.

For the love of all that is holy. I grit my teeth. Either she's completely oblivious to the awkwardness of being in the same bed, or she's fully aware and just wants to torture me.

"Don't sleep with wings? That seems wise," I muse aloud.

She grunts.

I roll my eyes and try again. "Where do the wings go? Like, are they on-demand?"

She sighs, exasperated. "Why are you so interested?"

I shrug. "Just making conversation. I like to know a bit about who I'm hopping into bed with." And it'll help distract me from this uncomfortable situation.

She shuffles slightly. "I can will the wings to appear and disappear on-demand, as you so eloquently put it."

I ignore her jab. "And your shadows? Will they be making an appearance while I'm sleeping?"

"Why—do my shadows make you uneasy?"

"Of course they do. They attacked me, remember?"

"They didn't attack you," she scoffs. "They were trying to bring you back to me."

"I don't see a difference," I sniff. I dare to peek at her from the corner of my eye. Her arms are crossed, and she has a sour look on her face.

Okay, clearly this isn't helping lighten the mood.

I roll my shoulders. "I'm not going to apologize for being wary of you. You are at the center of something very traumatic for me. I blame you for why my life has been so...unfulfilling." I take a deep breath. "But you didn't have to bargain my freedom with me. So, if you're operating out of good faith with me, then I can do the same with you. And, again, I'm sorry for what happened yesterday—at the site. I didn't mean for my magic to do that." I twist to face her. "I'm willing to put aside the shit between us so we can figure out what happened to the missing covens."

She looks sidelong at me, suspicion in her dark eyes. "Not much of a grudge holder?"

I shrug. "I've learned I don't have time to hold grudges. I'm much more of a 'forgive but never forget' person—I'm happy to forgive someone if they own up to what they did, but I won't forget how someone made me feel."

Which is why this is so difficult, I think to myself.

It's as if she hears that unspoken thought because she uncrosses her arms and nods. "My shadows are mine to command, too. I can make sure they...behave while around you."

My lips quirk at her olive branch. It's not much, but it's better than nothing.

"Deal," I tell her. "We'll be, like, colleagues or something."

She seems to fight back a smile herself. "Deal."

It seems we're entering into a lot of deals together.

Feeling content with that—at least for tonight—I flop over onto my other side, place my noise machine on the nightstand, press 'bird noises,' and throw my eye mask on.

"Looking forward to working with you tomorrow, partner," I say before I drift to sleep.

Chapter Eleven
The Dark Lady

I slept like shit.

Partially because of Vivian's ridiculous sound machine. Who listens to bird calls to fall asleep? And partially because she was so close to me. Vulnerable. I was tempted to just reach over and take her soul all night. Her magic was like a siren's song, pulling me to take what is rightfully mine.

Let us be united, her magic seemed to say. *Just think of what we could do together.*

Taking a witch's soul provides them with a lot of benefits, but it benefits me as well. It allows me access to their magic—within reason. I learned what could happen when I siphon too much from a witch too quickly. I've gotten better at controlling myself.

They don't lose whatever magic they gift to me, of course. It replenishes quickly without issue.

It's reassuring to know her magic wants to be with me, even if the bubblegum brat herself is fighting it at every turn. It won't matter anyway, I remind myself. Her soul still belongs to me, and I'll be getting it by any means necessary.

And, alright, maybe I was feeling a bit of guilt all night. She truly believes I'll keep up my end of the deal we struck in her apartment. I haven't felt guilt for anything in…a very long time. I don't see the point in it. I'm the ruler of Hell. I have to do things that aren't nice, or pretty, or always fair. Life isn't fair, is it? So, I see no reason to be swallowed by this feeling.

Still, it's finding its way to me. I try to shove it down, but it seems to take root in the back of my mind, not currently vying for my attention but just waiting to sprout whenever it pleases.

Vivian awoke exactly at 8 a.m., bounding out of bed like a golden retriever, and headed into the bathroom without a word. That was an hour ago. I'd wonder if she was dead if I didn't hear her fiddling around in there.

Her scent was sweet last night, no ounce of fear to be found. Her scent, not marred by fear or anger, made my mouth water.

I sigh and throw a pillow over my face to get her scent out of my nose. This wouldn't be an issue if I had her soul—I wouldn't be so tempted, like a green youth.

Finally, I hear her open the door to the bathroom and remove the pillow from my eyes. She steps into the bedroom, looking fresh as a daisy. She's in tight, ripped blue jeans, a white flowy top, and a shaggy periwinkle cropped sweater. She has glossy boots on her feet and her hair is pulled back into a high ponytail. Her makeup, of course, looks flawless.

"Nice," I comment before I can think better of it.

She blinks at me, surprise in her hazel eyes, before she smiles tentatively. "I'm done in there if you need it."

I wave her off. "I'm ready to go whenever you are."

She finally seems to notice that I'm already dressed and nods. Suddenly I'm pissed at myself. How has someone so unobservant been able to evade me for a decade?

Vivian doesn't seem to notice my switch in thought, which isn't surprising, because she simply chirps, "I'm ready, then. Let's stop somewhere along the way for food."

I nod jerkily and rise from the bed, following her out of the suite. We make our way down the stairs and through the cluttered lobby. The owner must be a hoarder, considering how much shit is littered throughout the place.

When we walk up to the car, I say, "I would prefer to drive, if that's alright."

She looks over at me with her brows lowered. "Why?"

"Because I saw how you drive, and it's horrendous."

She gapes at me. "It is not! I've only been in"—she considers for a moment—"three car accidents. Not counting the time I drove into a building. And they were all minor!"

I shoot her an incredulous look. "You drove into a building?"

She waves her hand dismissively. "I barely caused any damage."

"Were you drunk?"

"No!" She has the gall to look offended. "I wasn't on my phone either. The building just...jumped out at me."

My eyebrows hike up with each word out of her mouth.

She huffs, throwing her ponytail over her shoulder. "Look, the rental is in my name, just like it was in Alton. There's no argument to be had here."

Without another word, she unlocks the door and slips into the driver's seat. I'm clenching my fists together tight enough to feel my nails dig into my palms.

This insolent little brat. It seems a temporary truce—although she doesn't know it's temporary—has led her to forget who I am and what power I possess.

I'm so lost in my agitation that I don't even consider the fact that I'm silently walking around to the passenger's side and climbing in. She turns the car on and lightly puts her hands on the wheel.

"See?" she says perkily. "Not so bad, after all. Let's get donuts."

❧──────❧

We're sitting in the Dunkin' Donuts parking lot with a box of a dozen donuts. Vivian, ever the princess, demanded all pink frosted. When she ordered a large, iced sugar coma drink, she turned to me and asked if I wanted anything.

"Coffee. Black."

She snorted and simply said, "Boring!" before telling the drive-thru operator. Then she paid with the credit card I gave her, shooting me a triumphant grin when she handed it to the cashier in the drive-thru.

I'm cursing myself for thinking this would be easy.

Now, she's sipping her creamer and syrup with a dash of coffee. "What's up with your name? You're named after the planet?" she asks out of nowhere.

I sip from my own coffee before I respond. "In a sense, yes."

She hums around the bite of a donut she now has in her mouth. "Why after that one? I always thought Venus was associated with goddesses of light and love."

I blink at her, surprise and something like pride filling me. I shove them down. "That's right."

She shoves the rest of the donut into her mouth. "That's ironic," she says, her words muffled.

She has no idea just how ironic it is.

I make a noncommittal noise and try to steer the conversation elsewhere. "I'm hoping today will be more successful than last time."

She frowns and looks down at her hands as if she can physically see her magic at her fingertips. Meanwhile, her magic perks up at my mention of it.

When she looks up, her eyes are almost...sad. I'm not sure what caused the shift, but something is upsetting her about what I said.

Before I can comment on it, she flips her ponytail and smiles prettily at me, although it doesn't quite reach her eyes. "Let's get going, partner!" With that, she revs the engine and throws the car into reverse. The coffee I'm holding splashes over the rim, narrowly missing me and landing on the car floor instead.

"For all that is unholy, woman!" I shove the coffee cup into the cup holder and grip the handle above the window.

"No time to waste!" she chirps and peels out of the parking lot.

We make it to the woods in record time. I think my nerves are shot.

Logically, I know I'm not in any genuine danger when she's behind the wheel—my magic allows for the quick healing of any wounds. My concern is what would happen to her if we got into a fender bender. When witches give over their souls, not only does it provide them with a long life, but they get access to quick healing.

Since Vivian's soul is not currently in my possession, she'll heal as slowly as a human. And die like one too.

I push those thoughts from my mind once we reach the spot where the commune is. I alter the wards to allow us in and out but keep the homes invisible to all others, and when we step out, I observe what's left of the space. The homes all seem to look nearly pristine from the outside—but the inside tells a different story.

Lead sits in my stomach the closer we get to the homes.

Witches are my loyal subjects. They sign over their loyalty to me, and in return, I provide them with long life and protection. I've failed them. I should've checked in more often. They're further from a summoning place, and they never raised any alarms, but I should've made myself available.

I failed these witches—I failed Elizabeth and George. I failed Mary and Sarah and Rebecca and—

A hand lightly touches my shoulder, and I shudder under the touch. I look down and see FUCK written across the nails.

"You okay?" Vivian asks me delicately.

I focus on the design on her dainty nails—it is clearly a dig at me. I breathe in and out, trying to get a hold of myself. Vivian doesn't remove her hand, as if she can sense my necessary fixation. She stays still as a statue while I get a grip. After what feels like an eternity, I nod and step away from her touch. Her arm falls limply to her side.

"I...it's just hitting me that this is my fault. I didn't let myself think about it in Alton, but now..." My voice is hoarse. My magic is pressing against my skin, letting me know it's desperate to get out, to defend me.

I let a bit of my shadows out—just enough. They swarm around me, assessing and investigating the perceived threat. Once they're convinced I'm safe, they slither towards the empty homes to get to work.

I turn to Vivian and her face is pale, her eyes tracking the moving shadows. "Sorry," I grit out. "I know they make you uneasy, but—"

"It's fine," she cuts me off. She rolls her shoulders back and a look of determination sets her features. "Let's get to work."

Chapter Twelve

Vivian

The coven grounds look similar to the one from yesterday: nearly identical homes spaced out in a semi-circle. We slowly approach the home in the middle of the line, looking for any sign of forced entry. I step onto the porch, noticing the front door is ajar.

I look within myself and notice my magic is roiling around inside of me, ready to do the Dark Lady's bidding. It's almost giddy to be so close to her. I want to roll my eyes—it's like it's horny for her or something.

I start to feel panicky. My magic is too strong, too eager to get out and do whatever it wants. I can't ruin this site like the last one.

I'm trying to clamp down on my magic, trying to get it to cooperate, but it doesn't listen. It simply presses harder against me, looking for a way out.

"Picture your magic," I hear Venus say behind me. "Think of it as an extension of you. You and your magic are one and the same."

"Doesn't feel like it," I say through my teeth. "Feels like it's trying to rip me apart from the inside."

"Talk to it," she coaxes.

I roll my eyes but figure if anyone knows what to do, it would be her.

So I look into myself, finding my magic thrashing against the hold I have on it.

Listen, I tell my magic. *I'm going to let some of you out.*

It flips at that, like an overeager otter is sitting inside me.

But, I tell it, *only a little, and you must come right back once I'm done.*

It flares in indignation at that but doesn't push. So I let some of it spool out of me. I picture my magic like a ball of yarn I'm letting go; it unravels out of me and into the world beyond. The yarn ball of magic rolls into the home, investigating, searching for anything dangerous that might try to harm us.

I can feel the Dark Lady's presence at my back, but I don't give her any of my attention. Keeping myself in charge of my magic is taking all of my concentration.

My magic has sniffed around the entire home and has deemed it safe enough to enter, so I do. Still holding onto that invisible tether, I push through the front door.

The place is a disaster—furniture upended, glass shattered across the floorboards, and a puddle of something that looks awfully similar to blood.

What's most worrying, though, are the large gouges in the wood floor by my feet.

"What happened?" I whisper, mostly to myself.

My magic is sweeping across the space, digging into the walls, the floorboards, and down into the earth beneath. It's as desperate to find answers as I am.

Tunneling into the earth, into the grass and dirt, my magic pauses. Sensing.

I see it then. Just like I did when I pressed my hand on the black stone monolith all those years ago.

Something swept into the clearing, past the magical wards this coven had put up. It was some other magical being and knew how to not trigger the alarms. It came in the night, on phantom winds, searching, searching for—

It snuck through their door, crept up the stairs, and swept into their rooms. It blinded them, gagged them so they couldn't scream. They tried fighting back, but it was no use—it just made their deaths more violent, more gruesome.

What it came searching for was not here. It was time to move.

But this was nothing compared to what it will do once it finds—

"Vivian."

My name snaps me back into my body.

The Dark Lady is standing in front of me, hands on my shoulders. Her onyx eyes are wild as she scans my face. Her wings are cocooned around us, her shadows swirling around our feet.

I blink and shake out of her grasp. She releases me and pulls her wings back. We both seem to master ourselves because she clears her throat and makes an effort to look around the trashed room we stand in.

"What happened?" Her voice is rougher than usual.

"I..." My magic has returned to me. It's curling in on itself, scared of what it discovered. I doubt it'll come out to inspect the other homes—not that I want it to.

"You're right, the witches didn't leave of their own accord. They were...murdered." I choke out the last word. "And I think fed upon somehow. It felt like their very souls were devoured. I couldn't see everything clearly, but..." I trail off. "Whatever it was, it was some form of magic. It slipped past their wards undetected, rendered them useless, and killed them."

Her wings rustle. "What else?"

I hesitate but finally say, "It was...looking for something. I didn't get a clear picture of what, but it was searching for something here. It thought whatever it was looking for would be here, but it wasn't."

Her gaze doesn't stray from my face. That intense, scary stare. I look everywhere but at her eyes. The serpent on her neck seems to slither in annoyance. I blink, but then it's back to its original position. Her shadows slither along the floor, searching for more information. She gives me her back and walks over to a frame that's on the floor, shattered glass all around it.

She removes the photo within the broken frame and looks down at it while she says to me, "This was a smaller coven—only five families. This home belonged to Elizabeth and George. They had been together for eighty years but still looked like they were in their twenties. Elizabeth had numerous miscarriages and they were unable to conceive a babe." She blows out a breath. "She thought I would punish them for their inability to bring a witchling into this world." Her tone seems sad. "But I would never do that. Never had I done that for others who couldn't conceive. It never made sense to."

Something nags at a forgotten memory at her words. She walks over to the fireplace and props the photo on the mantle.

"Their souls never came to me. They were good, loyal servants—and now they don't get to reap the rewards of that," she says.

She finally turns to me, and her expression catches me off guard.

It's pure wrath.

Her shadows seem to respond to this shift because they return to her and gather around her shoulders, her wings, her legs. As if in protection of a threat.

I stagger back a step, that primal fear filling my veins.

"I want whatever did this to be punished," she growls at me. "I want to rip them limb from limb."

I nod jerkily, unsure of what I'm supposed to do in this situation.

She closes her eyes and inhales through her nose. Her shadows swirl in her hair, making it difficult to see which is shadow and which is strands. "I've frightened you."

I open my mouth, but nothing comes out. I close it, take a breath, and try again. "How do you—"

"I can smell it on you," she responds, as if that's a totally normal response.

Before I can puzzle over it further, she clears her throat. "Let's move on to the next house. Maybe there's more we can uncover."

"Um," I say meekly. "My magic..."

She tilts her head, sending some of her shadows scattering.

"Your magic is also frightened," she guesses.

"Whatever it was, it freaked my magic out. I don't think it'll come out anytime soon," I tell her.

Venus nods. "Well, there's no use standing here, then. Let's get back to our accommodations and start again tomorrow."

I start. "Accommodations?" I ask dumbly.

Despite the horrible circumstances, she smirks at me. "Did you think I'd let you stay all by your lonesome? I'll be staying with you. Again."

"You are *not* staying with me. Again." Not only because she scares me, but because I'm suddenly afraid of how this proximity is affecting me. It's starting to make me feel…tingly.

"Yes, I am."

"Why can't you get your own room? I know you can afford it."

"I know you know," she grumbles. "Because you spent a fortune on that rental and on your little girl's day, but it doesn't matter. We should stay close to one another."

I bite my lower lip. "Does that mean I'm a target for whatever this thing is? I never gave you my soul though. Does that mean I'm somehow immune?"

We turn towards the door and exit the trashed and abandoned home, making our way back to the car. She walks in-line with me, peering down at me from the corner of her eye. "Doubtful. I don't know of any witches that don't swear fealty to me, so I can't be sure, but I doubt you'd be any safer than any other witch."

I consider this as we make our way to the car. We both start towards the driver's side. We look at each other with disbelief before I step around and plant my back against the door of the car. "The rental is under my name. There's no way I'm letting you drive."

Her wings shift in annoyance. "I'm not in the mood, Vivian."

My name on her lips makes my magic stir and my stomach flip, but I ignore both sensations.

"Can't you just, like, fly there?"

She rolls her eyes, clearly not budging on this.

I sigh. "Look, we can drive together, but I will be the one to operate the vehicle. Can we please just go?"

She looks perfectly content to stand here and argue with me but closes her eyes for a beat and grits out, "Fine." She stalks to the passenger's side and grips the door handle a bit too tightly as we pile into the beautiful car.

We visit the coven site again the next day, Venus feeling confident my magic is manageable.

By the time we've swept through all five homes, both my magic and I are exhausted. I sit on the porch of the last house we scoped. The story appears to be the same. The creature—whatever it is—swept into each home, looking for something, and destroyed everything in sight when it didn't find what it wanted. It seemed to feed on the witches somehow. When I tried to push for more, to see what type of being this was, I was met with...a wall of some kind. Like I couldn't get through because whoever or whatever it is doesn't want others to know.

I rub my temples, a headache beginning to form.

I hear Venus's footsteps behind me, but I don't look up. She seems to pause before coming to sit next to me on the step. We're quiet for several moments.

She panicked yesterday—that much I know. She seemed to get overwhelmed by being back here. I can't blame her. I'm sure she feels responsible for what happened, even if it isn't her fault.

"Mary and Sarah lived in this house," she mumbles. I drop my hands and look at her. She looks pained. "They were twins. And that house"—she points to the home closest to us—"belonged to Susannah and Roger. Their witchling, Lydia, was seven." My heart drops at her words. "Alice and John lived next to them, and Rebecca and Percy lived on the other side. And, of course, Elizabeth and George."

I nod when she gestures to the house we inspected yesterday.

"I should've come out here more often. They rarely had any soul ceremonies—Lydia was the only witchling in recent years. They would rarely call on me for anything. I haven't been here in so long."

"I'm sorry," I say, because there's nothing else to say.

She looks at me with pain and sorrow and guilt—so much guilt in her onyx eyes that my heart nearly cracks. It cracks for the witches that died here, but it also cracks for Venus. For the guilt she must carry.

"We'll find out who did this," I tell her confidently, even if I don't feel it. She doesn't look convinced but nods anyway. "What do we do with the homes here?" I ask, looking around the clearing. "I doubt any other covens will be interested in using this land."

She hums her agreement. "We'll burn everything down. The land can belong to itself again."

My magic seems to like that idea as it flips in my stomach before it spins a few times and lays back down. I stand, dust myself off, and then offer my hand to Venus. She looks at it with a heavy level of skepticism.

"Let's find this fucker."

One corner of her mouth quirks up at my language and takes my hand in hers.

Venus made quick work of the clearing—all homes and barns destroyed, their rubble cleared away with a wave of her hand. She seems lost in her thoughts as we drive back to the B&B. She doesn't even comment on my driving. A few of her shadows are still out, perched on her shoulders. I try to hide my discomfort. I know she's not leaving them out to frighten me. Still, it feels like they're watching me. I keep one eye on them and one eye on the road.

We pull into the parking space and wordlessly walk into the B&B. I order us something to eat while Venus sits on the bed, staring straight ahead, her shadows swirling around her. When the pizzas arrive, I pay the driver and shut our door behind me.

"Food's here!" I say merrily, trying to snap her out of her thoughts. She doesn't even acknowledge me. Her shadows vibrate, as if annoyed I would dare disturb her.

I place the pizzas on the desk and turn to inspect her shadows. We didn't exactly have the greatest introduction ten years ago, but they've mostly kept out of sight or away from me.

I can tell they're curious about me—they seem to be watching me—and I hate to admit it, but I'm a bit curious about them, too. I tilt my head as I observe them.

One seems to become brave because it slithers down her arm, down across the floor, and approaches me.

I still.

It seems to consider me before silently slithering up my leg. I watch it with wide eyes, trying to calm my breathing. It moves up my torso slowly until it reaches my collarbone, goes over my shoulder, and hooks around the other. It's like I'm wearing a scarf. It doesn't feel cold like I expected, it just feels like gentle pressure.

A memory flashes through my mind of a dream I had just nights ago. Of being touched intimately, of writhing against something that felt just like this. I gasp and wave my arms, trying to dislodge the shadow from me.

That seems to snap Venus out of her thoughts because she looks over at me. "What?" she asks.

The shadow runs back to her as if I've scolded it and wants protection from me.

This must be a coincidence. There's no way—

"Did you..." I suck in a breath. "How did you get into my apartment that night?"

She slides off the bed. "I have my ways."

"And by that, do you mean you broke in with your shadows?"

Her brows furrow. "Why are you asking?"

My hands feel clammy. "Did you send your shadows into my apartment?" I demand, my voice sounding a bit hysterical.

"Vivian, I'm not sure why you'd be asking that."

A laugh bubbles out of me. "I can't believe it. I can't believe you sat there and accepted my words of acting in good faith when you've been lying to me!"

It's her turn to go still. It's almost eerie how she goes so still. "What do you mean?" she asks in a dark tone, but I'm not backing down now. I'm too angry.

"Don't play dumb! You sent your shadows into my apartment, where they found me naked and asleep, and fucked me!"

Her expression is now carefully blank.

"You did, didn't you?" I'm shrieking, unable to control the volume of my voice anymore. I don't even care;

I hope everyone in the building hears me. "You and your shadows are, just..." I sputter, feeling heat rise to my face. They saw me naked—she saw me naked. She pleasured me in my sleep. Too many emotions are running through me—anger at her for doing that to me, a bit of horror that she had been so close and I had no idea, embarrassment that a part of me is turned on by what she did, and confusion for being turned on by that in the first place.

She crosses her arms. "I wasn't aware it was so bad for you."

I choke. "That is just not the point!" I scream. "You and your perverted shadows can't just enter me whenever you all feel like it!"

Her chuckle is dark, and it skitters across my bones. My magic purrs at the sound. I grit my teeth, trying to get everything to obey me.

"Don't worry," she says calmly. The shadows around her neck disappear. "They won't bother you anymore. Unless you ask." She winks.

My mouth hangs open as she prowls toward me, taking up space, too much space. She leans down until her mouth is at the shell of my ear.

"Because, if I remember correctly, you enjoyed it."

A small whimper escapes my lips. My face is red hot.

"I look forward to hearing you beg for it." She pulls back, smirking at me, and reaches toward the pizza box.

I can't move, can't get my body to cooperate with me. I stand there, breathing heavy, trying to ignore the wave of arousal I felt when she approached me.

How did everything go so haywire?

"I'm going to use the bathroom," I push out, scrambling towards the other room.

I quickly shut the door and press my back into the wood.

I breathe in for four beats, out for four beats. I do this seven times until my body seems to calm. My magic, on the other hand, is apparently horny as Hell. It's jerking around inside of me, wanting out.

"Stop it," I hiss at it and at myself. "Get a grip on yourself."

It kicks my bladder in response.

"I know," I whisper, "but you gotta calm down."

My magic seems to settle back down, but my body is as taut as a live wire. I feel ready to explode, my arousal beginning to pool at my center. I try my breathing exercises again, but the feeling doesn't completely go away.

Apparently, I need to get laid if I'm so turned on by that.

Chapter Thirteen
The Dark Lady

When Vivian said I had been lying to her, I was worried she knew I had destroyed her precious forest from her childhood.

When my shadows were unable to retrieve Vivian after she made a run for it, her mother had fallen to her knees in front of me, blabbering her apologies, wishing I could show her mercy even if she didn't deserve it. It had been irritating, but I decided to spare her—after a lengthy interrogation, of course.

Where would Vivian go? Has she been planning this? Did you secretly aid in her escape?

Her mother had known nothing. No one in the coven had either.

From what the coven told me, Vivian was a bit of an airhead—she would do well in her lessons but always seemed to get distracted by a butterfly or a uniquely colored rock. She apparently loved to spend time in the wilderness that surrounded the commune, disappearing for hours and nearly giving her mother an aneurysm every time she went. She wasn't close with the other witchlings; they viewed her as strange, too scatterbrained, too bubbly.

I dismissed her as easily as they did at first, thinking I would catch her easily, but days turned to weeks, then months, and then to ten years, and she always evaded me. I realized then that I had underestimated her.

I tried different ways to lure her, hoping she would reveal herself.

By destroying her beloved forest. She doesn't seem to know the forest that helped her escape my clutches is no longer, scattered to the wind. Her magic would have felt it, no doubt, but she keeps such a tight leash on it. She had never shown herself.

It drove me mad at first, how she had kept out of my reach for so long. I was convinced someone was harboring her, some coven that was disgruntled or downright defying me. I had all covens on alert and sent demons scouring the world in search of her.

And they always came up empty.

I haven't told her what I did in the initial moments of rage. It's not really relevant anyway, but for a moment, I felt...worried. Nervous even.

What would happen if she found out her sacred wilderness is gone? I doubt she'll continue this investigation with me. Not only do I need her, but I find myself...wanting her close.

I can't tell if it's because I want to possess her soul or if there's something else at play here.

I shake the train of thought from me as I sit down on the loveseat and take a bite of my pizza. My shadows seem a bit disgruntled at being caught though. They're curious about her, just like I am. Maybe I should feel guilty that I sent them into her home to touch her, but for whatever reason, I don't. I know I shouldn't have. I know she didn't give me her explicit consent to be touched. But I was curious.

I wanted to touch her myself.

My shadows curl around my shoulders with a smug aura. I snort at them. Show-offs.

So many emotions seemed to run through her when she was shrieking like a banshee at me. Anger, fear, confusion, and...I couldn't be sure, but I thought I caught embarrassment.

And definitely arousal.

I knew she enjoyed herself in the moment that night, but when she realized it was me...seeing all of those emotions flash across her face and smelling them on her has me on edge. I'm not even sure why.

I shouldn't even be thinking about any of this, anyway. All Vivian is to me is a thorn in my side that I will remove eventually.

I won't entertain any other options.

I've spirited my shadows away and am absentmindedly flipping through the channels on the television when Vivian exits the bathroom. Her face is flushed and her eyes dart nervously around the room. She removes her crop sweater and the top underneath, revealing a tight tank top as if she got overheated and needed to cool down.

Her cherry blossom and pomegranate scent caresses me and my mouth waters. It seems even stronger now than it did just a few minutes ago. This is what she smells like when she's aroused.

My stomach tightens, and I dig my nails into my palms.

She clears her throat as she stalks over to the open pizza boxes, delicately takes a slice, and tiptoes over to the bed. My eyes track every movement. How she seats herself amongst the pillows. How she lifts the pizza to her mouth, chewing slowly before swallowing. My eyes dip to her throat, down to her exposed collarbones. Her tight tank top cups her breasts perfectly—like two perfect pomegranates, ready to devour.

My eyes skate down her abdomen—which looks so soft, so warm—when her eyes snap to mine. Confusion is written across her face, but her breathing has deepened, her scent blooming even more under my gaze. It takes all my self-control to not launch myself across the bed and expose her body to me, to drink her in, to hear what noises she makes. She lets out a little pant, her pupils dilating, as if she can also sense the direction of my thoughts.

I grit my teeth and stand abruptly.

"I need to stretch my wings," I grit out, my voice sounding like gravel. We don't take our eyes off each other. "I'll be back later."

She inhales sharply, her breasts rising with the intake of breath. I swallow, and before I can do something incredibly stupid and irresponsible, I dart out of the room.

I race down the stairs, as if I can outrun her intoxicating scent, and nearly knock over some of the hideous gnomes sitting in the lobby as I make my escape. I'm barely out the door when I summon my wings and shoot into the sky. I barrel towards the sunset, leaving the ghost town and the desire roiling in my veins behind.

Chapter Fourteen
Vivian

Venus has been gone for hours. Which is perfectly fine with me—I'm in desperate need of alone time. She's been affecting me in ways I didn't really imagine. I hate how she affects me. That she makes my blood heat. I can't do this. I can't...be attracted to her.

Trying to shake all the strange feelings from my body, I turn my attention to my phone, which I have been dutifully ignoring ever since I left my apartment. I have a few texts from coworkers sharing their condolences.

There's also one from Michael:

I heard you're out of town for your uncle's death. I'm so sorry to hear. Let me know if you need anything.

I groan and close out of my phone. I should be a good, nice person and respond, but I can't bring myself to. There's nothing wrong with him. Maybe if I was normal and not embroiled in all the shit I am with the literal Devil, we'd be able to see if something could blossom between us, but I can't drag him into my fucked up shit.

I'm not meant to have nice things like love.

So, I ignore his message, pull myself off the bed, and head into the bathroom. I splash some cold water on my face, then pat my face dry and decide to just start my bedtime routine. After about an hour of getting myself together, I hear the suite door open. I creak open the bathroom door just enough to peek through. Venus swaggers over to the bed, wings still out, and climbs up. Wings flared, she settles against the headboard and closes her eyes. I realize the feathers aren't completely black—they're an array of black, gray, and even hints of silver. Her wings rustle a bit as if trying to get comfortable as she shuts her eyes. They finally droop, framing her body, acting as a shield. She looks windswept, the braids down the side of her head loose, spilling stray hairs out in all directions, her golden skin flushed.

"I know you're watching me," she says without opening her eyes.

I let out a little squeak of surprise, accidentally dropping the hairbrush I have in my hand. I scoop it up, place it back in my toiletries bag, and shuffle into the room as if I'm a child who got caught with their hand in the cookie jar. I say nothing as I approach and climb onto the bed. She still doesn't open her eyes, but her wings fold inward, as if to give me space to settle in.

"So," I say, trying to sound cheery, but it falls flat to my ears. I'm determined to ignore what happened earlier. Mostly out of embarrassment. "What's next? We know the witches were killed and...eaten somehow. We know the creature that attacked them was searching for something, but we don't know what it is or what they want. Plus, we burned down the crime scene. So, what do we do now?"

Her eyes open and she peeks at me, her onyx eyes absorbing the light. "We continue looking. We go to the next coven that was attacked. There's one that was attacked a few hours from here. We leave here tomorrow morning."

I blink in surprise. "I can't just keep traveling."

She quirks an eyebrow. "Funny, that's all you've done the past ten years to evade me."

"I have a job that I actually like," I argue.

"Sure you do. Does this have anything to do with the human male I found you with?"

My eyes widen, and I blink innocently at her. "What makes you say that?"

Her own eyes narrow. "If it is, I'll make a quick stop there and kill him."

"Leave him out of this," I growl.

She chuckles darkly. "You wear every emotion on your face."

I bare my teeth at her. "And here I was, thinking you had moved on to wanting to fuck me instead."

So much for pretending it hadn't happened.

She leans forward, her wings shifting to cocoon us both. The surrounding light dims, unable to break through the storm of dark feathers. Her vision dips to my lips, then to my throat. The snake on her neck seems to open its mouth wider, as if it would love nothing more than to sink its fangs into my skin and rip out my jugular.

"Is this your attempt at flirting?" she asks.

"Is this yours?" I throw back at her.

She simply breathes in deeply. "You smell intoxicating."

"I forgot you can smell me," I whisper, sweat beading on my brow.

She hums, her chest vibrating. Her eyes track a bead of sweat I can feel forming at my temple and she leans forward slowly. Before I can ask what she's doing, she licks the sweat from my skin.

My insides turn molten. A small whimper escapes my lips before I can stop it. My magic is pushing against my skin, demanding to be let out, to play with the Devil, to finally be united—

Suddenly, light explodes in my vision, and I hiss, covering my eyes. I blink a few times and notice Venus has stashed her wings away to wherever they go. She's now leaning back against the headboard, hands propped behind her head.

"You better figure out whatever you need to tomorrow," she notes casually, as if she's completely unaffected by what just occurred. "We leave tomorrow morning."

Without saying a word, I flip over onto my side, giving her my back, and try to calm myself. So much for trying to manage my confusing feelings.

Somehow, I'm able to sleep through the night. The bird calls really come in clutch.

I'm dressed in a pink plaid top tucked into a brown corduroy mini skirt, knee-high white socks, and tall brown boots. My hair is blow-dried to perfection and frames my face with golden strands. I went for more subtle makeup, just some eyeliner with pink mascara and matching pink lipstick.

I look adorable.

I scheduled for the rental car to get picked up from the B&B and called off work again. I know I should just quit, but for some reason, I just can't do it. Maybe it's because this job gives me a sense of normalcy. I've been on the run for so long, always having to uproot whatever life I've created for myself. Maybe it's because I haven't had much of a life until now.

I'm not unfriendly; quite the opposite. I can make friends anywhere I go. Some people are put off by my bubbly nature, but I can usually win them over eventually. The problem is that I feared keeping them. I feared what would happen to someone I'm close with when I finally got caught by Venus.

Now that I've been caught, and she's entered into this deal with me allowing me freedom, I have a real shot at a life. Having friends I don't ghost. Maybe even a lover like Michael.

Having a normal life feels closer than ever.

So I don't quit my job.

I'm tossing the last of my toiletries into my bag when Venus storms in. She's been gone since I woke up. Her eyes travel over my outfit for a bit longer than necessary, gaze snagging on my high socks.

I clear my throat. "My eyes are up here," I quip.

Her eyes snap up to meet mine and her eyebrows narrow. "Are you nearly ready?"

I turn from her to zip up my duffel. "I'm all set!"

"Good. Although…" Her pause makes me turn back around to face her. "Your outfit isn't suitable for flying."

I blink and look down at myself. "I thought you said it was only a few hours from here."

"It is, but you aren't driving," she informs me. "We're flying."

"Well, I've never had an issue before." I ponder it for a moment. "There was one time the TSA agents lined up to pat search me, but I think that's hardly my fault for looking so cute."

"What? No." She shakes her head. "We're flying," she emphasizes with a rustle of her wings.

Horror immediately douses my good mood. "No," I say, determination coloring my voice. "Absolutely no way."

She tilts her head, studying me. "Why not? Afraid your hair will get ruined?"

"That, or that you'll drop me to my death."

She snorts. "You're too valuable for me to kill you."

I don't like that both my magic and my heart jump a bit at that. "I'm not doing it."

"Yes, you are."

"Am not."

"Can we"—she sighs, closing her eyes for a moment. The serpent on her neck seems to mimic the movement—"please just have one moment where we aren't constantly at each other's throats?"

I'm about to argue that we are not constantly at each other's throats when she gives me a pointed look. I close my mouth. Seeming to take that as agreement, she nods.

"Good. Let's get moving." She snaps her fingers, and my bag disappears.

Before I can ask what she did to my precious clothes, her wings also disappear, and she gestures with her hand to the door. I obediently head towards the exit, Venus on my heels.

"Too bad we didn't get to use the tub," I throw over my shoulder, hoping to inject some levity into this situation.

It seems to be the wrong thing to say though, because she doesn't respond. Once we've both exited the room, I slow my pace to walk next to her. We rush down the hallway, down the stairs, and past the empty check-in desk.

I pause, but Venus breezes past me toward the front door. "Don't we have to check out?" I ask, pointing.

"Already done," Venus states.

I shrug and follow along.

The streets are empty, which I find strange for a Thursday morning. I'm about to comment on it when I feel Venus wrap her arm around my waist. I jump and try to pull out of her grasp, but she simply holds fast. I look up at her face. Nothing but lethal focus is in her expression, and it's all directed at me. If this had been a few days ago, I would've dissolved into a terrified baby, but today, I see it as a challenge. I square my shoulders and hold my head high. Not shrinking away this time.

A smile laced with approval snakes across her mouth. "Ready?" she croons.

Oh, right. Flying.

I swallow. "Is—"

Her wings unfurl and we shoot into the sky.

My scream gets lodged in my throat as my stomach tries to fall out of my ass. We're gaining altitude so quickly that I wonder if I'll get the bends like scuba divers do—that's possible in the air, right? My arms wrap around Venus's neck, and I bury my face in the crook of her shoulder. Her arms wind around my shoulders and under my knees, so I'm being held like a child. Which I sort of feel like. I dare a peek over her shoulder to see her wings beating, pushing us forward. The feathers shift with the wind, reminding me how her wings might be powerful as a unit, but as individual feathers, they're surprisingly delicate. Without thinking, I unhook my claws from Venus and reach a tentative finger towards the powerful wings beating just behind us.

"Don't look down," she says, snapping me back to reality—and the fact that we're actually flying, and one wrong move could result in me being splattered against the ground that's very far below.

Oh god, I looked down.

"I'm gonna be sick," I moan before shutting my eyes and burying my face in her neck again, nausea churning my stomach.

Her chuckle rumbles against my forehead as it snakes up her throat. "Try to aim it downward."

"It's not funny."

"Absolutely not. Could you imagine, you're a normal person, just going about your business, when you're suddenly hit over the head with vomit? The impact would probably kill them. It would be such an embarrassing way to die."

I rasp out a laugh despite myself. "Everyone would talk about it."

"Indeed. There would be investigations into every airline that flew over at that moment. And when that proved not to be fruitful, people will argue if it was aliens or some religious phenomena, or if it was actually vomit to begin with."

"I'll have to send my condolences to the family," I respond into her neck, swallowing down my nausea.

She snorts. "It's the least you could do, seeing as your vomit is the cause of this fictitious person's death."

We both laugh and I feel a bit lighter. I'm still petrified, but Venus—surprisingly—is making it more manageable. I loosen my hold on her a degree and pull back a bit to look up at her. Her hair flows behind her like dark waves, her eyes watching the horizon. The beat of her wings is starting to feel melodic, rhythmic. She's warm, which seems to be the first time I register this. In fact, I don't feel cold at all, considering I'm in a miniskirt.

"Are you using magic?" I ask.

Her gaze flicks down at me for a moment before going back to the skies ahead. "Of course. We're shielded from sight and sound. Think of it like we're traveling in a large, invisible bubble—we're protected from the elements, and everyone is protected against seeing us."

"Can't you just, I don't know, jump from place to place?"

"My magic doesn't work like that. There are different summoning places across the planet, but it takes considerable work to transport using them. Flying is a lot less strenuous."

I consider that for a moment. So, it must mean she isn't all-powerful, like I had once feared. Her magic has limits. The snake's tongue slips past its mouth at me lazily. I narrow my eyes at it. "Why does your tattoo move?"

The serpent has the audacity to look affronted that I would refer to it directly.

"Magic," she replies. I wait for more, but she doesn't expand on that.

"That's it?" I push. "So, I could have a moving tattoo if I wanted?"

My mind begins rifling through what I could do if I could give myself moving tattoos when her voice interrupts me.

"No. Your magic is earth magic—and while it is basically unheard of in witches, that is all it is."

"So I won't turn into The Last Airbender?" I provide.

Her eyebrows furrow. "The last what?"

I shake my head, my hair shifting with the movement. "Never mind. I forgot you're the fearsome Devil for a moment."

"You seem to forget that constantly," she mutters.

I gape at her. "Are you joking? I was on the run from you for years. I could never forget what you are."

"Quiet down. You'll disrupt the magic and scare all the birds with your screeching."

Pouting, I look back over her shoulder again. "I never forgot who you were. You kept me from having a normal life, you know."

"Why would you want a normal life? You're a witch. You would have had all the pleasures of signing your soul over to me. Why throw all that away?"

"You wouldn't understand," I counter.

"Try me."

I take a breath, whoosh it out. I do that four times before speaking. Surprisingly, Venus doesn't interrupt my breathing technique.

"My whole life, I never felt connected to the coven. The other kids my age always thought I was too *'other.'* Which, honestly, was okay because I didn't really care for any of them either." The other children in the coven were always two-faced, always angling for a better position with the elder witches. "The adults thought the same of me—why would a witch like pink and be more interested in chasing butterflies than practicing spell incantations?" I laugh, but it comes out hollow. "My mother thought I would grow out of it, become more like everyone else, but I never did. She was always ashamed of me, feeling like I was a failure of a daughter to her." Pangs of grief reverberate through my chest.

"But," I continue before my heart can crack, "her twin, my aunt Judith, always understood me." A soft smile tugs at the corner of my lips. Venus stays quiet, so I continue. "She knew I was different too, but she didn't shy away from it or try to make me into someone I wasn't. She accepted me and even bought me frilly tutus that would lead to arguments between her and my mother. We walked in the woods behind our coven's land and tried to see how many types of flowers we could find. Sometimes, I think my time in the forest with Judith was the happiest I've ever been."

Venus goes rigid against me, her grip on my body bordering on painful. I pull back and look at her face, but her expression is unreadable.

"What is it?" I ask, following her gaze. Maybe we're flying towards something dangerous. Like a massive airplane.

She shakes her head but doesn't relax against me. "It's nothing."

I want to press her further, but she changes the subject by saying something that surprises me. "I could give you a tattoo if you'd like. That's the way you could have one like mine."

I choke out a laugh. "Oh, yeah? Wanna get matching ones? I want a little heart on my ass."

She throws me a bemused look. "I'm not doing that," she scoffs.

I throw her a half-hearted scowl, which makes her chuckle. She seems to relax again, as if the tension from a few moments ago has melted away. We fly in silence for a while. I don't dare look down again, so I keep my eyes glued to Venus.

I hate to admit it, but she is beautiful like this. She's not beautiful in a classic or conventional way but in a severe way. In a commanding way. In a way that steals your breath as if you'll be kept under her spell for the rest of your existence.

Her eyes are so dark, you can't see any pupils. That used to terrify me, but now...now I just find them intriguing. How they seem to both suck light into them and shine at the same time. They're framed by long lashes that seem to tangle together. Her skin is a gorgeous golden tone, looking like she's never had a pimple in her entire existence. She probably hasn't. Her mouth is wide, her bottom lip a bit too big for her top one. They're a slightly darker tone than her skin, like she's wearing lipstick, although I doubt she does. The sheer power of her could intoxicate others, I suppose. Could become addicting. My magic always seems more than happy to be with her, to be near her. I can see how witches readily agree to serve her, even if they didn't reap the rewards of such a decision.

"I want to discuss this coven before we get there," she says, interrupting my ogling. I startle a bit when I realize—I had been ogling, hadn't I? Staring at her profile like some horny teenager.

I clear my throat awkwardly, my face burning.

Luckily, she doesn't look down at me as she continues, "They're also a smaller coven of seven families. Another remote coven that was mostly self-sufficient. The last time I was called to them was when their youngest witch, Alina, turned eighteen. That was about thirteen years ago."

My mind sorts through this information, trying to understand the similarities between this coven and the others.

"So," I say, mostly thinking aloud, "all of these covens are further from summoning sites, and you consider them to be mostly self-sufficient. How would they reach you if they needed your help?"

"Every coven has a calling stone—it's made of the same obsidian stone as the monoliths. If they need me, they are to use it. It's a direct line to me."

"Wait, really?" I ask, surprised to hear this.

She nods. "Because your coven lived so close to a site, there was no need for them to have one."

I shake my head. "Why didn't you say anything while we were at the other location? I didn't see anything that resembled a summoning stone when we were there."

"I didn't think of it until now."

I gape at her. "You forgot, didn't you?" When she doesn't answer, I know I'm right. "Holy shit, that's incredible," I sneer. "You forgot about these covens, didn't you? Took their souls and immediately left them behind."

Her grip tightens on me. "It's complicated."

I laugh incredulously. "How old are you? Do you have no object permanence?" My laugh borders on hysterical.

"I have a lot of responsibilities," she growls. "I'm the ruler of Hell. Do you know how much I have to juggle?"

"Sure, sure." My tone drips with sarcasm. "Clearly too much, if you're only paying attention to covens once they've been murdered under mysterious circumstances."

I know it's a low blow. Venus was distraught when we were at the other coven site; I know she feels guilty for what happened, and I tried to erase that guilt when I saw it in her. Told her we'd find out what happened.

But maybe she deserves that guilt.

I remove my arms from around her neck and cross them over my chest. I don't want to touch her any more than necessary. I can't believe I was just studying how beautiful she is.

"I—"

"Save it," I snap at her, my anger building inside me. My magic seems, for once, to agree with me. We're both pissed.

"I don't need to explain or apologize to you," she growls.

"You do, though," I counter angrily. "We're supposed to be working together on this. Aside from how fucked it is that you forgot about them, you forgot this important detail that could help us solve this mystery. No detail is too small—it could be the difference between another coven being murdered."

I shuffle in her arms, daring myself to look out into the horizon. "And you don't need to apologize to me for their deaths. I don't deserve that apology. They do, though."

Chapter Fifteen
Vivian

It feels like we're racing against the sun. Venus keeps a consistent pace, but the Earth continues its cycle, where the sun is beginning to set ahead of us.

"We'll stop at our accommodations for the night," Venus says to me. The first thing either of us has said for the past few hours. "Then head out to the commune location tomorrow."

"Fine."

"Fine."

I roll my eyes. It appears age has no impact on pettiness.

She begins her descent, tipping us to the right, her wings working to stop us from landing too quickly. Her magic bubble doesn't stop the wind from whipping past us—as we land, the wind tosses my hair all over my face, skewing my vision. My organs don't seem happy to be dropping out of the sky. I let go of my pride to wrap my arms around her neck again. I shut my eyes and try to gulp down air, but it moves too quickly past me to get enough down. I pull myself closer to Venus, hoping to get some respite. I press my face into her neck completely, my lips brushing against her skin. The snake tattoo seems to hiss at me, but I ignore it—I need air, I can't get any—

I take a deep inhale and find this position is blocking the gusts of wind from assaulting my lungs. I fill them with air greedily, letting my ribs expand almost to the point of pain, and let it out against her throat. I can't hold onto my anger at her in this moment. At this point, this is a matter of not passing out from lack of oxygen. I continue my deep breaths into her skin, feeling it cool and heat as I continue.

She doesn't say anything, but I swear I feel her arms hold me a little closer to her body.

After a lifetime, we're stationary on the ground. I keep breathing—in, out, in, out.

"Whenever you're ready," Venus drawls, but she doesn't drop me to the ground like I expect her to.

Once I'm sure my body will obey me and not drop like a bag of rocks, I slowly untangle myself from her grip. She lightly places me on my feet. I stare down at my shoes pressing into the soft earth beneath me. My magic leaps out of me and burrows into the ground, testing, stretching—I yelp and try to reel it back in, but it's too late. It's ground into the soil, finding flowers and earthworms and soil mites...

Back, back, back, I'm scolding it, barreling over onto all fours and pressing my hands into the grass, trying to pull it back into me. It seems to strain against me, and I grit my teeth, commanding it to *get back here this instant.*

Reluctantly, it acquiesces, spooling back towards me. I angrily receive it, gathering it back into myself. Once my magic is firmly back in my body, I slowly shudder out a breath and stand.

"Interesting," Venus murmurs from behind me.

I look over my shoulder at her, but she's not looking at me.

She's looking at the space around us. I turn to follow her eyes and my breath catches in my throat.

The world has come alive.

Grass now stands as tall as my knees, swaying gently as a breeze passes. Dandelions scattered throughout the grounds are as big as my head, some seeds drifting through the surrounding air. Smaller wildlife has scurried out to enjoy the changed scenery—mice dart through the thick blades of tall grass and birds swoop to catch worms that now wiggle along the ground. Even the trees in the distance seem to stand taller, prouder, their leaves sparkling.

"I—" I choke, left nearly speechless.

"Beautiful," she whispers into my ear. I nearly jump out of my skin. I hadn't heard her approach.

Her front is lightly pressed into my back, heat radiating from her and seeping into me. I find myself leaning into her, seeking her out.

"Look at what your magic can do. It's extraordinary," she tells me. Her wings curl slightly around us, blocking my peripheral vision. She lightly strokes my braided hair and my eyelids flutter.

"Yes," I breathe, because it's the only thing I can think to say.

It is *extraordinary*.

For the briefest of moments, I don't hate my magic. I want it to drive deep into the earth and let it rework this entire planet. I want it to transform everything. *I* want to transform everything.

My magic and I have always felt separate, but...maybe I don't want that anymore.

Venus's hands continue stroking my hair, and I nearly start purring. My back arches and I press my legs together for some friction.

"We could do so much together," she croons in my ear.

Yes, I think. *Yes, yes, yes*—

"All you have to do is say it." Her lips caress the shell of my ear. "Say it's mine and we will remake this world."

It's like a bucket of ice water being thrown in my face. My eyes fly open, and I nearly trip to get out of her grasp, spinning to face her.

"Are you really trying to manipulate me into giving you my soul?" My eyes are wide and I'm panting—whether it's from arousal or anger or a mixture of both, I don't know.

She crosses her arms over her chest, her wings rustling in agitation. "Why are you so resistant? Look at what you can do." She extends her arms to gesture to the surrounding greenery. "I can make you *more*. I can make you the most powerful witch who has ever walked this silly, floating rock. Don't you want that?"

"Not at the expense of my soul!" I shout back at her, my hands balling into fists at my sides.

She rolls her eyes. "What do you even want your soul for? To never use your magic and live a boring, temporary life? Find some mortal man to pump a few children into you, grow old, and die, without doing anything of real importance?"

"Stop," I tell her quietly.

"You're wasting your potential," she growls as she points a finger at me. "You're going to let yourself live a mediocre life—and for what? Just to spite me?"

"Stop," I say again, louder this time.

"All you're doing is hurting yourself by living this way." She looks down her nose at me. Her voice sounds just like it did at my failed ceremony—like it's coming from all directions, foreboding and powerful.

"You are the reason I'm living like this!" I shout at her. My anger is building inside of me, too quickly for me to tamp down. "You have caused me to live a lonely, sad life with no genuine connections to it because I am *terrified* of you taking *everything* from me!"

She snorts, dismissive. "All I would do is provide you with the life you deserve."

The leash I keep on my anger snaps. I rush her, my palms outstretched, slamming into her chest. She stumbles back, shock registering on her face, but I don't have time to think about it—I push her again, and again, and again.

"Do you know what my life has been like because of you?" I cry out, my hands now gripping her shirt, pulling her face close to mine as I shout. "I have no real friends and no romantic partners because I am scared shitless that you will appear and make them suffer for getting close to me. I have hated my magic because of you." My voice cracks and I hate that it cracks. I stare into her depthless eyes and say quietly, "But I choose the life I made over the one I was nearly forced to live because I'm not shackled to *you*. I get to decide who I am—what I wear, what I like. I can be whoever I want to be. And I swear, if you try to trick me into giving that up, I will *destroy* you."

Her face is slack with shock—whether at my words or my actions, I don't particularly care.

So I bring her even closer until our noses are touching. "I have agreed to help you, but I will not play these power games with you. You have one last chance with me. If you ruin that last chance, then us working together is *done*. I don't care about the deal we made—I will walk away from that and this investigation if you fuck this up. Am I understood?"

Something sparks in her eyes at my tone, but it's quickly replaced with a blank expression. "Yes," she mutters. "You're understood."

I release her shirt and step back. We look at each other in silence for a beat, assessing one another. Her shirt is crumpled, but she makes no move to straighten herself out.

"The cabin we're staying in isn't far from here." Her voice is rough, as if she's trying to keep herself under control.

Good.

I nod at her. "Lead the way."

The cabin is secluded in the forest—the road isn't even paved and there are no streetlights, throwing the entire area into darkness. I'm fighting to not trip over my own feet, but Venus doesn't slow her pace as she approaches the dark home. I'm about to joke if she booked this place on Airbnb, just to ease some of the tension that I feel partially responsible for, but she simply waltzes through the front door and begins turning on lights.

I stand in the doorway hesitantly.

The place is cute, albeit old-fashioned. There's a plaid couch facing a small TV to my left, a fireplace against the far wall, a desk against the closest wall, and a hallway ahead of me that must lead to the rest of the home. Venus disappears down that hallway without a word, her wings having to curl inward to stop them from brushing against the confined space.

I step into the entry and heave a sigh. I feel physically and emotionally exhausted. My magic seems to feel the same, after its little stunt earlier. I slowly, so slowly, drag myself over to the couch and sink into it. Looking down at my shoes, I will them to just remove themselves without my physical intervention. Unfortunately, they stay on my feet.

I'm starting to push myself forward to take them off when Venus appears out of the corner of my eye. I don't bother turning to look at her—I'm not ready for round two. Without a word, she walks around and kneels in front of me. I freeze, unsure of what she's doing until she gently grips one foot and slips my boot off then does the same to the other. She keeps her gaze on my feet as I keep mine on her. She starts to rub my feet, massaging her thumb into my soles and I bite down on my tongue to stop myself from moaning at the sensation.

I lean back and nearly melt into the couch—the Devil is giving me a foot massage.

Her dark hair cascades around her face, her eyes intently monitoring my foot that she's working. Her wings drift forward, their tips folding inwards to touch the couch on either side of me. Keeping me caged in.

She hits a ticklish spot and I let out a little giggle, trying to pull my foot from her grasp, but she holds tight. I see the corners of her mouth lift at my reaction, and she presses into that same spot again.

I'm thrown into a fit of giggles. "Stop, that tickles!" I try to wrestle myself out of her grip, but she refuses to release me as I squirm.

She stops messing with that spot and moves on to the other foot.

"You were right," she says to my feet. "I know I'm the reason you've been living the way you have."

My ears burn thinking about what I revealed during my little outburst.

"I mean, I didn't know for sure, but I could have guessed." Her fingers dig into my arches firmly and my toes splay out. "I know you must want an apology from me, but I don't think I can give one to you. At least, not a sincere one." She looks up at me then.

"I cannot apologize because I do not understand. I do not understand why you are so resistant to this. What I can give you. How we can work together. You said you enjoyed getting to choose who you are in your life now, but...are you really living?"

Her question pins me to the spot.

"Are you really living?" she repeats. "You have no friends, no lovers. You've been looking over your shoulder every moment, worried I'm going to steal you away. What is so wrong with wanting to give your soul to me?"

She's...hurt.

My mouth parts in surprise and I blink at her a few times.

"What is so wrong with that?" she whispers hoarsely.

"I'd never decided anything for myself before," I stammer out. "Every single thing in my life was chosen for me. I wasn't my own person."

"I would have let you be whoever you wanted to be."

"Would you?" I push. "Would you have allowed me to traipse around in pink and sparkles and tutus?"

Her mouth flattens into a hard line.

"I didn't think so," I scoff. "And time with you has only proven what I've always been afraid of: you don't protect those who have been nothing but loyal to you. You hadn't checked in with either coven that has disappeared."

Guilt swirls in her eyes. As it should.

"You're the ruler of Hell. You don't deserve the blind loyalty you're given." I lean down and remove her hands from my foot but hold firm. "But you could be." My tone is urgent now. "You could be," I repeat before loosening my grip, but she grips my hands tighter.

Her eyes search mine, her wings moving to lightly caress my cheeks. "I will be. I will make mistakes along the way, but I will be better." With one last squeeze, she releases my hands and her wings pull back, letting the dim light of the cabin reach my eyes again.

I smile tentatively at her. "I think that's a good place to start."

Chapter Sixteen
The Dark Lady

Vivian is in the shower as I sit at the cabin's dining room table. I tap my tattoo once, twice, zapping a bit of magic into it. I feel it disappear from my skin. As I wait for it to return, my thoughts drift to my new favorite thing to think about.

If I wasn't going to let Vivian go before, I certainly am not going to now.

No one has ever spoken to me the way she has. When she raged at me, I was so shocked, I couldn't even do anything but stand there and let her. She sees me. She wants me to be better. I'm not sure I even *can* get better, but for the first time, I want to try. I want to be the being she thinks I can be—one that cares, one that has earned loyalty—and if I show her I'm willing to be a better ruler, then she'll want to give me her soul, and maybe even more.

Now I'm pleasantly surprised that I've underestimated her. She has always been slippery, staying out of my grasp for so long, but if she wasn't a challenge, I realize I would be bored. I want her to keep challenging me.

And she's right—I've neglected my responsibilities. When she ran from me all those years ago, I became obsessed with finding her. It was all I could think about. I stopped doing anything that didn't involve hunting her.

I feel my tattoo return, snapping me from my thoughts. Then an arch demon appears across the room from me.

Luke seems to take in the tiny dining room around us. He bows his head as a sign of respect. His red skin and pitch-black horns look startling under the dim cabin lights.

"Your Grace," his gravelly voice travels to me.

"Any news?" I say to him instead of a greeting.

He shakes his head, his black horns glittering in the artificial light. "No new covens have been attacked, and there are no signs of malcontent within any of the covens."

I hum, drumming my fingers on the table. His eyes seem to track the movement, although it's difficult to truly know—his eyes are pure black with no irises and no whites.

Luke is my second-in-command, a powerful arch demon who had risen through the ranks by pure cunning. He uses his skills as a soldier to deal with enemies, but his mind is the real weapon.

"My concern is not that the witches are stirring up trouble against me," I say to him, thinking about how Vivian's magic reacted to the creature that killed the coven. "My concern is that a certain someone has awoken and wants to take what is ours."

He nods. "I agree. I've reached out to the other arch demons throughout the realm, and they fear the same. They sense something is amiss, but they can't tell what."

"Once I'm done here, I'll gather the arch demons and the High Priestesses, and we'll determine what to do from there."

"And when will that be?" he asks, his head turning slightly to the sound of the shower shutting off.

"I will let you know," I reply, my tone laced with warning at his questioning me.

He dips his head. "Apologies, Your Grace. I was merely curious."

"Hmm," I say noncommittally, lifting my hand to examine my nails. "I'll summon you after seeing the site of this next coven."

He says nothing else as I tap my tattoo again, and I watch it slither down my body towards Luke. It wraps itself around him, growing larger and larger until it encompasses his whole body, and transports them from sight. I could've told my serpent to wrap him tight enough to break some bones, but I didn't.

See, Vivian is rubbing off on me already. I think she'd be proud of that moment.

My tattoo has reappeared just as Vivian exits the bathroom, a towel wrapped around her body and another around her head. She pads into the room, her eyebrows furrowed. "Were you talking to someone?"

"I was not," I lie smoothly and gesture to the chair to the right of me. "Sit. Let's discuss tomorrow."

She hesitates, most likely so she doesn't have to sit next to me in just a towel, but she obeys. She grips the top of her towel as she lowers herself into the seat. "Okay. Let's discuss, then."

"You'll need to do what you did in Missouri, but you'll need to push further. No new covens have been attacked, so this is our last chance to catch who—or whatever—this is before they can hurt anyone else."

She nods, chewing on her lip absentmindedly. "So, my magic needs to figure out what is attacking the witches tomorrow. No pressure."

"You need to stop thinking that you and your magic are separate beings. You're one and the same. Don't let it run away from you like you did tonight."

She looks at me, scrutinizing me, and a look of concern flashes across her face. After a beat of silence, her expression smooths out and she heaves a sigh. "Alright. I'll get to the bottom of it tomorrow."

I grin at her. "Good girl. Now," I say, standing and heading into the attached kitchen, "I'm assuming you're hungry. What would you like?"

She snorts. "I doubt you can get delivery all the way out here...wherever we are."

"I'm not ordering anything," I say as I inspect the contents of the cupboards. "I made sure the owners of this place stocked up before we arrived."

Surprise splashes across her face. "So you *did* book this place on Airbnb."

"What? No." I find uncooked rice and an array of spices in some of the cabinets. "Some old friends live here. I sent word ahead of time that I would be in town and they offered to let us stay." I walk across the room to the fridge and begin rummaging through, spotting a few vegetables and uncooked chicken.

"You have friends?" she asks boldly.

I bark out a laugh as I load up my arms and slam the fridge shut. "Is that so hard to believe?"

She taps her index finger against her chin in faux thought. "Hmmm, let me see. Uh, yes, it is. How do you know them?"

I set everything down on the counter. "They're less friends and more...underlings," I admit as I search for bowls and a cutting board.

"Underlings," she echoes, sounding confused.

I line up all the equipment and get to work. "Demons," I clarify.

"I wasn't aware demons were allowed to live in this realm," she responds thoughtfully.

I shrug, beginning to cut into the raw chicken. "Only the most advanced ones can. They go through a rigorous clearance process—I can't have a lower-level demon coming into this realm, going into a frenzy, and eating everyone in sight."

She goes quiet for a moment and when I sneak a peek at her, she's stroking her amulet.

"What are you thinking?" I blurt out.

"I was always told not to go to the summoning place by myself because I could accidentally summon a demon."

"Ah," I respond. "I'll let you in on a secret. That's just something matrons tell witchlings to scare them. The monolith is a direct line to me and me only. Also, demons can enter the realm without a summoning stone—but only if I allow them access."

She's quiet for a moment, most likely digesting that information. I continue cooking in silence for a few minutes when she randomly asks, "You had said one of the couples that was murdered didn't have children and they weren't punished for it. Why didn't you punish them?"

I furrow my brows. "Why would I do that?"

"I..." She trails off, causing me to look over at her again. She looks confused and upset. "I thought it was required for witches to have offspring."

"I've never required that."

"Oh."

She lowers her eyes to the table and lightly touches her necklace again as if to make sure it's still there.

"That is a belief elder witches sometimes push. It makes sense, I suppose, to require it," I say as I turn my attention back to dinner. "There's always the worry that witch numbers will dwindle, but that's not what I'm concerned with. In fact, I'm concerned with the exact opposite. If witches reproduce too much, they might risk exposing themselves to humans. This has happened throughout history, as I'm sure you know. A witch exposing their magic, leading to their death or the death of innocent mortals.

"There's also the concern of magic depleting, watering down as it passes down generations. Which, unfortunately, has already been happening," I admit. I shouldn't tell her these things, but I can't seem to stop myself. "A thousand years ago, witches were some of the most powerful beings to walk this planet. Even one hundred years ago, they were still full of power. But now?" I sigh. "It is no longer the same."

I fight the urge to look over at her, to gauge her reactions to my words. Her scent isn't drifting over to me, so I'm completely blind to how this information is sitting with her, but I keep my eyes on the food in front of me.

"Why do I have earth magic?" she asks suddenly.

I still. Instead of answering her question, I give her a question in return. "Why do you ask that?"

"Because no one in my coven has it, and my mother and aunt never mentioned anyone having that type of magic. We never learned about this type of magic growing up."

I force my body to move, to act natural. I know I'm not a convincing enough actor to pull it off. The ingredients simmer in the pan atop the stove and I place a lid over it before turning to face her.

"It is incredibly rare, your magic," I offer, trying to sound nonchalant. "It has not been seen since the first witches walked the earth."

Her eyes widen at that.

I should stop. She doesn't need to know this. I don't want her to know this, but my mouth keeps moving anyway.

"The most powerful witch with earth magic was named Lilith. She could raise mountains and create fissures in the earth leading straight down to the planet's core. Everywhere she walked, the earth responded to her. Flowers bloomed and trees twisted to reach her as if she were the source of life. She could even cause entire forests to up and move to a location of her choosing."

Much like you, I nearly say.

Her eyes are as wide as saucers. She's picturing her escape from me ten years ago, much like I am.

"Lilith managed to find other witches with extraordinary magic and created the first coven. That was when she called upon me."

Lilith's face flits in front of my eyes, her long wine-red hair and deep forest-green eyes. I suck in a breath. I haven't pictured Lilith in so long—I was worried I forgot how she looked, the tone of her hair, or where every freckle on her face sat.

"Wait, she called on you? I thought you always ruled over the witches?" Vivian asks, pulling me from Lilith's smiling, ethereal beauty.

"I had no interest in witches. At least not at first. They were mortal, after all."

She shakes her head, confusion all over her face. "That's not what we're taught," she responds, as if I don't know my own history. "We're taught that you found the witches and had them pledge their loyalty to you, which included working alongside demons, using our magic for nefarious purposes, et cetera."

"Nefarious purposes?" I ask with a smirk. "What nefarious purposes can you think of, Vivian?"

She clears her throat delicately. "Oh, you know. Just..." She waves her hand dismissively and a blush creeps up her cheeks.

I snicker but let her off the hook. "No, that's not how it happened. I might have altered the stories passed down through covens over the centuries."

"Why?" she pushes.

I ignore her question and continue, "Before Lilith, I was content to be amongst the souls and the cruel and wicked creatures. Demons had finally begun to evolve and create their own hierarchy, and I felt Hell was progressing in the way I wanted. That is, until Lilith came knocking." I smile at the memory.

"She somehow managed to create a portal to Hell through her magic—I'm still not quite sure how, but her magic created the summoning stones. She waltzed right into Hell as if she owned the place."

"How did she know who she was looking for?" Vivian asks.

"She was always curious where the dead went." I shrug, turning my attention back to the food. "She saw what I created and wanted to be of assistance. If I would help her with something in return." I know Vivian is a curious, little creature, so I answer her question before she can even ask it. "Before the history you're taught began, a completely different world existed. A world of torture and pain and suffering. Humans were mere chattel to the gods—celestial beings who used to revel in the suffering they caused. Lilith came to me, hoping I would help her overthrow them. In return, she would willingly hand over her soul. I laughed at her proposal—I was meant to overthrow numerous beings as powerful as me, all for one soul? It seemed like a terrible bargain to me, so I sent her away.

"She wasn't deterred, though. She kept coming back every day, demanding an audience, becoming a real thorn in my side. I went to the realm of the living and destroyed the monolith, but somehow, she still managed to show up the next day. When I went back to the realm, she had created two in its place."

"Let me guess," Vivian pipes up. "She created all the summoning places—and then you decided to take the bargain."

I grin down at the food I'm now putting onto two plates. "She sweetened the deal. For my assistance, all witches would hand over their souls while they're alive and would become my subjects."

I pick up both plates and walk them into the dining room, placing one in front of Vivian, but she doesn't even look down at the stir fry that's steaming on her plate—instead, her eyes are glued to me.

"Was there a war?" she breathes.

I sit down across from her and nod to her plate as if to say, *eat and I'll keep talking*.

She picks up her fork and shovels a mouthful in, not even reacting to how hot the food must be on her tongue.

"There was," I say, my bones feeling weary. "It was the witches, demons, and myself on one side; gods of the earth and sky on the other. It was brutal. There was much bloodshed and death—innumerable losses on both sides. We were able to rid the world of most of the gods, except one. Think of him as my mirror opposite; he creates the souls of the living while I receive them after death. We could not defeat each other. To defeat one is to destroy all, but it didn't stop him from trying," I hiss.

I see Vivian's hand dart out and lightly brush her fingertips against the back of my hand. I stiffen under her warm touch but don't pull away. When I look at her, her eyes look so sad. She's trying to comfort me, I realize.

"What happened?" she asks gently, her thumb stroking across my skin.

Her touch helps me push the rest out. "He knew Lilith and I were...close. He took her and removed her soul from her—I didn't have it yet, you see, as that was how our bargain was worded. Instead of allowing her eternal peace, he destroyed it. Her soul no longer exists, and it never will again."

Vivian lightly holds my hand in hers. Her sympathy is overpowering now, her eyes filling with tears. For me. I can't stand the sight or the stench of it. I don't deserve it.

So I pull out of her grasp and pull my walls back up.

"He also damned all witches. When they die, their souls will have the same fate as Lilith's, so they pledge their souls to me."

She's looking down at her hand, still outstretched, as if confused as to why she's no longer touching me. Then she blinks and looks up at me. "So when I die," she whispers, "I will cease to exist completely?"

"If you die before giving me your soul," I respond, "your soul will be destroyed upon your death. You will be no more."

Chapter Seventeen
Vivian

I lie in bed, staring up at the ceiling. Luckily, I have my own room in this cabin.

Dinner ended in awkward silence after Venus admitted what will happen once I die.

If you die before giving me your soul, your soul will be destroyed upon your death. You will be no more.

My mind plays those words over and over and over until they blur together and are no longer actual words.

Ifyoudiebeforegivingmeyoursoulyoursoulwillbedestroyeduponyourdeathyouwillbenomore.

I try to think about this like a rational person instead of spiraling into an anxiety attack. On the one hand, I'll be dead when my soul is destroyed, right? So why should I care what happens after that? I doubt I'll even know what's happening to me once I'm gone.

But...what if I do? What if I'm fully aware of what's happening to me when I die? The witches always say we're given immortality once our soul descends to Hell. Is that what I'll be missing out on?

My stomach turns to lead. I made a deal with her where my soul will be kept out of her grasp, but if the cost is my soul's resting place...

Things would be easier if Hell wasn't ruled by Venus, I decide. I'm suddenly angry at her. I feel like she kept vital information from me when she entered into our deal. She's made things much more complicated, and it got even more complicated when she spoke of Lilith. It's clear Venus had a thing for her. They might've even been in love. And now Lilith will forever be kept from her.

I stare up at my ceiling fan that's slowly making its rotation.

Then something dawns on me. Does Venus want my soul so badly because my magic is so similar to Lilith's? It would make sense, I guess. Her lost love's magic hasn't been seen since she died, and here it reappears in me. I'm not even sure how that's possible either.

I huff, irritated, and shuffle to lie on my side.

I shouldn't let my feelings change about Venus, anyway. Especially not after learning her negligence plays a role in these dead covens. Witches bound themselves to her after she lost her lover, and yet, she can't be bothered to make sure they're safe.

But...maybe she just needs help. I remember how guilt had gripped her at the coven sites. I'm sure it would be similar when we venture out tomorrow too. She's just one...being. I could be, like, her assistant or something—keep track of all the covens, file her paperwork, get her boring black coffees every morning...

Spend late nights in the office—because this fantasy includes an office space, obviously— where we'd be the only two around. She'd call me into her office, asking where I'm at on some mundane project, when her shadows would silently shut the door. Sealing us in the room together. I'd boldly walk around to her side of the desk and perch myself in front of her, spreading my legs—

I squeeze my eyes shut, trying to banish the little porno my mind is coming up with. What the Hell is wrong with me? She just basically admitted she was in love with someone—and is most likely still in love with them—and that I'm damned if I don't give up my soul.

Surprisingly, my magic has been quiet since dinner—no nudging, no attempt to reach out to the Dark Lady like it usually seems to do. I look within myself and wonder if it's asleep, but it isn't. It's awake and alert but seems to have an edge to it.

Like it's weary. Maybe even sad.

I let out a little groan of frustration and throw the pillow over my head. Between my magic and my lizard brain, I'm confused and annoyed and a bit turned on. Which I shouldn't be—turned on, that is. The other emotions are totally valid.

Venus is the last...being I should ever be attracted to. She's dangerous and selfish and greedy. I can't let myself forget the torment she's put me through just because I think she's attractive. I press the pillow into my face a bit harder. This investigation has become more fucked up than I ever thought possible.

The next morning, Venus makes it clear that we are to fly to the coven location, but I tell her I want to go myself. She's, understandably, very confused. I tell her I looked up a small car rental place that I can walk to and that I'd like to do some exploring of the town after we're done. She's clearly ready to argue, but I refuse to back down until she lets out a long sigh and says she'll meet me there.

I don't tell her the real reason I want to travel separately. I think space between us is a must. Getting too close would not only mess up this entire investigation, but it would also mess up my head even more than it already is.

So, after a nice ten-minute walk down the one paved road to the car rental business, I peel out of their parking lot in the cutest little car they had.

Venus is gonna be so pissed.

Chapter Eighteen
The Dark Lady

I've been at the commune for twenty minutes and I already know there are no traces of the witches that dwelled here. I disabled all wards around the land, took a few steps onto the property, and just knew. I feel like I'm going to be sick.

All of these lives, gone. Taken. All because I was too wrapped up in finding Vivian that I lost sight of my true purpose. Lilith would be so disappointed in me if she could see me. See how far I've fallen off the pedestal that has been crafted for me. But she can't see me, and she will never get to.

I cannot decide if that's a blessing or a curse.

I walk for an eternity down the gravel road, unsure of where I'm going. All I know is I need a minute, an hour. I feel myself spiraling, my shadows swarming around me. I try to suck in air, but my lungs can't seem to fill. I gasp, again and again, trying to get my lungs to work.

And then, I hear it. A car driving up the road.

I know it's Vivian—somehow, I just know.

Something was different about her this morning. What I shared with her last night must have upset her or confused her. Maybe even angered her. This morning I couldn't get a read on her. Even her scent wouldn't tell me what she was thinking. Maybe she's figured out how to hide her true feelings from me.

I doubt it.

My shadows pull back, swirling around my shoulders and my wings as she approaches. She pulls up in a bright pink Volkswagen buggy and honks the horn at me—multiple times. I'm too busy being shocked that she would pick the most ostentatious car possible to be annoyed.

As she rolls down the window, a dazzling smile brightens her face, though dark sunglasses hide her eyes from me. One hand rests lightly on the steering wheel. "Like what you see?"

I sigh through my nose. "We don't have time for this. Get out. I'm driving us to the site," I say, realizing I've walked a few miles away from where we need to be.

She slowly places her free hand on the rim of her sunglasses and lowers them just enough for me to see her beautiful hazel eyes.

Right now, they're alight with mischief.

"Do you have a license to operate a motor vehicle?" she asks innocently, but I know she is anything but. She's riling me up on purpose. I clench my jaw but don't deign to respond. She knows I don't. She gives me a saccharine smile, something like mock pity entering her gaze. "That's too bad," she hums as she pushes her sunglasses back into place. "Looks like I'll be driving, considering I'm the only one of us who is legally allowed to."

My teeth grind down hard enough that they might break.

Without thinking, I reach in and grasp the car door through the open window. I yank once and the door comes dislodged from the car with the loud groaning of metal bending and breaking. I hold the door in my hand as if it weighs nothing. It really doesn't weigh much to me.

I take one look at her and all I see is shock—and rage—on her face. Sunglasses ripped off and eyes wide with mouth agape, she sits there, stunned for a moment, before trying to launch herself out of the car. She gets trapped by the seatbelt and battles it for dominance to get free.

I chuckle under my breath and turn on my heel, carrying the car door.

I hear her angry little footsteps behind me. "What do you think you're *doing*?!" she screeches.

I don't turn around. Instead, I merely plant my feet, swing my arm back, and toss the door. It shoots across the sky, seeming to gain momentum the longer it's in the air, until it finally flies out of sight. A quiet thud hits our ears a few moments later. Birds squawk and fly off in different directions.

She's reached my side now, and I glance sideways at her. She's breathing heavily, staring off at where the car door flew. "You—I—what are you—" she sputters, seemingly at a loss for words, which is new for her. Then she spins to me, her face contorted in anger. "This is a *rental*!"

I lift my hand to examine my nails. "You wanted to test my patience. This is the consequence."

Her mouth hangs open, gaping at me like a fish. The expression has laughter bubbling inside of me, but I push it down. I can't even remember the last time I laughed.

I'm driving the ruined buggy, Vivian in the passenger seat. We're in an awkward, angry silence—minus the sound of the outdoors, which is extra loud without a door. My shadows are working to stop any debris from flying at me, but it doesn't stop the wind from rustling them and making it quite loud in here. Vivian sits there, arms crossed, pointedly staring out the windshield with a permanent scowl on her face.

I'll admit, I might have reacted brashly, ripping the car door off its hinges like that, but I've never been known to be patient, and Vivian should know that. I clear my throat loudly, but she doesn't look at me.

"Maybe we should play some music," I yell over the wind. Still no response, not even a hint of movement. I don't think she's even blinking.

I press the volume button on the car radio and heavy metal blares through the speakers. I jolt, caught off-guard by the loud screaming that's filling the space and leaking out into the world beyond. I quickly switch it off and throw Vivian a bewildered look.

"Is that what you were listening to?"

She shrugs delicately.

I scoff. "You'll blow out your eardrums listening to music that loud."

"It's supposed to be listened to that loud," she spits.

"Uh-huh."

She twists towards me. "Who do you think you are, my mother?"

I chuckle. "I'm certainly not your mother."

"No," she responds bitterly, "although, you're not much worse than she was."

I think back to the tidbits of information Vivian shared about her mother. It seems Jessica was not the most warm or caring. I don't comment on it, though—I'm not a fucking therapist.

She's on one today. From this morning to now, she's seemed off. Part of me wants to comment on it. The other doesn't want to touch it with a ten-foot pole. I know it's related to our conversation last night.

She can have her issues—it's not my problem, seeing as I have more important things to deal with.

We pull up to the coven site, the trees thinning out as I maneuver the car onto the side of the road. Vivian climbs out without a word, her brows still furrowed on her pretty face, and I follow after her. She stalks into the clearing, her shoulders raised, her hands balled into fists. I keep back, not wanting to distract her. She continues until she's walking directly into one of the homes.

The houses are positioned similarly to the previous coven. Seven homes in a semi-circle, all of Victorian style. Each has its front doors ripped off its hinges, but otherwise, they all look normal. It's as if they've been abandoned instead of violated.

Vivian stops suddenly in the house's doorway, a pretty blue two-story. She places a hand on the door frame, as if searching for something. Sensing. I can feel her magic before I see it. It feels hungry, powerful, near bloodthirsty. As if the few times it was let out of its cage has woken the inner beast that it intended to be. The ground beneath my feet vibrates, the grass shifting, rolling. I look up to find the trees swaying violently, leaves and branches raining down. I hear the house groan under the might of her power. As if the building is an intruder and she's ready to destroy it.

I take a step toward her but pause once she lowers her hand and turns to face me.

Her eyes are open, but they aren't hers.

They're completely white.

A monster, perhaps nearly as wicked and vile as I, is staring back out at me.

Chapter Nineteen
Vivian

There is nothing but darkness in this place.

Despite my magic's panic, it's trying to keep the darkness at bay.

I'm not sure what's happening. I remember walking up to one of the coven's homes, letting my magic spool out of me like a ball of yarn, and seep into the earth. My magic was searching, searching until I saw flashes of what happened—like before. An evil creature, also searching for something and angry that it was not found here. It devoured the magic inside the witches and then killed them. Then...darkness.

I try pulling my magic back, but it creates a bubble around me.

Protecting me.

What has come searching for me?

I gasp and spin around, trying to locate the sound of the voice. It's dark and foreboding, but not in the way Venus's voice can be. This is the voice of a different kind of evil.

A lovely, little protective ward, the voice says again. I turn again, trying to track it, until I realize the voice is inside my head.

Horror sluices through me. I go ramrod straight.

I was curious who would come poking around. It seems my work has not been in vain.

Sweat slides down the back of my neck. My magic shudders but holds firm. Whatever it's doing, it's keeping us away from whoever is in the darkness.

Tell me, little witch, did you find what you were searching for?

"Let's go," I whisper to it, but I know it's useless. I don't know where we are or how we even get back.

Because I think I found what I was, the voice purrs in my mind.

"What's that?" I ask the voice.

It simply chuckles in answer.

I'm trembling from head to toe. My magic begins to press inward.

I know now, it answers vaguely. *Child of the earth.*

My magic races back into me, but it's too late—blackness has swept in.

I open my eyes to see a clear blue sky. A few birds fly overhead, and a gentle breeze touches my cheek.

I blink a few times and look around. Venus is leaning over me, her hands on my shoulders. I go to sit up, but I find my body feels sore. Like I just did a hot yoga workout the morning after eating three pizzas in one sitting. Venus gently pushes me, so I give in and lay back down on the grass.

"What happened? Did I pass out?"

Venus's shadows are swirling around my body, lightly pressing into various areas, as if checking for any damage. I ignore them and stare up at Venus. Her midnight eyes are alight with panic.

"What happened?" I demand again, more forcefully.

"You—I've never—"

"You're freaking me out," I tell her. "Tell me what happened."

The grip on my shoulders tightens. "Everything was fine at first. Your magic seemed to assess the home—I felt it working." Her throat works as she swallows. "But then your body was possessed by something else. By some*one* else. I could see it in your eyes—they transformed, turned completely white."

"Someone talked to me," I tell her, eyebrows furrowing. "My magic worked to protect me, but I could hear this voice in my head." I shudder.

"What did it say?" she demands.

"It said that it was curious who would come looking to see what it did, and that it knew who I was. It called me..." I pause. I force the next words out, "It called me a child of the earth." Venus's shadows wrap around my arms, my legs, my torso. They slither along my skin, making me feel trapped. I buck against them, trying to dislodge them.

"Shh," Venus soothes, her hand going to my forehead and stroking my hair back from my face. "They're just frightened for you. They'll relax in a moment."

I want to say something cutting, but my mind can't conjure anything. The shadows continue to swirl around me, but they don't press into me. I try to keep as still as possible.

"I think," I say hoarsely, "that whatever—whoever has been attacking covens knew you would investigate. It seemed like it was waiting, and by investigating, we've alerted it to our presence."

Venus's eyes say she's come to the same conclusion.

The shadows seem satisfied that I'm not harmed and dissipate. I raise myself to a seated position, and, after throwing me a disapproving look, Venus lets me.

"Why would it call me a child of the earth?" I ask.

Her jaw twitches. "I don't know."

"Don't lie," I snarl at her. "Some weird, evil being just entered my brain and said that to me. So don't you dare lie."

"I'm not," she says, her eyes wide, her hands open. "I truly don't know what it means. I'm assuming it's connected to your magic, somehow, but I honestly don't know what it means."

For some reason, I believe her. For now.

I sigh and run my fingers over my amulet absentmindedly. "Okay," I sigh, weariness seeping into my bones. My magic seems to be exhausted too. I reach inward and stroke a hand over it, to which it pushes into my touch. I smile a bit and bring myself back to the surface.

"We need to leave here," Venus says. "Right now."

"We aren't done—" I begin to argue, but she holds up a hand.

"The creature hunting witches knows who you are. We cannot risk poking around more until we know what we're up against."

I nod, suddenly feeling too tired to argue. My eyes begin to droop closed as Venus slides her arms around me, lifting me to her chest. I feel her walking, but I can't keep my eyes open.

"The car," I push out.

"I'll deal with it later," she says. The last thing I hear is her say, "Go to sleep. I'll protect you."

I wake up in one of the softest beds I've ever slept in—which is impressive, seeing as I'm a total snob when it comes to my beauty sleep. I stretch out like a cat napping in the sunlight when I realize there actually isn't any light hitting my closed eyelids. I peel them back and stare up at dark feathers. Venus has her wing draped over me. It shifts up and down as she breathes.

I look over and I inhale a sharp breath at the sight of her.

She's a force, even when she's in a deep sleep. She's face down on the bed, face smooshed into the pillow, with her mouth slightly ajar and drool trailing down. Her eyes flicker back and forth underneath her eyelids. I can't bring myself to wake her—I just keep looking at her face.

I've never seen her so relaxed. Of course, it's not like we're normal people, just going on a relaxing vacation, but still—I didn't realize it before, but she holds a lot of tension in her face, in her stance. She needs a spa day.

Although I doubt one spa day will alleviate the weight that she carries.

I mull over what the creepy voice told me when it possessed me. It seems, by trying to uncover this mystery, it's led the perpetrator right to us. It seems to know who I am—it might even know more about me than either Venus or I know about me. I chew on my bottom lip nervously. If Venus doesn't know what the creeper was talking about, we're screwed. We need to figure out what's going on, and how to get our answers without somehow awakening the creature again.

If only I could type *Witches have been disappearing and some creepy thing spoke to me in my mind. What do I do?* into the Google search bar.

Suddenly, the wing pulls back from me. I wasn't aware of how warm she was keeping me. I shiver as the room's coldness touches my skin, and when I look over, Venus is blinking blearily at me. Then, as if remembering who I am and what the fuck just happened earlier today, her eyes immediately sharpen, and she's running her eyes all over me, inspecting me for any new injuries.

I clamp down on my smirk. "Good morning, sunshine," I chirp at her. "I didn't know you drooled in your sleep."

She wipes the back of her hand across her mouth self-consciously.

"So," I say, shuffling to lie on my side and prop myself up on my hand. "What's on the agenda for the rest of the day? Rob some graves? Maybe find some dead people to bother? I'm feeling extra lucky today."

She throws me a withering glare, which makes me want to giggle. "I can't believe you can joke after what happened this afternoon."

I give a half-shrug. "I was scared shitless earlier, but now it's time for action. So...what do we do now?"

She positions herself as a mirror of me, her wings drooping behind her, and the snake on her neck seems to size me up.

"I need to figure out what we're dealing with," she responds.

"We," I correct. "We're in this together now. The creepy voice spoke to me, and you're, like, probably my best chance at survival now. So we need to stick together." She looks ready to argue with me, but I continue. "Look, a lot of bombs have been unloaded on me the past couple of days, and whether you like it or not, we're a team now. Wherever you go, I go." My stomach flips a bit at that, but I try to ignore it.

Her mouth parts as she licks the corner of her mouth absentmindedly. As if she's also reacting the same way that I am. I track the movement of her tongue with my eyes, not taking them off her mouth. I suddenly feel breathless. I feel too hot, like I'm wearing a puffy winter coat in the middle of summer. I swallow roughly and try to drag my eyes away from her mouth. They end up just landing on her eyes instead.

Her eyelids are heavy, her eyes glassy, like she's tired. I start to puzzle over it—wasn't she just asleep?—when she says roughly to me, "I want to touch you."

My brain doesn't register her words immediately. Why would she want to touch me? She seems to sense my confusion because I feel her hand lightly caress my hip. "I want to touch you," she repeats, her voice low.

My breath hitches when my brain finally catches up. "Oh," I sigh. Her fingers draw circles on my hip where my shirt has ridden up, exposing my skin to her.

"I, um..." I say, trying to get myself together. Heat is building inside of me at an alarming rate.

"I just need to know you're here." Her voice sounds almost desperate.

Swallowing, I look into her eyes and say, "No."

Her fingers still against my skin. She looks at me with a bemused expression. I doubt anyone has said no to her before. I'm probably the only one brave enough—or stupid enough—to do that.

"I—I think it's a bad idea," I say breathlessly. "We're both terrified after what happened today. It's just our hormones messing with us. We'll regret it later—"

"You don't know anything about how I feel," she growls, her shadows peeking over her shoulders at the sudden shift in atmosphere. "I was so worried when that creature took you. I thought it would hold your mind and never give you back."

I place a gentle hand on her shoulder. "I know," I respond. "It was horrible, but we have to figure out what's going on before we even consider fucking each other."

Her eyes widen at my boldness. "So you're saying I might get to touch you at some point?"

Looking at her, her sudden vulnerability in expressing her desire for me, I do what I told myself I would never do.

"If you take me to Hell, I'll let you touch me."

She stiffens. "Absolutely not."

"It seems like the logical next step. You said you don't know why the voice would call me a child of the earth, but I bet it's connected to Lilith somehow. If I have the same type of magic, it *has* to be connected to her. The problem is, no one seems to have any information on her, but I bet there's some place in Hell that might have the information, isn't there? Like a library or archives or something." It's more of a rhetorical question, but Venus nods anyway. "So you take me down to Hell. We look through whatever texts they might have on Lilith or what this manner of creature is and see if it can point us in the right direction."

She seems to mull it over, her eyes looking off into the distance, as if she can see the archives in her memory. After a few long beats of silence, she relents. "Fine. I'll take you, but you must be on your guard at all times. Do not talk to anyone there, do not leave my side. You aren't dead, and your soul hasn't been signed over to me, so demons might get some ideas about your availability."

I snort. "Won't being by your side be enough of a deterrent?"

"Demons are beasts. Even the most advanced can become a slave to their own impulses. I'm not taking any chances."

Shrugging, I say, "Okay, then I won't talk out of turn or give any demon my award-winning smile." I flash my teeth at her.

She doesn't bite. "You should also wear all black."

"What? No, thanks. Not my style."

"It's for your own safety."

"I'd rather die in my favorite pink pumps than die in combat boots."

"You're not going to die," she sighs, exasperated.

"Only if we get down to Hell and find out what we need to," I remind her.

She rolls her eyes but doesn't press me anymore.

Looks like I'm finally going to Hell.

Chapter Twenty
Vivian

Venus refused to let me out of her sight all evening and into the next morning. Even when I had to pee. Even when I sat on the toilet and asked in a sickly-sweet tone if she secretly had some kind of piss kink. She hadn't taken the bait, though, and simply stood in the doorway. She made us breakfast—some scrambled eggs, potatoes, and crispy bacon—before telling me that we were leaving for Hell in the next hour.

Now, exactly sixty minutes later, we're currently standing in the living room of the cabin. I'm fidgeting, unable to stand still, nerves trying to worm their way out of me.

Going to Hell was my brilliant idea, but I'm still anxious.

Elder witches have spun us stories of Hell; it's like a mirror of Earth, only much more ancient, with cities and castles. Except everyone is dead.

The hierarchy of witches is quite rigid. Every coven has a matron who is the leader of their coven. Once they die, those matrons act somewhat as nobles in Hell, presiding over the souls of fellow departed witches. The High Priestesses rule over all witches, including the matrons, both dead and alive. According to my mother, it's fraught with tensions that date all the way back to when witches first joined forces with the Dark Lady.

Now, standing next to said Dark Lady, I wonder how much of that is true.

I'm fiddling with my amulet when I finally ask after a few minutes of tense silence, "What are we waiting for?"

Venus tilts her head from side to side, as if releasing some built-up tension. Her neck tattoo ripples with the movement, its eyes slowly blinking at me. I slow blink back at it. I once heard you can do that with cats, and it makes them think they can trust you.

From the slight hiss it gives me in response, I'd say snakes don't communicate the same way.

"We're waiting for me," she finally responds. She rolls her shoulders back. "I need to teleport us there, but it takes considerable effort to do so. Especially if I'm carrying someone. So please, just stand there silently and look pretty."

I open my mouth to argue but then close it, my face heating. It's not even a good compliment, but it warms my insides all the same.

Venus shuts her eyes and begins breathing deeply, her hands loose at her sides.

I take the time to drink her in, a bit greedily. I'm struck by how attractive I find her—whether it's when she's flying or sleeping or now.

Her sharp cheekbones could slice through the air and her dark eyelashes nearly brush her cheeks. Her lips are slightly parted as she continues to breathe deeply. They're a nice, full dark tone that looks so beautiful to me. I wonder what they feel like against my fingertips, against my own mouth. Against other, more secret places.

I'm too fixated on her mouth to notice her eyes have opened and she's observing me too.

She clears her throat and I jump a bit, startled and slightly embarrassed at being caught daydreaming about her.

"I'm ready," she says after a beat of awkward silence.

"Right, yes, sure. Let's do it!" I squeak out, knowing I sound completely flustered. The tips of my ears are burning.

A light grin graces Venus's face, but she simply holds out her hands. "Shall we?"

I take them both in mine without hesitating. I've never teleported before, and I realize with a start that I should have asked more questions because Venus's serpent slithers down her arm.

"What's happening?" I ask, my voice lowered to a whisper.

Venus doesn't answer. Instead, the serpent continues its descent down her arm and slides over my skin. It feels like an actual snake is moving across my flesh. I gasp as its scales lightly scrape against my arm until it winds its way up, across my shoulders, and down my other arm. It crosses back to Venus, continuing its movement again and again, wrapping around our bodies, winding us together.

The tattooed snake forces our bodies closer and closer until the front of my body is flush with hers. I feel its scales across my arms, my back, my legs. I look up at her, alarmed and concerned about what is happening, but that fear dissipates as I take in Venus's midnight eyes.

They're relaxed, placid. As if she's done this millions of times before.

"It will feel better if you are calm," she murmurs, her breath fanning across my face. "If you're too tense, not all of you will teleport. I don't want to have to search for your limbs." Well, that certainly won't help me relax.

I narrow my eyes at her, about to snap a retort, but the snake grips us tighter, as if it's trying to merge us into one person.

Venus squeezes our conjoined hands gently, reminding me I need to chill out. "Just focus on me," she says, her eyes soft. "Focus on how I feel."

I swallow and nod shallowly. With every breath in, it pushes my chest into hers. The warmth of her body seeps into me.

With every breath out, I find myself wanting to be closer.

I watch her as she dips her head until her mouth is at the shell of my ear. "Focus on how it will feel when I finally get to have you." Her breath tickles my ear as my toes curl in my pink heels. Her thumbs trace circles on the backs of my hands. "I'll make sure you enjoy it. I'll have you begging for more." Her tone is rich and deep.

A small whimper passes my lips before I can stop it. My eyelids flutter closed as she lightly presses a kiss to the hollow of my throat. The bridge of her nose slides against my jawline as if she's scenting me, getting her fill of me while she can. She inhales deeply and pulls away. My body reacts to her movement by shifting forward, seeking that warmth, that growing pressure under my skin.

My eyes fly open, and we're no longer in the cabin.

The room around me is a dark bedroom fit for royalty. There's a canopy four-poster bed with deep red curtains pulled back to reveal black silk pillows and a matching duvet. It faces an entire wall of windows, which shows a pitch-black night—no stars, no moon. Twin nightstands are set on either side, with candelabras tastefully placed on both. A black armoire and vanity table are set against the far wall while a writer's desk and massive bookshelves are to my right. The room is dimly lit by a large overhead chandelier.

We're in Hell.

And this must be Venus's private bedroom.

The serpent binding us slithers once more around me until it has completed its cycle, settling back into its original size and location on Venus's neck.

I drop her hands and take a step back. The coldness it brings nearly slaps me in the face.

Clearing my throat, I make a show of circling the room and let out a whistle. "Fancy place."

Venus snorts and crosses her arms. "It suits me."

I walk over to the bookshelves, perusing the titles. They all look like historical works. Boring.

"I'm sure it does. Although," I say as I lightly run a finger down the spine of a large volume, "it's a bit bare." I turn back to her and shoot her a grin. "Could really use a woman's touch."

She hums, her wings twitching. I realize now that either means she's annoyed or turned on. Frankly, I'm okay with either option.

"Where is the library?" I ask.

She crosses her arms. "You can't just go into the archives."

"Do I need to get a library card before entering?"

"It's more complicated than that. And it's not a library."

"Have you tried getting a library card? Some places make it really difficult."

She gives me a look that says, *are you done?*

I lace my fingers behind my back and clamp my lips shut dramatically. I might also have pushed out my boobs a bit more. If she wants to rile me up, I can easily do the same. Her gaze dips to my chest before slowly reaching my eyes again.

"I'll be unable to take you into the archives." I open my mouth to argue, but she presses forward. "While I hate the idea of you being out of my sight, I fear I will put you in graver danger by bringing you along. So I will have someone escort you to and from. You are not to give them trouble. Is that understood?"

I nod obediently, even though I'll raise Hell whenever and to whomever I want. She should know that by now.

She seems to hear my thoughts because she pinches the bridge of her nose dramatically.

"I will be back for you once I am done. The room—and this palace—is warded against those who want to cause harm to me. And, by extension, to you, but you are not free to wander on your own."

This time I nod and mean it. I can't wait to look through all of Venus's shit.

Her wings unfurl as she prowls toward me. I hold my ground. She cocoons us in, throwing us into darkness. All I can see is a faint outline of her features.

"Once I return," her words curl around me like shadows, "I'll make good on your promise."

"My what?" I ask, breathless.

"I get to touch you if I brought you to Hell. I've done my part. Now it is time for you to uphold your end."

Without a word, she peels her wings back, beating them powerfully, and soars through the open windows.

❧ ❧

I'm unabashedly rifling through Venus's underwear drawer when the door opens and a demon steps into the room. At least, I'm assuming he's a demon, with his pitch-black eyes and the horns on his head.

I quickly shove the drawer closed as he strolls into the middle of the room. We observe each other for a few beats. Then, to my complete surprise, he bows slightly. "Vivian," he says in greeting. His voice is like granite.

"Uh, hello," I respond awkwardly. I flip my hair over my shoulder, remembering to channel my confident, bad bitch energy. Squaring my shoulders, I say, "Are you the one who will be taking me to the archives?"

He nods, clasping his hands behind his back. "Her Grace has requested I escort you and to not let you out of my sight."

I roll my eyes. Of course.

"Well, let's get to it, then!" My tone is chipper, which seems to make him cringe. He nods and steps to the side, letting me lead the way, which is incredibly silly because I have literally never been here before and he must know that.

Regardless, I plaster a smile on my face and strut confidently out into the hallway.

This place is like a castle. The walls are made of large, black stone, similar to the summoning monoliths. The hallway is lit by candles mounted on the wall, throwing creepy shadows in their wake. I make a snap decision and turn left, my heels click-clacking against the stone floor, the demon right on my heels. We reach the end of the hall, with options to turn right or left again. I opt for right this time, not letting myself hesitate. We carry on for a few minutes until I get tired of pretending I know where we're going and spin around. The demon stops a few feet away from me.

"Okay," I huff impatiently. "We both know I've never been here before. Can you *please* lead the way?"

He snickers as he passes me. "You were actually on the right track. We're almost there."

I flip off his back and follow behind him.

The corridors are all decorated with various pieces of art—depictions of people having sex, of winged creatures, of battlefields. It's like walking through an art museum. Finally, the demon stops in front of a set of double doors and places his palm upon them. I hear a *click* and the doors slowly swing open.

The demon gestures to the open doors. "After you."

I narrow my eyes at him before stepping into the room. We're standing on a small balcony with a spiral staircase on either side of us. I walk over to the railing and peer in, seeing levels upon levels of shelves, tables, comfortable-looking love seats, and armchairs, all lit to perfection by various chandeliers.

This is a librarian's wet dream.

I look over my shoulder at the demon. "Did Ven—did the Dark Lady inform you of what I'm looking for?"

"She did," he replies as he steps up next to me. "I spoke to the archivist before receiving you. She's pulled all the texts that she can find on the subjects."

I nod. "Well, lead the way down."

About an hour later, I'm sitting at a table surrounded by books. The archivist, a soul that died about 2,000 years ago, greeted us and showed us the texts she pulled. As she drifted next to us, she told me she could only find a handful of writings that might be useful to me, but to call for her if needed. I had given her one of my dazzling smiles before digging in.

So far, I've gotten nowhere.

Most of the texts give the same story I was taught. Venus had recruited the witches, not the other way around, and there's been no mention of Lilith.

I close the book with a frustrated grunt.

The demon looks over at me curiously. He's made himself comfortable in an armchair, although he has offered no help and is merely sitting there in silence.

I flip my hair over my shoulder. "So, what's your name?"

His eyes narrow. "My name is Luke. I am Her Grace's Second."

"Ooh, fancy."

He grunts, "And I know who you are."

"I bet you do," I say as I bat my eyelashes at him.

"Your womanly charms won't work on me, witch."

"Are you not into women?"

"I'm not into witches."

"Neither am I," I retort. "How long have you been the Dark Lady's Second?"

He crosses his arms, as if weighing the pros and cons of speaking to me. Finally, he relents and says, "Ever since the Great War."

"Ah," I reply, sucking on a tooth. "So, a long time."

He nods. Considering his eyes are entirely black, it's hard to read his expressions. "Yes, a very long time. It is the greatest honor anyone—demon or otherwise—could be imposed."

I hum noncommittally at that. "You became her Second after the witches joined Hell, then."

"Yes. I was a soldier in her army for many years before the Great War."

"So you were around when Lilith died."

"Yes."

"Did you know her?" I ask.

"Not personally," he answers, propping his ankle over his knee. "I never spent time with her. I was just a commander then—not important enough to get close to the Dark Lady—and Lilith was either with the witches or with Her Grace."

My own sick curiosity moves through me. "What happened to the Dark Lady after Lilith died?"

He casts his eyes downward for a moment before looking at me. "It's not polite to discuss someone's affairs without their knowledge."

"Hey, I'll have you know that gossip was a way for women to be in community until men came and ruined it—"

"I believe she would rather share that information with you when she is ready. It is simply not my place."

I chew on my bottom lip and let it go. "I guess I wouldn't want someone else telling people about my lost love, either. Not that I've had one, but still."

His mouth twitches upward.

"Why do you think Lilith is erased from history?" I ask, propping my arms on the table and leaning forward. "The witches don't teach us about her—we're taught some bastardized version of the story. Why?"

He shakes his head. "I don't know. Demons do not lie about what happened during the War. We receive extensive education about it."

I blink. "The demons go to school?"

Luke throws me a bemused look. "The most advanced of us do, yes."

"How do you become more advanced?"

"We eat souls." He says it so nonchalantly. "The more souls we eat, the more advanced we become. We can eat any kind of soul. I was a soldier, so I had access to many demon souls as I killed enemy soldiers. I rose to the status of an archdemon quite quickly."

I scrunch my nose. "That sounds disgusting."

He shrugs. I guess this is normal for him.

"So demons know the truth—about the War and about Lilith?"

He nods. "She had a great and terrible power none had ever seen. While demons hate witches, they feared Lilith."

"Why does that distinction matter?" I ask.

"Because demons fear little. It also shows that we respected her, despite what she was."

"I have the same magic she does," I admit. My magic perks up at me mentioning it. Since the creepy voice had infiltrated my mind and my magic worked to protect me, it's been somber, closed off. Despite myself, I'm happy to feel it stir within me.

"I know," he replies. "I will admit, I was relieved when you didn't provide Her Grace with your soul."

I blink in surprise. "Why?"

"Because I fear a new war is imminent."

Furrowing my brows, I ask, "But wasn't the War against you guys and...gods? Gods don't exist. Not anymore anyway."

"Most don't," he corrects, "but one does remain. The one who destroyed Lilith's soul."

I think back to my conversation with Venus just the other day. "She said the last remaining god and her could not destroy one another. That, by destroying one, they would destroy everything."

Luke nods. "Life and Death—the Dark Lady represents Death and he represents Life," he spits, as if claiming such a thing is abhorrent to him. "If they work to destroy one, the balance of the world will forever be tipped one way."

"So why bother even starting a war against them in the first place?" I ask. "It seems counterintuitive for Lilith and the Dark Lady to work on eradicating the gods if destroying them ends up destroying everything."

He shakes his head. "I cannot provide you with those answers. You must ask the Dark Lady."

I roll my shoulders. "What was even the point of bringing me to the archives if none of these books have the answers?"

"I suspect," he replies, his tone light with humor, "that it was to distract you long enough for Her Grace to take care of a few things."

Chapter Twenty-One
The Dark Lady

It has, admittedly, been far too long since I've summoned the council, but that's because the meetings always end in everyone threatening to kill one another. It's simply not worth the headache.

I strut into the war room and am greeted by six individuals sitting around the large table. Three witches—the High Priestesses—on one side, three archdemons on the other. Luke is usually the fourth demon in attendance, but I have him on babysitting duty.

They all rise from their seats at my entrance, and I slowly make my way to the head of the table, letting my wings unfurl casually and my shadows dance around the room.

Everyone stays still, but I can smell the fear radiating off them. It never hurts to remind them how much power I have.

I take my seat and, after a few tense beats, I wave my hand at them to be seated. The tension subsides, but there's a tang of it still hanging in the air as they wait for me to speak.

"You all know why I gathered you here. Three witch covens were attacked, and I suspect more will be soon. After investigating, it's clear that all covens are in danger."

"What happened to them?" Aradia, one of the High Priestesses, asks.

"They were murdered, their magic sucked right out of them." Horrified murmurs rise from the witches. "The wards to their communes were not disturbed, so whoever did it was familiar with them. They left no bodies."

"Do you know who did it?" Marie, another High Priestess, inquires.

"It was probably demons," the usually near-silent High Priestess, Isobel, hisses, provoking growls from the demons across the table.

"This was not an act of a demon," I inform them all. "I believe the wards are failing, and that Phanes is to blame."

Everyone is stunned into silence.

"But, my Lady," one of the demons named Grigor responds, "we have not heard from him since the Great War. Why would he reappear now?"

"Because a witch with the same magic as Lilith has finally walked the earth, and he knows it. He wants another chance at retaking this realm."

Nervous rumblings fill the room.

"A witch with Lilith's magic?" Marie asks incredulously. "You're sure?"

I nod. "When we were at the location of an attacked coven, a strange form of magic seemed to overtake her—it infiltrated her mind. Told her things. Called her a child of the earth."

The High Priestesses are stunned into silence.

"That's not possible," Marie whispers.

"What isn't?" a demon named Kali asks.

"I'll admit, I'm not sure what it means," I tell the room.

Gesturing to the three witches around the table, I say, "I was hoping you could enlighten us on the meaning."

The High Priestesses share nervous glances, a silent conversation passing between the three. Aradia, Isobel, and Marie are the most powerful witches that ever lived mortal lives—minus Lilith. Upon their deaths, I appointed them as the High Priestesses of Hell.

I would have made Lilith a High Priestess, had her soul not been destroyed.

"As you know," Aradia nods to me, "Lilith was the only witch ever recorded to have earth magic. Her magic was an anomaly."

"But her magic was not new," Marie picks up the line of thought. "Her magic was unique—legend has it that the earth itself created it, as a protection of sorts."

"Protection from what?" I ask, leaning forward.

Isobel shrugs as Marie continues, "Protection from harm, we assume. A way to keep itself alive if it was being actively destroyed."

The gods destroyed much of the physical world during the War, and now humans are destroying their own home.

"Some also argue it's actually the power of the original Goddess of Life, but all texts were destroyed eons ago," Isobel explains quietly.

I blink at her. Isobel is always near-silent, but her power is truly staggering. She could lift oceans with half a thought. During the War, she drowned entire battlefields—while they were on dry land.

"Regardless," Aradia continues, "the magic is completely unique. Witches consider this rare form of magic as being interconnected to the earth—to the trees, to the flowers, to the dirt. If this young witch has the same magic as Lilith, I'm not surprised to hear Phanes would show an interest."

My shadows curl like snakes, ready to strike. They don't like the sound of Phanes even knowing Vivian exists, nor do I.

"What do we do?" the third demon, Azrael, asks. "We've tried replicating the wards the witches placed after the War to no avail. If Phanes can get through, how can we stop him from destroying everything in his wake?"

"We created the wards before Lilith died—she used some of her own blood to bind them. I'm assuming the blood of a witch with the same form of magic will do the trick," I respond. Unease churns my stomach, but I shove it down. "I will bring the young witch to you three," I say, nodding to the High Priestesses, "when the time is right."

The three witches share a look among themselves, seeming uneasy, but they nod their agreement.

"But, Your Grace," Grigor interjects.

I silence him with a look. "I know what the risks are, and what must be done. For the sake of our realm, I will make sure it is done. Does anyone else dare to question me?"

I'm met with silence.

"Good," I say, rising from my seat. My shadows purr from my shoulders. "Then we shall prepare as we did during the Great War."

A few hours later, I find Vivian exactly where I expected her to be.

What I didn't expect to find is a crowd of spirits gathered around her table, cooing and fussing over her.

I let some of my magic out, alerting everyone to my presence. The spirits startle and begin to move away, but Vivian appears oblivious to my entrance and continues speaking. "—so this guy—I think he was, like, a CEO of some huge company, I don't know—offered to let me drive his new Aston Martin and I was all like, 'yeah, sure!' Problem was, he was, like, *so* rude to the server and that's a red flag for me. So, I managed to pickpocket him, steal his keys and his wallet. When he went to the restroom, I gave the server all the cash in his wallet. I think it was, like, five thousand dollars. It's so tacky to carry cash anymore. Anyway, then I drove his car for a little joy ride!"

The spirits are sucked back into her story, their faces alight with curiosity as she speaks to them. I find myself standing a few feet away silently, wondering how this story is going to end.

"Now I didn't *mean* to, but I *did* drive the car into a Chanel store. No one was hurt, except for a few man-nequins. I don't even know how I managed to do that—I wasn't even that drunk! The building, like, jumped out in front of me or something. So, I guess I 'fled the scene' or whatever, but I was moving the next day anyway, so they never caught me, but I'm probably banned from the state of California now." She shrugs as if that's not a big deal.

My mouth is agape. I hadn't realized I fixated on such an unhinged woman. Do I even want her soul?

Who am I kidding? I definitely do, but it might be something to seriously reconsider.

The spirits begin asking her rapid-fire questions. It seems she has made fast friends down here.

I clear my throat and Vivian peers over her shoulder at me, her impeccable blonde hair shifting with the movement. "Can I help you?" she asks, batting her eyelashes.

My nostrils flare, both at her indignation and at her cherry blossom and pomegranate scent reaching me. "I see you made friends."

Floating above the ground, the spirits all bow to me before floating off in different directions.

"Ugh," Vivian groans as everyone leaves. "We were just getting into my twenties."

I ignore her and look around the space for Luke. I do a double take when I see him seated on a chair, head crooked to the side, fast asleep. I growl as two shadows slither over and poke him. He jumps awake, eyes flying open and immediately landing on me. He shoots up from his resting spot, back ramrod straight. "Your Grace," he breathes, his voice sounding groggy.

"Babysitting duty boring you?" I ask, eyebrows flicking up.

He works to pull himself together, smoothing down his button-down black shirt and clearing his throat. "I apologize, Your Grace. She seemed to be in the company of many spirits—they would have woken me if anything was amiss."

"Hmmm," I respond before turning back to Vivian.

She's looking at me with her eyebrows furrowed. Her scent has turned tart—it makes me want to smack my lips together.

"I don't need a babysitter," she snaps.

"I don't trust you to be alone in my realm," I respond. "You've been known to run off. I need to make sure you stay exactly where I put you."

"What was so important that you needed me trapped down here?"

"Last I checked, you were the one who wanted to come down here," I remind her. "It was the perfect opportunity to take care of a few things."

"Like what?" she demands.

I cross my arms, irritation worming its way into my stomach. "Nothing that concerns you," I lie. I'm not sure why I do. Maybe because, as much as her stubbornness drives me up the walls, the thought of our dynamic shifting has me hesitating. It's safe to assume she won't jump at the chance to use her magic, especially if it benefits me. Using her magic at the coven sites seemed to make her uneasy, and I think we're both anxious after what happened last time.

She narrows her eyes at me, clearly unhappy with my response—whether it's because I'm dismissing her or because she can tell I'm lying, I'm not sure.

I try to keep my face mildly annoyed, not letting her see the nerves and dread bubbling underneath the surface. "Any luck down here?"

"Yes," she says, pivoting to show her back to me, dismissing me in a way. I grind my teeth together. "I met a bunch of cool people down here. I seem to have a way with ghosts." When I don't bite, she continues. "In terms of finding out more about the covens and creepy voice that invaded my brain, not so much."

I walk around to the other side of the table, shifting my shoulders back and flexing the muscles in my wings. Sitting in the seat across from her, I take in the texts that are spread across the table.

"These books have been useless," she grumbles at me, as if it's my fault, "but your loudmouth archdemon over there gave me some good intel."

Luke has the good sense to look worried. Itching one of his horns, he says, "I wasn't aware of what information she should and should not have."

I close my eyes for a moment, trying to rein in my annoyance. "And what, exactly, did my 'loudmouth archdemon'"—I throw a glare his way—"share with you?"

She shrugs, pretending to be nonchalant, but she's clearly pleased with herself. "Just that I won't find any texts about Lilith down here."

I blink at her. Much to my own chagrin, I don't spend much time in the archives. "I'm not a scholar. I don't know every piece of text that is housed here."

"Interesting," she drawls. "Considering you're such a control freak, I figured you kept tabs on when everyone breathes."

"Not everyone. Just you."

Her cheeks turn a beautiful shade of pink as her scent wraps around me. She tries to keep her expression carefully blank, bordering on disinterested, but I know the truth—I can smell it on her.

"Anyway," she replies, clearly wanting to change the subject. I smirk at her. "Luke said you are the one with the answers on what's going on. It sounded like you sent me on a wild goose chase."

Unholy gods, this woman. "First, let me remind you *again* that coming to the archives was *your* idea." She opens her mouth to argue, but I hold up my hand to stop her. "Second, despite what you've been told, I don't know everything."

"So you don't know why the Great War happened?"

Fucking Luke and his big mouth. "Of course I know why it happened."

She leans back in her seat, a smug look etched on her face. "Go on, then."

I bristle at her casual demand. "It isn't relevant," I lie again. I can't seem to stop.

She snorts. "I thought we agreed to work together. We can't work together if you're keeping things from me."

I hate that she's right. "Can we just…" I sigh, suddenly overcome with exhaustion. "Can we discuss this tomorrow? We've done so much today. I'm tired."

She considers me for a moment before mumbling, "Fine," and getting up from the table.

I follow suit, throwing a look at Luke, who is hovering just within earshot, that says *we'll discuss this later.*

I follow behind Vivian, her hips swishing back and forth as we make our way out of the archives. Her brightly colored outfits no longer offend me—at this point, I've come to expect them. She's in an oversized pink plaid top that's tucked into black high-waisted jeans and matching pink heels. Her heels click against the stone floors as we make our way back to my rooms.

I can't believe I've started cataloging her damn outfits.

Biting my tongue, I try to shift my thoughts to something—anything—else but how gorgeous her legs look in those jeans. My mind wanders to how I'm going to get her ready to remake the wards. And why I lied to her about it just now. Maybe I feel she isn't ready to know the truth yet—she and her magic still operate as separate entities. They need to merge more to be at full capacity.

Thinking about her magic gives me a new form of anxiety after what the High Priestesses shared. If her magic is as unique as they claim, maybe they're right—maybe that's why Phanes wants her. But for what? What would he want with her magic? I'm puzzling over it as we approach my door. I absentmindedly press the door open, stepping into the space.

The wind from the open windows floats cherry blossoms and pomegranates to my nostrils, and my body goes rigid. I turn slowly to face Vivian. She's glided closer to the windows, looking lost in her own thoughts. She seems to sense my stare and glances over at me.

My heart rate picks up a bit. How could I forget? It's time to call in on her bargain.

Chapter Twenty-Two
Vivian

The walk back to Venus's rooms is quiet except for the sound of our shoes against the floor, both of us clearly in our own heads. After Luke essentially revealed her secret and stated that I was sent on a futile search to the archives—even though it was, technically, my idea—I can't help but feel angry at myself. I assumed that would be the best place for answers instead of asking the one person I've been forced to spend all my time with.

I think over what Luke shared, and more importantly, what he didn't.

The Great War was between Venus's army and the gods. All but one was destroyed and that god is the God of Life. If he or Venus is destroyed, that would basically destroy the entire world. I sigh as I stop my pacing and peer out the large windows. Why would the God of Life want to murder witches? You'd think their whole thing would be about, like...living?

Maybe it's a way to get back at the witches for siding with Venus. I can safely assume that's why Lilith was destroyed in the end.

A part of me isn't convinced the answers aren't written *somewhere*. Luke said himself he was a soldier during the War—surely someone had the brilliant idea of documenting what happened. Venus can't be the only source of this information.

I feel like I have even more questions than answers at this point. My mother used to say I was so stubborn it bordered on stupidity. That used to upset me, but now, I'm going to use my borderline stupidity to untangle this whole mess.

The wind around me shuffles through the open window. As it tosses my hair around me, I turn and look at Venus. Her face is grave, her eyes intense. I blink at her, surprise—and then panic—rising within me.

"What?" I ask.

She prowls toward me, her gaze slowly sweeping up and down my body. I open my mouth to ask what's wrong, but she presses her body against mine. Her midnight eyes pierce into mine as she croons, "It's time to call in on our bargain."

"I—what?" I'm suddenly breathless, my mind struggling to grasp the meaning of her words until she lifts a hand to my hair and gently tucks it behind an ear. She doesn't drop her hand. Instead, she places it against the side of my neck. My pulse skitters against her warm palm.

"I get to touch you," she says, her tone low and rough. As if she's holding herself back from throwing me onto the bed.

That thought alone emboldens me. "I did agree to that," I purr. Surprise lights her eyes at my response.

A challenge.

Her hand travels to grip my neck as if she's about to choke me, but her touch stays gentle. Just showing me she could hurt me if she wanted to.

I push myself into her hand, grinning devilishly at her. "Go on, then. Or is this all you got?"

Before my mind can register what's happening, I'm thrown onto the bed like a ragdoll. I land with a whoosh as air leaves my lungs and my hair fans out beneath me. In a flash, Venus is straddling me, her wings spirited away. There is also no sign of her shadows. As if she wants it to be just me and her for this first encounter.

"I should've known you'd be a brat," she growls, her hand going to my throat again and squeezing.

All I do is laugh and say, "I think you like my bratty side."

Before she can see my plan forming, I throw her weight off me. Surprised, she grunts as she lands splayed underneath me.

I straddle her, pinning her arms underneath me. She squirms under my weight, clearly angry the tables have turned.

I can't help it—I laugh again. Her face contorts as she snarls up at me.

I grip her face, pinching her cheeks as I lean down. Nose to nose, I whisper, "Who do you think you're growling at?" She clenches her jaw, refusing to answer me. I snicker. "You don't like this—me being in charge—do you? You're such a control freak, so I'm not surprised. You thought you'd fly in here and I'd immediately spread my pretty legs for you, didn't you?"

Her eyes narrow, which gives me all the confirmation I need.

I lean down until my lips reach the shell of her ear. "But what you don't understand is," I say into her ear, "I'm already in charge."

I lick the curve of her ear and pull back, staring down at her, triumphant.

She snaps her teeth at me, a feral beast, angry at being restrained.

I laugh sadistically again as she tries to dislodge me from on top of her. "Maybe you should call me Daddy."

The imaginary tether around her snaps. In a blur, I'm thrown and land back on the bed. This time, Venus has thought ahead. Her shadows have whipped out and are snaking around my wrists and ankles—my arms are being pulled overhead and my legs are being spread wide.

She begins to unbutton my top as her shadows pull me spread eagle. "It would be in your best interest to behave," she snarls. "I can go for a very long time. How long do you think you can last?"

In a matter of moments, she's stripped me down, baring my naked body to her and her pervy shadows. A few slither around my body, trying to get their fill of my exposed curves.

I keep my mouth shut, not letting her get any satisfaction out of what she's doing to me. Inside, I'm giddy, my body heating from the inside out with desire.

She looks down at my body, a look of carnal pleasure written across her face. "You're even better than I imagined."

A small whimper escapes my lips.

Venus seems unsure of where to start, where to touch me first. I know exactly where she should start—I buck my hips, making it clear where she's needed.

She chuckles. "I know what you need. I'll get there, eventually."

Part of me regrets pushing her. The other part of me can't wait to see what she does.

Chapter Twenty-Three
The Dark Lady

She's even more beautiful than I could have dreamed.

Her blonde hair frames her face, which is currently pink with desire. Her creamy skin feels too soft for my hands. She breathes heavily when I trail my fingertips down her throat to her collarbones. They jut out slightly and move with each deep breath she takes. I trace them both slowly, eager to take in every inch of her.

I'm trying to go slow—to torture her, but also to torture myself.

I finally get to touch her.

My fingers dip to her breasts, which causes her breath to hitch. I circle a nipple with my finger, watching it pebble under my soft touch. I do the same to the other, trying to keep control over myself—drinking in the sight of her pretty, pink nipples, now looking ready to be devoured.

I hold back. *Savor it,* I remind myself.

I take her breasts in my hands, feeling their heavy weight in my palms. They're nearly too big to fit, but I'm not complaining. Vivian mewls underneath me, and I know she's struggling against the shadowy restraints. I flick her nipples with my thumbs, and I feel her body tense. I do it again, watching her face transform. Vivian always has her emotions splashed across her face. It would take an idiot not to see what she's really thinking and feeling in the moment. And in this moment, all her face says is that she's aroused. Her eyelids are heavy, her mouth parted, her cheeks flushed.

"Venus," she pleads breathlessly, and I nearly lose my composure at hearing her say my name in that way. Like I'm not the one who made her life miserable and is dragging her into this universal nightmare, but like I'm the only one she wants to be touching her right now.

"Patience," I grit out, flicking her nipples once more, causing her to cry out. The sound is like music to my ears.

I move down, running my hands greedily against her stomach, her waist, her hips. My mouth waters at the perfect specimen I have underneath me, completely at my mercy.

Just how I have been at her mercy since I found her.

Continuing my descent down her body, I position myself between her luscious thighs. I can't stop myself from placing a kiss on the inside of both. Vivian trembles like a leaf underneath me. I look up at her from between her legs, and that's when her scent hits me like a freight train. My muscles coil, ready to devour her whole, but I keep a leash on my baser instincts—just for a moment longer.

I lick my lips as our eyes connect. Her pupils are blown wide. She bucks her hips again, trying to make it explicitly clear where she wants me. I let out a chuckle and say, "As you wish, princess."

Her taste bursts against my tongue at my first slide through her folds. I groan into her—she tastes even better than I thought possible. I'm ravenous, unable to control myself anymore, diving, lapping, sucking at her center, unable to stop. I move up to her clit and give a few delicate circles of my tongue.

She cries out above me, squirming against the shadows holding her still.

I dive back in. Now that I've had her, I never want to do anything else. I will never touch another. Wanting her before was nothing compared to this feeling now, this basic need to have her. I drink her in and take every drop she gives me. She's moaning, her hips gyrating, telling me she wants more.

I lift my hand and lightly circle her opening with my finger. She's so wet, so pliant, that it fits in easily. She's so tight, so snug, but it feels right. Like she was made to have me inside her.

I move my mouth up to her clit as I pump my finger in and out of her. Her channel tightens around my finger, making me desperate to get her to her climax. My shadows are winding all around her now—circling her hips, her waist, her breasts.

My tongue swirls over her, my finger moving in and out of her, making obscene, filthy noises that I never want another soul to hear. She tightens to the point I think her body wants to keep me in her forever, and when she moans out my name, I see stars.

She comes apart against me, because of me, for me, her orgasm finally cresting as she goes rigid on the bed. I continue through the throes of it, pumping into her, sucking her, claiming her.

I refuse to let her relax, though. Surely, she can handle release more than once, right?

The noise of my finger fucking her is so erotic, the sound of my flesh drenched in her arousal. It's the most erotic thing I've ever heard. One of my shadows slithers down her breasts, lightly circling her hard nipples, as I fuck her hard. She cries out, her back bowing off the bed, but I don't stop. I keep going, thrusting in and out, pushing another finger into her. She's stretched around me, struggling to take them all.

"Venus, please..." she mewls, her hands fisting the bed sheets underneath us. I chuckle against her skin before lapping at her clit.

I will never tire of this taste. I need to save it, to bottle it up and cherish it for the rest of eternity.

"Can you do it?" I murmur against her center. "Can you come again for me?"

"Yes, yes..." she pleads, her channel tightening around my fingers.

"Go on, then," I encourage, lightly scraping my teeth over her clit.

She falls over the edge with a scream, electricity lighting up her body from within as she works through her orgasm. Finally, she relaxes on the bed, sweaty and docile. It's the most beautiful version I've seen of her yet.

I remove my fingers from her channel slowly, relishing in the feeling of her clamping down on me. I raise my eyes to hers and place my fingers in my mouth, cleaning them.

We both shiver.

I prowl up her body, not able to get enough, never able to get my fill now that I've had a taste. I press light kisses to her hip, her stomach, her breasts, her collarbone.

She moans, a satisfied sound, as I reach the top of her.

Her eyes are glassy, her face calm. I've never seen her so relaxed. I only want to see this expression on her face.

"Is it my turn?" she asks sleepily.

I blink at her, confused for a moment, until I read the lust in her gaze.

"Ah," I say, a bit awkwardly. "No need to reciprocate tonight."

She pouts. "But I want to."

My dead heart pounds at that. "We can make another deal," I chuckle, settling into bed next to her.

My shadows release her limbs, but she doesn't move. She simply closes her eyes and sighs, content.

"Tomorrow then," she slurs before drifting off to sleep.

⁂

The next morning, Vivian is adamant she must go back down to the archives. I try to push her on it, but she simply flicks her hair over her shoulder and says, "You'll see."

So, here I am, sitting across from Vivian at a large table in the archives. She's in a bright pink jumpsuit that both assaults my eyes and brings a smile to my face. We're quite a pair, sitting here together, me in my usual all black, her in all pink.

It makes me wonder again...would she have flourished under my care? Witches rarely stray from the status quo.

I'd like to think I would foster differences, letting her be the person she was meant to be, but I can't fool myself. I would've taken one look at her outfit and demanded she burn it.

Shame washes over me as she twirls a strand of blonde hair around her finger, engrossed in whatever text she requested from the archivist. I would have crushed any individuality, any sign of difference from her.

She claims I ruined her life, but I don't think that's accurate. I think I would have ruined her life if I had caught her and dragged her back all those years ago.

Vivian taps a slender finger twice on the page she's reading, nodding to herself. It snaps me from my self-pity. "What is it?"

She looks up at me, a triumphant grin on her face. "I knew someone would have written the true story of Lilith somewhere. Why wouldn't they? She was the one who aligned the witches with you and the demons. You were her...lover." She chokes out the last word, her eyes falling to the book. Her cheeks are flushed.

I lean forward, noting her sudden uncomfortable nature at mentioning Lilith as my former lover. Is she jealous? My chest swells with satisfaction at the thought. I like that.

Lilith and I were lovers, it's true, and I mourned her for so long, but recently, I've found that sharp pain of losing her has dulled. It is still there, deep in my chest, my heart, but it no longer takes my breath away.

And I would wager it has to do with the witch across from me.

Vivian continues, "But I realized maybe the answers are in a different place." She taps the page again. "So, I asked for all texts on the God of Life."

The wind rushes out of me.

"Granted, my request alarmed the archivist, but she pulled the only text there was—and I think I found the answer."

My shadows peek over my shoulder, concerned. I'm struggling to get another breath into my lungs.

"The God of Life, Phanes, is said to have created the universe. He was, like, hatched from an egg or something and was the ruler over everything. Until," she pauses for dramatic effect, as if I'm unaware of the story, "someone challenged him. They grew tired of his cruelty and his blood lust. His cronies—the other gods—weren't much better. Humans were nothing but slaves. Witches were abused for their magic and discarded once it dried out. So, one witch met with the ruler of Hell, and they worked to rid the world of the gods and the God of Life himself, but it didn't work. You cannot get rid of Life and Death."

She tilts her head at me, her hazel eyes surprisingly soft.

She twists the book to face me, pushing it across the table and tapping the page for a third time. I look down. On the page is a portrait of Phanes. His white beard and long hair surround him like a halo. He's naked, aside from the gigantic serpent that coils around his muscular frame.

"Tell me why Phanes had one daughter who was considered the Goddess of Night, but there's no record of what happened to her?"

Panic is working to claw its way out of my throat.

She's figured it out. The little brat has somehow figured out what I have tried to keep hidden for so long. Waiting for an answer, she tilts her head. She doesn't push, but she won't let this go.

"Because," I choke out the words, "Phanes is my father."

Chapter Twenty-Four
Vivian

I'm trying not to bounce in my seat.

I knew it. I fucking knew it. I'm basically a genius.

It felt strange not having written texts about Lilith or even about Venus. It was her realm—you'd think every damn text down here would talk about her and how great she is.

Phanes, the God of Life, is depicted with an enormous snake around himself. It's nearly identical to the snake wrapped around Venus's neck. Even though I'm bursting at the seams with excitement that I figured it out, I keep my face calm as Venus wrestles with what I've shared.

"You're the Goddess of the Night," I say to her, as if she's unaware. She merely nods, her eyes glued to the image of her father. "Who was so lonely," I continue softly. "You were alone in the darkness. You were so excited when other life began, but so many feared you—feared the darkness. Even though there was more, you were still alone. Even after the most vile creatures came knocking on your door, looking for their new home after Phanes created them and kicked them out."

She closes her eyes, sadness etched into her face as if it is the only emotion she has ever felt. My heart strains, but I continue.

"You saw what your father was doing, what the other gods were doing, and you hated it. You hated them. They took companionship for granted, took humans for granted. You heard that many hated your father the same way you did. So, when Lilith graced your doorstep, you finally felt hope." I'm mostly guessing at this point, but Venus doesn't stop me. "At first, it worked. The other gods—your own brothers and sisters—were dead, but your father couldn't be destroyed. He knew it too. He figured, if he couldn't physically destroy you, he could destroy what you loved most."

Venus's snake tattoo hisses at me. I know I've hit my mark.

I continue, "So now, even though you have witches indebted to you, it still isn't enough to kill him. Because he cannot be killed."

Her eyes slowly open and land on me. They're hollow, broken. I force myself to breathe steadily, to weather the despair.

"Your father is the one attacking the covens. He's the one who attacked me, who got into my head that day."

Venus simply nods. My breath hitches. Gone is the excitement of figuring out this puzzle—now I'm left with only dread.

She says quietly, "Before Lilith died, she figured out a way to protect us from him. It was a warding spell. He couldn't reach this realm, but as time has passed, the wards have been failing." She heaves a sigh, weary and full of exhaustion. "The wards used Lilith's blood to seal. Her blood, laced with her earth magic, kept the realm from being attacked."

I blink at her. I hadn't guessed that part.

"We need a witch with the same magic as Lilith to bind them together again."

Horror washes over me. "And I'm the only known witch with Lilith's type of magic."

She nods, solemn. "You will need to work with me to strengthen the wards again. You and your magic. The High Priestesses will get you prepared."

I learned all about the High Priestesses—they are the three most powerful witches to ever live, now ruling over all witches. The only one above them is Venus. They answer to no one else.

"Will I die?" I ask, my thoughts quickly spiraling into panic.

"No," Venus argues, her jaw ticking. "Lilith did not die by forging the wards, and neither will you."

"Were you ever going to tell me?"

Venus narrows her eyes. "I...I knew I had to, but I didn't want to," she admits.

"So I don't have a choice," I realize out loud. I will assist with this, even if I don't want to. "This whole time—needing my help figuring out who killed the covens—was all a lie? You already knew?"

Venus doesn't respond.

She knew. She knew all of this and refused to tell me. Knew how I played a role—a really important fucking role—in the balance of the entire world and said nothing. Her father is attacking the covens, and she already knew. All she has done is lie to me. I never get a choice here—not really.

I have never been given a choice when it comes to Venus.

I'm stunned into silence. Then, without thinking, I rise from my chair, walk over to Venus's side of the table, and slap her across the face. The sound of my palm connecting with her cheek radiates through the silent room.

I pivot and speed walk out of the archives, refusing to look back.

Angry tears pool in my eyes as I navigate the halls back to Venus's room. Then they spill down my cheeks when I realize I have no other place to go. I thought last night changed something between us. I'm not sure what I thought it meant for us, but I thought maybe she was more interested in who I was and not just my magic, not just my soul.

All I am to her is a possession, a thing to use, no matter the consequences to me. She's shown it repeatedly how little she regards witches, how little she regards me. What happened to the goddess of the night who just want-ed companionship? What happened to the goddess who wanted everyone to live in peace, no longer under the thumb of a tyrannical ruler?

Maybe she died when Lilith's heart stopped beating.

I reach Venus's room and yank the door open. Slam-ming it shut behind me, I stare around the space. All I want is to go home, but...

Where is that? I don't think I've ever had a home.

I lean against the door and slide down until I'm seated. I hate to admit it, but Venus and I have so many similarities. We were both so lonely, controlled by the life we were forced into, but she made my life the way it was. She took her newly found freedom and used it to forge cages for others.

My tears keep coming, and I don't stop them. I don't wipe them away. They flow down my cheeks, staining them, branding me with my despair.

Venus isn't good for me. I know that. No amount of therapy would fix how fucked up she is.

And that isn't my problem.

I chew on my lip, wondering how the Hell I get out of Hell.

She must have some summoning stones around here. My coven is right by a summoning monolith. Nerves wind through me. The last place she would expect me to go is back there, which makes it the safest place to be.

I rise from my seat and begin searching the room—her drawers, her bookshelves, her mess of papers on the desk. After about twenty minutes of searching, I have found nothing that resembles a summoning stone. I deflate and drag myself over to the bed when a light catches my attention from the corner of my eye. I turn, looking for the source. A book on the bookshelf is shimmering. I blink and rub my eyes, trying to get myself right, but the shimmer is still there. Slowly, I approach it. The light is gentle, soft, like the first few rays of sunrise. I lick my lips and hesitantly reach my hand towards the book. I can't read the spine—the words are too faded. It's like someone has opened this book many times before.

I pull the book from the shelf, and I'm falling through air, being torn apart, piece by piece, atom by atom—

Before I can scream, I land with a thud on the soft earth.

Groaning, I roll over and reach for the book, which was thrown from my hand on impact. I feel around, but I don't make contact. I open my eyes and look around, but it's gone. I push myself up, standing on shaky legs. In front of me stands the monolith I've seen in my nightmares. It looms over me, threatening to suck me back in.

I take a deep breath once, twice, and a third time before looking around. Here is where my beloved forest is. My magic, surprisingly, doesn't seem very excited about seeing it.

And that's when I realize the forest is gone.

Chapter Twenty-Five
The Dark Lady

My cheek stings, but that pain is nothing compared to the feeling of my chest caving in on itself. Vivian left a few minutes ago—or maybe hours or days or years ago—and I continue to sit here, looking down at my hands in my lap. I can't move. I can't seem to do anything.

Maybe because I've already done enough.

Keeping things from Vivian felt like the right thing to do. It felt like the safest thing to do. I didn't trust her and she didn't trust me. Until the other night. Something shifted in me when I finally got to have her, when she finally let those powerful walls down.

Now we'll never get that chance. Her walls will be impenetrable now.

"Your Grace?"

I look up to see the archivist hovering at my side, her face the portrait of concern. "I'm sorry to disturb you," she says. "Your companion, Miss Vivian...well, she's vacated the premises."

"Yes," I reply, my tone sounding flat, "I'm pretty sure everyone in the entire realm saw her leave."

"No," she says, her voice now bordering on urgent. "She's left the realm, Your Grace."

Surprise rushes through me. "What? How do you know this?"

She gestures to Luke, who is waiting at the top of the stairs.

I rush out of my chair, wings flaring, and fly up to the landing.

"Guards saw her enter your room, and then felt magic push through," Luke says, not bothering with niceties. "When the guards entered, they found the room ransacked."

I don't even respond—I simply rush to my chambers, yanking the heavy door open. The space is a mess. Books and keepsakes litter the room.

Did Vivian manage to leave on her own? She doesn't have the magic to transport between realms—no one besides me has that ability.

Or was she taken?

I suddenly feel sick. My father hasn't been able to get into the realm since Lilith created the wards, but with them failing...

Guards rush in behind me along with Luke.

"Get the High Priestesses here now!" I shout, hoping they can sense where she's gone—or where she's been taken.

Luke barks orders at the guards, but I'm too lost in my panic to hear it. I rummage through my things, looking for any other signs of struggle. There's no blood, I notice with a bit of relief.

I feel Luke place a hand on my shoulder—assumingly in comfort—and I snarl at him. He releases me and staggers back a step.

"My apologies," he murmurs, his eyes wide. "The High Priestesses will be here shortly."

I don't respond—I simply continue picking through my things, trying to find any clues.

Vivian was right about me. I was always a lonely creature, something created that could never have true companionship. An Angel of Death. I was so lonely, but for the first time since Lilith, I felt...less alone. Vivian made me feel like that—she always seemed to see through me. Her unwavering confidence, her snark, her ability to see who and what I truly am.

And all I've done is ruin that.

I kneel on the floor, not seeing, not hearing, locked in my mind. My shadows swirl menacingly around me, showing others not to approach.

Is this a self-fulfilling prophecy? I see myself as horrible, therefore I am horrible. I wanted Vivian to fear me, therefore she can no longer be close to me.

No longer, I tell myself. No longer will I allow that to happen. I want to keep Vivian, but I realize I can only keep her if she wants to be kept.

Bustling behind me rouses me from my thoughts. I take a deep breath and rise, rolling my shoulders back and turning.

Aradia, Isobel, and Marie stand before me. They bow at once. "Your Grace," Aradia, the eldest of the three, greets me. "We understand there is a pressing matter for which we are needed."

"Indeed, there is," I say. "Vivian, the young witch accompanying me, has gone missing. As you know, no one besides me has the ability to simply come and go from Hell. I need to know if she was taken and to where."

They all nod and begin moving about the room, feeling for remnants of magic. I could have done this myself, but I'm not thinking clearly. Marie stops by the bookshelf and tilts her head as she reaches to examine a book. "Your Grace," she says, her voice soft and light. "Are there summoning stones in this space?"

I blink at her. "I keep them in various places, but there is one in this room..."

I move to stand behind her, noticing which book has caught her attention.

It's the book where I keep the summoning stone to Vivian's coven.

That little witch.

A laugh bubbles out of me, startling Marie enough to back up a few paces.

Vivian wasn't taken, I realize. She knew I'd be searching for her the moment I found her missing. She managed to use the summoning stone and head back to the one place I would never have thought to look for her.

Relief floods me so quickly that I nearly keel over.

I rein myself in and turn to Marie, whose piercing blue eyes look frightened. They dart to the shadows perched on my shoulders with a start. I know I must be a sight, so I attempt to relax my face enough to communicate that the crisis has been averted.

"Thank you for your help," I tell the witches, letting my voice carry across the room. "I have it under control from here."

Marie's eyes flit to the book that held the summoning stone and then back up to me. "The witch used the stone?" she asks.

I sigh. "It would appear so."

She blinks, surprise lighting her face. "That takes an immense amount of power. Even the strongest of witches have never been able to travel *through* a summoning stone."

I'm well aware of this, but I nod. I always knew Vivian was stronger than she knew. She might even be stronger than Lilith had been. The thought causes dread to curl up my body. With Phanes on the loose, what will happen if he learns of her power? I swallow down the rising panic at not having her close. Now isn't the time to lose myself to hypotheticals.

The High Priestesses are still staring at me, waiting for an explanation as to why the one witch who has thwarted me also happens to be powerful enough to use a summoning stone as a travel device. As if it isn't obvious.

"Vivian has proven to be quite the extraordinary witch," I hedge. "We have yet to uncover the true depths of her power."

Aradia steps closer. "My lady, if this witch is as powerful as you say...her power will only grow once her soul is signed over to you. She will be unstoppable—and you along with her. She might be the key to stopping Phanes for a final time."

"I'm well aware," I grit out. "Vivian's soul is of no concern to anyone but me."

"My lady, forgive me," Marie chirps hesitantly, "but if you two were to unite, and it is a true chance of defeating Phanes, then it is everyone's concern."

"Phanes cannot be defeated," I say slowly. "Not in any true manner, anyway. He must always live, just as I must."

Marie chews on her lower lip. "In theory, it is true that a God of Life must exist. That has always been Phanes. It has never been questioned..."

Aradia seems to pick up on Marie's thoughts because she finishes her sentence. "But it is possible another could overthrow him, taking his place."

I blink. "Are you suggesting I kill my own father and take his throne, becoming the God of Death and Life?"

Marie shrugs one shoulder. "You are the only deity left in this world. I see no better alternative for the role."

I nearly burst into hysterical laughter. This whole conversation has taken a wrong turn.

"I don't have time to discuss silly theories," I scold. "Vivian has left the realm, and with Phanes on the loose, she's in danger. You are all dismissed."

They leave without another word, although Isobel, ever the quiet one, throws me a curious glance over her shoulder. I ignore her and stare down at the book in my hands. Shame from my last conversation with Vivian washes over me again. There is so much for me to make up for. She makes me want to do that. I gnaw on my lower lip as I pull the summoning stone from the book.

It feels depleted of magic. I sigh as I make my way over to my bed and plunk down, stone still in hand. It will need a few days to recharge with magic. I've tried to infuse more of my magic into one before, and the results were not pleasant—it became too powerful, and it shot me through time and space too quickly. I nearly lost my head when I arrived at my destination from the sheer force.

Luckily, I have more than one way of getting to where I need to be. I tap my tattoo three times, feeling it slither along my bones. I'm going to let Vivian cool down first. Let her hate me a little less before I barge in, but I cannot leave her—she must be in my sight at all times. So I will arrive at her coven's land and will watch from a distance.

The snake has wrapped itself around me, and I'm traveling through space and time. When I land at the remains of Vivian's forest outside of her coven's land, I blanch. I forgot how devastating it looks. There's no sign of life for miles.

Nausea churns as I remember—she didn't know. I didn't tell her of the most egregious things I could ever do.

But now she knows.

Chapter Twenty-Six

Vivian

The forest is gone. The trees have been reduced to stumps in the ground and the grass under me is dead.

Everything is dead.

Air won't enter my lungs. I'm hunched over, hyperventilating, trying to get my lungs to work, just work…

Suddenly I'm vomiting, my body wracked with tremors as tears stream down my face. My stomach empties, but I don't stop crying. I curl into a ball and cry and cry and cry. I cry because I am sad and alone. I cry for the life I was forced to have. I cry for the freedom I never truly got to experience. I cry for the part of me that felt attached to Venus, who thought there was a different side to her.

There isn't. There's nothing but hate in her.

She took and took and continues to take from me at every turn. I forgave her, hoping I wasn't imagining the goodness that I felt from her. That my magic felt from her. I don't have the energy to hold my magic in once it pushes against me. It frees itself, folding itself over me, comforting me. Protecting me, like it did when Phanes got into my head. It wraps itself around me, providing warmth. And it cries too.

It cries at the loss of life all around us.

Our tears flow from us and seep deep into the dead earth. For the first time, my magic and I are truly one as we mourn the loss of our most cherished place.

I don't remember falling asleep, but it's dark when I wake up on the cold ground. I pick myself up off the dead forest floor and walk along the path to where the coven—my coven—lives. My magic and I are both tired. A tiredness that has seeped into my bones and feels as if it will never lessen. I drag my feet along on autopilot, my body wanting to just lie down for a little bit more. I don't have to think about any of this while I'm sleeping.

A few minutes later, homes come into view, and I pause at the outskirts of the forest. I turn back around and face the death at my back.

I touch the closest tree stump to me and murmur, "I'm sorry. This is all my fault and I'm so sorry."

My magic agrees with me, lightly pressing itself onto the tree stump with my hand.

After a beat, I cradle my hand to my chest and walk away from what had felt like my home towards the house that always felt like a stranger's.

There are no lights on, no sign of anyone being home. I look at the other homes and notice the same thing—no lights, no noise, no sign of anyone being here.

My heart sputters and I run towards my mother's house.

What if Phanes has come here? What if everyone is dead?

I race to the front door and yank it open. I take a few steps into the foyer and let my magic spool out of me, driving it deep into the earth. It searches for any sign of danger, any sign of an attack. I'm in a panic—I'm no longer thinking clearly. What if everyone is dead? What if my aunt is dead and I never get to tell her how much I love her? What if my mother is dead, and I never get the chance to tell her what a massive bitch she was my entire childhood?

My magic barrels back into me with enough force that I double over. There's no sign of death. No Phanes. No scary monster lurking in the shadows.

I breathe a sigh of relief, taking in the state of the place.

It looks like a frat house in here. Stacks of books piled on the floor, clothes and trinkets strewn throughout, and other belongings scattered carelessly. I eye the various piles of clutter before calling out, "Hello?"

Only silence greets me.

Slowly, I climb the front spiral staircase up to the second floor. My body is moving on autopilot—I'm not even fully aware I'm standing in front of my old bedroom until I'm there. I stare at the closed door with a mixture of curiosity and horror. This is a bad idea. There are only two options I will find behind this door. Either my mother collected all my belongings and burned them while dancing over the ashes and converted my room into a shrine of Venus, or she...didn't and left it untouched.

I'm not really sure which option would be worse.

With a shaky hand, I turn the knob and push the door open.

Everything looks the same. She even left my posters of Britney Spears and the Backstreet Boys on the walls, even though she would screech at me to turn my music off any time she felt it was too loud. I enter the room slowly, as if worried it's a mirage and will disappear if I make any sudden movements. Everything is the same. As if it hasn't been touched since I left. Somehow, that feels worse than her destroying it and pretending I never existed. Like she couldn't even bother to do anything about it.

I make my way over to my bed and sit on the edge. This room had bits and pieces of me in it, but I never used it as a place where I could fully be myself. My mother usually refused to let me decorate other than the posters; she nearly fainted when I asked about getting a pink dresser.

Instead, this room is nearly identical to every other witch's room in the coven. Black furniture, black sheets on the bed, and deep red paint on the walls. It's gloomy, just like everything else.

The only place I could truly be myself was the forest just behind this house, and that has been destroyed.

By Venus.

Tears well in my eyes again, hot and angry. I was a fool to believe she could be anything other than a self-serving, dangerous psychopath who only sees me as a game to be won.

Yet part of me knows that isn't right. There is more to her than I once believed. She is also lonely and sad and desperate for someone to love her. Instead of embracing her hurt, she lashes out at others, wanting them to hurt just as much as she hurts.

But I was already hurting.

I blink my tears away, suddenly overcome with the resolve to not shed another tear over Venus. This is bigger than me, bigger than her issues. We have a God who is currently Hell-bent on destroying everything.

My magic nudges me, showing me it's still there. As if to say, *we'll figure it out together.*

Venus was right about one thing: my magic and I aren't two separate beings. We feed off one another and can work together. I smile inwardly at this thing that felt so foreign and that I sometimes blamed for the life I was given.

I'm sorry, I say to it. *We're in this together now—I'm sorry it took me so long.*

My magic extends out of me, brushing against my cheeks to wipe away the newly spilled tears, and I laugh a bit breathlessly as it curls back into me like a cat ready for a nap.

Chapter Twenty-Seven
The Dark Lady

The forest looks worse than it does in my memory. A lot of that night is a blur. I remember my shadows returning to me, empty-handed, and the rest was just flashes of movement. I leveled the forest with a few blasts of my otherworldly magic. Then I spent the next several days interrogating the coven, demanding they tell me any minute detail that could help me catch Vivian. No one had known anything. No one really seemed to like her. Even her own mother was desperate to make it known she had no part in this stunt.

Looking back now, a pang of sadness radiates through me. Vivian was always an outsider amongst her people—something I know far too intimately.

There's no life here anymore.

I feel like I'm trespassing on this land by even daring to walk here. I quickly pump my wings and get airborne, too ashamed and afraid to face what I've done. Although I know I will have to do just that once I'm in front of Vivian again.

I fly towards the commune, hidden from sight by my magic. I see the homes grow closer and swoop down, landing right past the tree line. My shadows work to conceal me as I approach the wards of the commune.

I don't want to risk detection—not yet. I just want to see her, to make sure she's unharmed.

My wings rustle in the cool breeze, my shadows shifting with them. The homes are dark except for one. Vivian's childhood home. The light from the top window is on. I'm assuming that's her bedroom. I stand here, waiting until I can get a glimpse of her.

How this witch has completely altered me. It makes me sick to even consider—and to think about how, even after I atone for my wrongdoings, she will want nothing to do with me.

I can't let her go, but I can't keep her against her will, either. The thought of hurting Vivian any more than I already have makes me feel physically ill. How else can I protect her if she refuses to be with me?

My thoughts drift back to what the High Priestesses said before I came here. Is it possible, a new God of Life? I know in my bones that responsibility should not fall to me. I can barely protect the ones I am already in charge of protecting—how could I protect every living soul?

But...maybe they wouldn't need protection if my father was gone.

My thoughts are moving so quickly they're making my head spin. I can't focus on anything other than Vivian now. She is my priority.

Suddenly, I see the curtains rustle. I stiffen, worried she might spot me—until I remember I'm hidden from sight.

The curtains shift, and there she is.

Seeing her hits me harder than I thought possible. She's alive—yes, she used the summoning stone and is actively trying to hide from me, but...she's alive and safe. Her blonde hair is pulled into a high ponytail that swishes as she pushes the curtains all the way back. She's in a tight black tank top and matching shorts. I've never seen her in all-black before, but it makes my mouth water. I know she gives me shit for wearing all black, but she should do it more often because she looks stunning.

She takes one look out the window, right at me. I hold my breath, worried my magic might not be working on her, but I see no recognition in her eyes. Only...sadness. She walks away from the window, and a moment later, the light in the room goes out.

Chapter Twenty-Eight
Vivian

The house is silent the next morning. No sign of my mother or Aunt Judith. I decide to make myself at home—considering it technically *is* my home—and scrounge for something to eat in the cluttered kitchen. I manage to find a bit of cereal and some milk that, luckily, isn't expired. I can't say the same for the other contents of the fridge. I'm not sure how they're surviving in this house—my mother especially.

She was always so orderly, snapping at me for leaving a hairbrush out of a drawer or becoming irate that a picture frame was hanging crooked on the wall. Judith was the messy one, although my mother always let it slide. It would be my aunt, leaving a mess in her wake and my mother grumbling about cleaning up after her.

Their relationship always confused me growing up. Mostly because when I started acting a lot like my aunt, my mother was always unhappy with that. If Judith left a mess, it was fine—but if I did it, I was a terrible child that needed disciplining. If I tried acting more like my mother, she'd simply ignore me. I never understood her.

I'm jolted out of my memories by the sound of the front door slamming. I freeze, the spoon of cereal halfway to my mouth, unsure of what to do. I hadn't really thought my plan all the way through. Do I hide? Pretend I'm not even here? The house is so big, I doubt my mother would notice I'm even here. I'm measuring the distance and how long it would take me to dart from the kitchen back upstairs when she enters the room.

I stay seated like a deer in headlights. An array of emotions is running through me—surprise, anger, sadness, worry. It's hard to keep track of them as I look at her. My mother has aged rapidly, which is nearly unheard of for witches. Her dark brown hair is streaked with gray. Her face has deep creases and her cheeks are sagging. She's hunched over a bit, as if her back is in a perpetual slump.

She's looking down at a piece of mail in her hands, her eyebrows furrowed as she shuffles into the kitchen. I hold my breath as she approaches, still unaware that I'm even here. Suddenly, her eyes snap up and lock with mine. Her hazel eyes widen with surprise. I don't dare move, but my hands begin to tremble—milk on my spoon dribbles down into the bowl.

Drip, drip, drip.

It's the only noise in the house, as if the entire world is waiting with bated breath.

I can't keep a hold on myself. I know my emotions are written all over my face. I open my mouth to say something, anything...

"How dare you show your face here?" My mother's face contorts with anger. Her hand crumples the piece of mail she's holding. The house seems to hiss—her magic winds around the space between us.

"I—" I start, but no words come out. I'm not even sure what I want to say. I'm not even sure what I want *her* to say. *Hey Vivian, it's so good to see you after a decade. You look great!*

Even a cool dismissal of me would be better than her anger. Fighting the urge to cringe, I swallow. "Hello, Mother."

She scoffs. "Is that all you have to say to me?" Her tone is freezing. I can't believe I was more afraid of Venus than I ever was of this crone before me. "You disgrace me, this entire coven, and disappear, only to show up now?" She laughs without feeling, without humor. I shiver. "You are not welcome in my home."

"But the Dark Lady—"

"Will be glad I finally found you," she interrupts, a horrifying smile slithering across her face. I rarely saw my mother smile growing up. The only times were when misfortune had befallen someone else. It's hateful and cold. "I will alert her to your presence at once. Maybe I will finally get the recognition I deserve for being her loyal servant. Even you, my errant daughter, cannot ruin that."

I slam the spoon down on the table, rattling the bowl. "You will do no such thing."

My mother's eyes light with surprise—then cloud with anger. "You embarrassed me, embarrassed the entire coven with your little stunt ten years ago. You don't get to show up now and demand anything from me."

An incredulous laugh bubbles up inside of me. My magic roils in my stomach, ready for a full-blown argument. "I didn't come back here for a heartfelt reunion, don't worry," I sneer. "I will be out of your hair soon. Then you can go back to pretending you never even had a daughter."

She opens her mouth to spew more acid, but a knock sounds against the front door. My mother's brow furrows as she moves towards the front door without another word to me. I stay where I am, both my magic and I fuming. I know I shouldn't be surprised. She never showed any inkling of love for me.

I hear my mother's voice reach a higher pitch, alerting me she's nervous. My ears perk up, but I'm unable to make out any words, just that she's speaking to someone who rattles her.

Dread washes through me. No fucking way.

Sure enough, my mother walks into the kitchen, Venus right on her heels.

The concept of bringing a romantic partner home to my mother was never something I imagined doing. Even as a child, I watched romance movies where couples would meet the parents and it never felt like an experience I could have.

I really didn't expect to be bringing the Dark Lady home to meet my mother. Granted, they've already met, and my mother will literally kiss the ground Venus walks on, but still. It's weird. And it isn't like I invited Venus home. She merely stalked me from Hell—like she's been doing for the past ten years.

Venus, my mother, and I are standing around her old oak table in the dining room. The space has gotten cluttered over time—cabinets full of old food, many dead plants hanging from planters drilled into the walls, and a mess of books and papers stacked on the table. My mother quickly shuffles things around, saying breathlessly to Venus, "I'm terribly sorry for the clutter, my lady. I haven't had company in quite some time," before she throws me a nasty look.

I flinch under her gaze. It brings me back to when I was a child and how quickly she would belittle me. Or simply ignore me.

Venus steps toward me and places her wing around my shoulder in comfort—or in solidarity—as she replies, "It is not a problem, Jessica. I had planned to let Vivian enjoy her solitude, but I saw you arrive home and figured it would be best for us all to speak. Please, let us all have a seat."

Here we were, one estranged mother-daughter pairing with the ruler of Hell.

"Your Grace, please believe me when I say I did not have any knowledge of her arrival. If I had, I would have called upon you immediately. I am not in the business of harboring fugitives."

Venus holds up her slender hand, a tiny shadow twisting around her fingers. "I'm well aware of that, Jessica, and that is not why I am here."

My mother blinks in surprise. Then a hideous smile blooms across her lips. "Are you here to select a new witch for your council? I feel I have done nothing but uphold the duties assigned to the coven."

My mother might have been beautiful once, but her true nature cannot be hidden. Her hazel eyes hold no warmth, her skin is as pale as someone who never sees the sun. Her fingers are wrinkled, and her joints bend in different directions.

Venus shakes her head at my mother's question. "The council does not need new leadership," she answers in a placid tone, although her eyes are sharp.

"Of course, my lady." My mother dips her head. "It's just that I have done all I could. I cannot help but feel I'm being punished for the faults of my daughter and my traitor sister."

I furrow my eyebrows in confusion. "What do you mean, traitor sister?"

My mother's laugh is more like a cackle. "My sister is the reason you were able to stay hidden for so long."

"I don't understand."

"She *hid* you from her." My mother's eyes are wild, crackling with a bit of magic. "Your beloved aunt hid you from our leader, our Dark Lady."

She points a hateful finger at my chest—no, at my necklace. "She bewitched the amulet," she spits. "She cast a protection spell on it to protect the wearer. To ward off evil." Her cackle sounds like a crow's caw.

"When you ran, I cornered her. She swore she knew nothing, but I knew, I *knew* she was lying. She wanted you to escape this coven, escape this world." My mother shakes her head in disgust. "I couldn't believe she disgraced the coven, disgraced me, like this. You were never worthy of all the effort she put forth to protect you."

Something salty hits my parted lips. I realize I'm tasting my tears.

"What did you do?" I demand in a whisper.

"I killed her," she snarls at me. "She received no burial, no honor upon her death. Not after what she did."

Tears are streaming down my face now.

"How could you?" I ask, my hands balled into fists. "She was your sister!"

She rolls her eyes and gives me a look of disdain. "You always were so naïve, Vivian. What did Judith do to help the coven? She was useless! My magic has always been stronger than hers. I have always been the better witch than her. She deserved what she got." She spits on the floor as if speaking of her dead sister is beneath her.

My magic presses against my skin, wanting out, wanting retribution.

"Enough." Venus's dark, foreboding voice rumbles through the house, causing a few planters to crash to the floor. Her midnight eyes fix on my mother. "You are in no position to execute a fellow witch, especially not one of your own."

The room darkens as she stands, her wings flexing, shadows swirling. The Dark Lady is here to enact the vengeance I desperately want. My magic and I are both gleeful at the sight, nearly foaming at the mouth for it.

"Witches who break this cardinal rule are sentenced to death."

My mother cowers in her seat, her own magic nowhere to be seen. Not against the might of the Dark Lady.

"Please," she begs, her voice no louder than a whisper. "Please, I have only done right by you—"

"Did I ask you to murder your own sister?" Venus snarls.

"N-no."

"No," she agrees. "You were meant to inform me of your sister's actions once you learned of them. And did you do that?"

"No." My mother sounds defeated.

"No, you did not." Venus's shadows dance around us. My mother flinches when one slithers over to her.

Venus turns to where I'm rooted in my seat. She jerks her chin at my mother cowering in her chair. "Seeing as your mother took matters into her own hands, justice would be best handed down by you."

I blink at her, a shadow drifting up my arm to scurry into my hair. "Me?"

Venus nods. "She murdered your aunt, her own sister, for her own gain. She clearly thought it would win my favor by taking matters into her own hands."

She's angry. She's nearly trembling with it.

Without thinking, I reach out and grab her hand in mine. She looks down at our joined hands for a moment, surprised I reached for her nearly as much as I am that I did it.

"She's not worth it," I tell her. "At least," I shoot a glare at my mother, who is watching us like a fly caught in a spider's web, "she isn't worth it right now. We have bigger things to deal with."

Venus nods once and turns her attention back to my mother, her hand still in mine. "You will be kept in Hell while we await a decision from your daughter." She taps her snake tattoo three times until it slithers down her arm and makes its way over to my mother.

"Until then," she continues as the serpent wraps around my mother's body, "you are forbidden from using magic and from speaking to any others." She turns to me again. "Any last words, darling?"

I look into my mother's eyes—a mirror of my own if I had simply been the daughter she wanted me to be. Fear and hatred swirl around in them. She will never get over the embarrassment of this moment, of her disappointment of a daughter deciding her fate.

A wicked smile graces my lips as I say, "We'll see you in Hell."

The serpent vanishes, taking her with it. I swear I hear her scream for me as she goes.

Chapter Twenty-Nine

Vivan

"I hope you know that throwing my mother in Hell jail isn't enough of an apology."

Venus teleporting my mother down to the dungeons of Hell was not on my bingo card for the year. Souls sent to the dungeons of Hell do not come back.

When I asked Venus about this, she simply shrugged and said, *"It's my realm—if a soul is worthy of being released, it will be done."*

When I asked if she'd ever released a soul, she replied with, *"Never. But, for you, I would make it happen."*

I'm not sure I want her to.

Once my mother was gone, I stomped up to my childhood room, needing a moment to collect myself after everything. The news that my aunt is dead felt like a kick to the gut. My free-spirited, loving aunt, gone from this realm. I had thought to ask Venus if that meant she was in Hell, floating around as a ghost now, but part of me doesn't want to know. Would that mean I get to see her again? What if I don't?

The scenarios play in my mind on a loop as I sit on my childhood bed, trying to get myself together.

Of course, Venus follows me upstairs. I shouldn't be surprised—she's like a hound on a scent when it comes to me. She's now standing in the doorway, her wings spirited away, her shadows peeking at me from her dark hair. Her midnight eyes are unreadable.

"I'm aware," she says, her tone gravelly. "Like I said, I had planned to leave you be—under my watchful gaze, of course, but once I saw your mother return home, I thought you would need the extra help."

The snake tattoo reappears on her neck, back from transporting my mother. The snake's tongue dips out slightly, as if to say, *you're welcome.*

I ignore it and Venus, flopping back on the bed and staring at the ceiling. "What happens to the coven now?" I ask.

"They'll need a new matron," Venus replies.

Snorting, I close my eyes. "I'm sure all the witches will be vying for that spot. They have been since I could remember."

"You will have to decide what to do with your mother," she responds.

I sigh, opening my eyes and sitting up. "My mother spent most of her time belittling me. It was a mercy when she would simply ignore me." I laugh, but it comes out hollow. "Sometimes I feel that growing up with so much conflict at home, I used up all of my ability to deal with conflict now. Whenever anyone is upset with me, I just clam up—I can't deal. My brain short circuits and my body freezes. So I keep to myself. I don't let anyone close enough because I don't want to let anyone down. Maybe that's why I'm so forgiving. Maybe I forgive so much because I had to forgive my mother over and over again."

I can't look at Venus. I can only imagine what I'll see on her face. Disappointment, judgment, perhaps even disgust. Or she'll simply laugh at me.

"Maybe it's time for me to forgive her one final time. That doesn't mean what she did was right, or that I'll forget what she's done, but I need to let go of her. Of how she treated me. Of how the entire coven treated me. It's like a festering wound that refuses to close, and I don't want it to poison me anymore."

A few beats of silence pass between us, but I still don't look over at Venus. "You did not grow up in a home full of conflict," she snaps. She sounds angry. I shrink into myself, shoulder hunching. "You grew up in a home full of abuse. Conflict and abuse are not the same thing."

I snap my gaze to her, and I was right—she's angry, but I can sense she isn't angry with me. "You deserve so much more than what you've had," she says, walking hesitantly over to me. "And I know I have caused a lot of the pain you have. I want to atone for how I've treated you. For keeping things from you. For not letting you go when I should have. I got swept away in the chase and forgot that you are an actual person who deserves more than you have been given."

She lowers herself down onto her knees, as if in prayer. The sight both surprises me and does funny things to my insides. "I'm sorry for all that I've done," she says, her head hanging. "I've always been alone. No one seeks out the night—it's too full of silence and horrors to be fully enjoyed." She sounds tired. "Lilith was the first person to not run from me, to not bow before me. I liked how she stood up to me, but also, I liked how she saw me. Like she knew all the parts of me, and she wasn't afraid."

She looks up at me now, her midnight eyes haunted. "When I lost her, I lost so much more than I thought. I lost my companion, my first chance at love. What's that saying? It's better to have loved and lost than to have never loved at all?" She laughs, but it's without humor. "Whoever said that has never lost love.

"And then I found you. You, the witch who defied me, who was so headstrong and courageous and brilliant and, sometimes, very stupid. You were afraid of me, yes, but the fear didn't control you in the way you think it did. It led you to live a life that was your own. I know I stopped you from having a true, normal life—and for that, I am sorry. You are extraordinary and you have always been honest with me."

She sucks in a rough breath. "My quest for you muddled my mind. I became obsessed. I was constantly on the hunt for you. Any sign of you appearing, and I dropped everything to get to you. My sole purpose was to find you. No witch had ever denied me their soul and you doing so made me feel...alive. I shirked my responsibilities as a ruler, as a leader. I destroyed your forest out of spite. I kept things from you when I should have told you the truth. I am sorry, and I will spend the rest of my existence repenting for it. For your forgiveness, I will do anything. I will cut out my own heart if that is what you wish. Just, please, tell me what to do and I will do it." She hangs her head again, her hair shifting like a curtain of night around her. My magic stirs inside of me but makes no move to interfere. As if it wants to see what I'll do with this fallen angel of death, this goddess of night on her knees before me.

I scoot over to the edge of the bed, placing my legs on either side of her, and tilt her chin up. Midnight eyes meet mine.

"I have always been quick to forgive," I start, "even with you. But," I say, tightening my fingers on her chin, "did you deserve any of the forgiveness I gave you?"

"No," she trembles. "I did not."

I nod. "I forgave you for hounding after me. I forgave you for forgetting the covens and for keeping things from me. I will even forgive you for destroying my beloved forest—eventually.

Some may say forgiveness is a weakness. But I am not weak, am I?"

"No." She tries to shake her head, but I hold firm. "You are one of the bravest I have ever known."

I always knew my ability to forgive was a strength. I could forgive, but I never forgot. I forgave my mother for emotionally abandoning me. I forgave the coven for ostracizing me. And I forgave Venus numerous times since we met all those years ago.

They acted this way towards me because of their own issues, not because of me.

"You're sad," I muse quietly but not gently. "So you make others sad. You hurt, so you make others hurt. You feel alone, so you make others feel alone." Her eyes shutter under the pressure of my words, but I continue. "You tried to make my life miserable because you were miserable. You became the exact thing that you fought so hard to eliminate. You are destined for so much more," I parrot the words she's used towards me back at her. "You could be a leader worthy of your people. Isn't that what you want?"

Her tongue darts out to lick her lips nervously. "Yes, I do. I just...don't know how."

I know she doesn't. She's never had a chance to.

"I will help you," I tell her, "but only if you finally prove you are worthy of my forgiveness." I give her a slight, mocking smile. "I want to know that you are willing to do what it takes to receive it."

"Yes," she breathes. "I will do anything."

I raise my eyebrows and say, "You will beg for it."

The rush of power I feel from having this goddess before me feels heady. Before I lose my nerve, I gesture to the bed.

"Get up." She quickly stands, as if worried I might change my mind. "Wings out," I instruct. Her face lights with surprise, but she doesn't argue. Her wings appear as she turns from me and climbs onto the bed. "Lay down," I say, and she does.

Watching her do whatever I say turns me on. I'm suddenly ravenous for her, for my chance to have her, but I squeeze my palms into fists to calm myself down. "Clothes off."

Immediately, all of her clothes disappear. She's lying there, her wings splayed out under her, completely naked. She is the most beautiful thing I have ever seen.

Our eyes meet, and I realize...she looks nervous.

Good. She should be nervous.

"I haven't been in this house since I was eighteen," I say conversationally, walking over to open the nightstand next to the bed. "Surprisingly, my room has been left untouched, which means..." I trail off as I rummage through the cluttered drawer. My hand closes around what I want, and I pull it out and show it to her.

A very large purple vibrator, shaped like a cock.

I show it to Venus, and she audibly swallows. I'm giddy with excitement now, unable to stop myself from making my way over to her. I position myself between her legs, not bothering to waste time. We both know what we want.

"I'm going to fuck you with this," I tell her from between her legs. She looks up at me and gives me the most vulnerable expression I've ever seen on her face, uncertainty bright in her dark eyes. I press a hand gently on the inside of her thigh as a form of comfort. "You're going to love it, and you're going to beg for it."

It wasn't a question, but she nods jerkily at me. I smirk before looking down at her body again. My mouth waters. Her golden skin, her dark pert nipples, and her full hips, all leading my eyes down to what's between her legs. A dark, small patch of hair greets me, and I lean forward to kiss her mound. Her hips buck and I press my palm against her stomach.

"Don't move," I say into her, causing her to tremble.

I position the vibrator at her opening. She's so aroused that she's dripping onto the duvet beneath her. I slowly tease her entrance, letting just the tip breach her. She gasps at the intrusion. I can feel how tight she is.

"Have you ever had someone in here before?" I ask, looking up from where the vibrator is teasing her.

She shakes her head, her eyes wide and something akin to fear enters them.

"Don't worry," I croon. "I'll take good care of you. I'm going to stretch out your pretty little pussy."

I lean forward and kiss her mound again, gently, lovingly, as I shove the entire vibrator into her. She tenses, her body going tight. I press another gentle kiss into her hair and whisper sweet nothings against her skin—how great she's doing, how good she is, how she was made for me to do exactly this to her. I move the vibrator in and out of her slowly, letting her get used to the sensation. After a moment, she settles back into the mattress, welcoming the intrusion. The noises she's making—both from her center and from her mouth—are erotic. My own arousal is spiraling, hoping for release.

She looks at me with a mixture of confusion and desire when I sit up and rip off my own clothes, her eyes trailing over my naked body. It spurs me on—I climb over her until my knees are on either side of her head, facing her glorious body.

"Do you want this?" I ask.

"Yes," she groans. "Yes, please, Vivian, please—"

I lower myself onto her mouth, making her face the cutest seat I've ever had the pleasure of sitting on. She laps at me hungrily, eagerly, her tongue swirling over my clit and making me see stars. I lean forward, draping my body over hers, and grip the end of the vibrator that's protruding out of her, pumping it in and out to the rhythm of her licks.

My orgasm is already building in me. This is what she does to me. She makes me a feral, bold, unrecognizable version of myself. I love it. I drink it up. I'll never be able to get enough of this.

I piston the toy in her and she's writhing underneath me, trying to guide it deeper into her. I laugh sadistically.

Maybe I make her feral with need too. She moans loudly against me, reverberating against my clit.

"Greedy whore," I growl at her, pumping faster, harder. "Falling apart all over my cock. Maybe next time I should strap it on, huh?"

Her pleas are garbled against my center.

I snicker. "Pathetic."

I'm reaching the pinnacle now, and I want her to go over the edge with me. I press my lips to her clit just as I feel my own pleasure cresting. I suck on her clit and her body tightens as she orgasms. She grips the toy so tightly, I wonder if she'll ever release it. I'm grinding myself into her face, no longer fully in my body. It feels like we're free-falling together, making animalistic noises as we fly through the open sky. Her wings splay out even more and circle around us, keeping me pressed up against her.

Once I come back into my body, I release all my weight against her. My sweat-slicked skin moves against hers as I gently pull the vibrator from her and lift myself off her face. I look down at her and am suddenly ready to go again—her eyes are glassy, and her mouth is wet from me.

I move forward and press my lips to hers, chasing my own taste against her tongue. I slip into her mouth easily and we're a clash of teeth and tongues, fighting for domi-nance, as we always are. By the time we break apart, we're breathless. She spirits her wings away and I lay down next to her, her head on my chest. I run my fingers through her glossy black hair absentmindedly as my eyes drift closed.

"Anything," I think I hear her whisper. "I will do anything for you."

Chapter Thirty
The Dark Lady

I feel utterly shattered and reformed. The being that entered this house the other night is not the same one that sits at this table, across from the most beautiful witch I have ever seen.

Vivian.

She's currently devouring the breakfast I made her after rummaging around the kitchen for anything edible. My shadows worked to clean up some of the clutter, being the neat freaks they are, and we sit across from each other at a newly cleared table.

The fate of her mother, and the coven, is still at the forefront of my mind, but I push it away. Vivian was right; her ability to forgive is a strength I could never understand. I don't know how she does it—if I think about it too long, I want to destroy everyone who has ever made her feel less than what she is, which is extraordinary.

Her offering to forgive me makes me feel like the weight of the world has been lifted off my chest.

"We should discuss what happens now," I say hesitantly, shuffling the food around my plate.

My stomach does a little flip when she looks up at me. Her hazel eyes are a kaleidoscope of colors in the morning light. A little content smile graces her lips before her tongue darts out to lick the corner of her mouth. It makes me think of where her lips were last night. My toes curl as I watch her mouth.

She chuckles deeply, clearly seeing where my mind has taken me. "With your daddy dearest?"

It feels like cold water is dumped over my head at the mention of my father. "Yes," I answer, "but also with this coven, and with your mother, and with the larger witch population."

"So basically the entire world," she quips, as if dealing with the weight of so many big decisions doesn't faze her.

"Basically," I echo. "The coven here should be dealt with first. Figure out where their allegiance truly lies, with your mother or with me. If they're smart, they'll quickly replace her."

She nods before spearing a potato with her fork. "They love my mother, but they would never go against you."

"How can you be so sure?" I ask, the guilt of being absent gnawing at me. "They must feel I abandoned them."

She waves her hand around. "Have you seen the state of this house? My mother could barely keep it together, let alone run the coven with any sort of care or efficiency. I don't think you have to worry about them rebelling. Plus," she adds, chewing with her mouth open as she continues talking around her food, "you could just, like, smite them or whatever."

"'Smite them or whatever?'"

"You know, get all scary on them."

"Ah, that clears it up, then."

She laughs and I can't stop myself from grinning back at her. "But really," she says, her tone light, "they still worship the ground you walk on. I wouldn't worry."

I try to take her words to heart, but I have a lot of work to do. "You could lead them, you know. Become the next matron."

Her eyebrows arch at my suggestion. "What makes you think that's a good idea?"

I shrug, trying to act nonchalant. "When you stole my summoning stone and left Hell," I give her a pointed look, which she just bats her eyelashes at with faux innocence, "the High Priestesses had come to see if they could figure out where you went. When we realized you had used the summoning stone, they were shocked. Witches can't use summoning stones to transport themselves. It is merely used to summon me—hence the name—but you managed to do it."

"So?"

"So," I say slowly, "you are an incredibly powerful witch. It would behoove you to step into a role of power."

"I thought I was going to help you remake Hell," she replies, cocking her head to the side. "Remake it in a way that you truly want it to be."

"You are and you will, but..." I trail off.

"I don't want to work with them, Venus. They've always treated me like some outsider, some freak. I doubt they'll look at me any differently now."

"But now you have me at your side."

"I said no." Her tone is final.

I sit back, trying to rein myself in. I don't want to push her too hard. I understand, I really do—the idea of these witches treating her badly makes me want to destroy things, but she's powerful and deserves to be recognized for that.

Still, I push it aside—it's a conversation for another time.

Changing the subject, I say, "Your mother shouldn't come back here. Besides the fact that she killed her sister"—a look of sadness and anger flashes across Vivian's face—"you're right; she's clearly not fit to run this coven."

"So, what do we do with her?" she asks, worrying her bottom lip. A shadow darts out to run itself against her lips. She gasps and jolts back, caught off-guard by the sudden movement.

"I'm sorry," I say quickly. "Sometimes, they do act on their own accord."

She eyes my shadows at my shoulders, but her look is full of curiosity. "They're dirty perverts, that's for sure," she murmurs.

In response, a shadow darts across and shoves itself down her shirt. She yelps and bats at it, but it's already exited and perches on my shoulder once again.

"See?" she says, pointing at the frisky shadow. "Like I said, dirty perverts."

It appears the little stunt from my shadows has cracked the tension in the room. Vivian's eyes are bright again as she says, "We'll figure it out together. Can we just, I don't know, do something fun today?"

What a strange word coming out of her mouth. "Fun?" I repeat.

"Well, no new covens have been attacked, right? We should take an afternoon just to be ourselves. There's this lake that's not far from here we could visit." Her eyes stare off into the distance, a gentle smile on her face. "I used to go there sometimes, cutting through—" She cuts off as devastation clouds her face.

It takes me a moment to realize. "You used to go through your forest to get there," I guess.

She nods, as if unable to respond verbally.

Shame clangs through me. "Vivian, I am forever sorry for what I did. I will make it right, I promise."

She nods, but her eyes are clouded, her scent upsetting my senses. She picks up her plate and walks over to the sink. "Maybe one day," she says in a tone that sounds light but is hollow inside. Guarded. "One day, you will."

Chapter Thirty-One
Vivian

I must be a masochist. Why else would I take Venus through my destroyed forest to get to my lake? I must enjoy hurting myself.

We arrive at the tree line, and I'm overcome with sadness and pure rage—both my own and my magic's. I know I said I would forgive her for this, but it's proving harder than I thought.

She must scent my emotions because she keeps back from me a bit. I try to breathe deeply, in and out, in and out, as we walk towards the lake. I feel it bubbling under my skin, my rage, my devastation. I feel like a teapot that's about to blow, a pot of boiling water that's about to spill over. I try to get a handle on myself, but I can't.

I stop walking and squeeze my eyes shut. Behind me, I hear Venus stop walking too.

"Viv," she says softly. I hold up a hand to say, *don't say another fucking word*. She ignores me, and I feel a shadow press itself against my calf. "I want you to try something," she murmurs.

My eyes fly open, and I spin around, glaring at her.

She holds her hands up in surrender. "I just want you to let your magic out," she whispers.

"Why?" I snarl. I'm wound so tight, I'm not even sure if we're arguing or what we're even talking about. All I know is that I feel like I'm drowning in my own emotions.

"You have a beautiful gift," she replies. "See if it will help with healing."

I'm not thinking clearly—I can't understand what she's saying. My magic presses against my skin, amplifying my anger. It wants out, it wants—I don't even think; I don't even command—my magic slips from my fingers and burrows into the ground around us. Deeper and deeper, all it feels is death and destruction and...sadness. So much sadness. I barrel over, dry heaving from the intensity.

The land, my sanctuary, is so alone.

I might be screaming or crying or cursing Venus and the world. I might even black out because the next thing I know, I'm on my knees. Venus is hovering in front of me, her midnight eyes wide in fright.

My throat is on fire. Sucking in a deep breath, I rasp, "What...what *was* that?"

Venus's eyes flash as she smiles down at me. "Look," she says.

I groan, my body feeling like I got hit by a semi-truck. What I see in front of me makes me blink a few times, unsure if I'm hallucinating. The grass around the two of us is no longer yellow with death—it's now a deep green. I gasp and run my hands through it, feeling the short little blades run between my fingers. This living grass circles us for a few feet before it abruptly ends in the yellow blades.

"How is this possible?" I ask breathlessly.

"Your magic," Venus replies, as if it's a simple and obvious answer.

"But I've never done this before," I argue. "I've never brought anything...back to life." Every time I've used my magic, it simply enhanced what was already living.

She strokes my hair that cascades down my back. "I've told you that you're extraordinary. It might take a lot of work, but I think you could restore this land, Vivian."

Hot, fresh tears pool in my eyes as I look at her. "I was so angry," I whisper. "I know I told you I would forgive you, but it just made me so angry."

She gives me a sad smile. "I know." She leans in and kisses my forehead. "I think I know how to help." Slowly, gently, she helps me to my feet. Dusting me off, she says, "The High Priestesses are some of the most powerful witches to have ever lived—and they're amazed by you. I think, maybe, they could help you channel your magic. Help you two become one, even more so than you already have. Maybe with a little help, the forest can be restored." She gestures to the fresh grass around us.

"The idea of spending time with witches—even dead ones—isn't exactly high on my priority list," I counter.

She nods. "I know. Just think about it. I would be more than happy to facilitate it for you."

I suck in a breath, the air feeling like fire as it drags down into my lungs. Tunneling into myself, I see my magic is slumbering—passed out from all the hard work. I grin up at Venus and say, "I'll think about it."

It takes about an hour to get to my lake. I spend most of the time pestering Venus for stories about her time as the Dark Lady.

Has she met any famous souls? *She doesn't pay attention to such frivolous things.*

Is the Illuminati real? *She isn't familiar with this*—which means no, they aren't.

Venus also seems very curious about my life.

What was college like? I don't remember; I was stoned for most of it.

What jobs did I work? Receptionist at a hair salon so I could get my hair done for free; dog walker; nanny; then different accounting firms and departments.

What do I do for fun? Spa days, shopping, watching reality TV.

Did I have any pets? I had a fish once, but it died after a few weeks.

I'm babbling on about how much I love my current nail artist and how I can't decide if I want butterflies or hearts next when we reach the lake. Instead of stopping my words, I begin to pull off my clothes to get in. "So I think butterflies would be super cute, you know? Like different colored ones, but I could also do different colored hearts too—"

"What are you doing?" Venus asks me.

I halt, my shirt already off and my shorts halfway down my legs.

"I'm getting in the lake," I say slowly. "That's why we're here."

She's staring at my chest, her dark eyes showing her feral hunger as she looks upon my naked chest. A breeze tickles my nipples, pebbling them under the caress, and I shiver.

Venus's tongue darts out to lick her lips before her eyes trail up to my face.

"I wasn't aware we were getting naked," she stammers.

I smirk, my confidence growing the longer she looks at me like she needs to have me, touch me. "I'm not swimming in my clothes. You can, though, if you want."

I shimmy out of my shorts and stand up straight, fully naked. With a flick of my hair, I saunter to the water's edge. I might swing my hips a bit more than I need to, for no particular reason. The water is nice and warm, heated by the sun beating down on the surface. Without a look behind me, I wade into the water until it reaches my chest. I sigh as it gently laps at my skin, dragging out the soreness from my magic's stunt earlier. The ends of my hair float around me like a gentle halo.

Turning, I see Venus standing on the shore, her eyes trained on my every move. A predator sizing up prey.

Even though we both know I can also be a predator.

I raise my hand out of the water and crook my finger at her. She raises an eyebrow but doesn't object. Her clothes instantly vanish, and her wings appear, unfurling from her back. Without her eyes leaving mine, she wades into the water.

Need forms in my stomach the closer she gets to me. Her glorious body is hidden under the water, but the mere thought of her naked form approaching me is enough to have my insides turn molten. She slowly wades over to me, her powerful wings propelling her forward. We meet in the middle, our arms and legs tangling around each other, our bodies molding together effortlessly. I shiver again, but not because I'm cold.

Her fingers slowly trail up and down my spine, causing me to arch into her. I close my eyes, soaking in the sensations of her fingers stroking me, her chest pressed against mine, the sun on my face, the water lapping all around us.

I could happily die here like this, I realize.

Lifting a hand, I run my fingertips along the upper curve of her wing. She shudders and a low moan passes between her lips.

"Sensitive?" I murmur. She simply nods, as if she can't quite form words. "Mmm," I hum into her ear, stroking my fingers over the spot on her wing again. She bucks her hips against me in answer.

Her body responding to what I do does something to me. The power I feel by having this goddess melting from a simple touch is otherworldly. I feel like I could remake the entire world with half a thought. I shift, opening my legs and positioning my center against hers. She gasps when our bodies meet, her eyes sparkling. I begin moving my hips, letting our most sensitive spaces glide against one another. Sparks of arousal glow between us, lighting both of us up from within.

Venus gyrates her hips to meet me, stroke for stroke, chasing her desire just like I'm chasing mine. We stare into each other's eyes, not blinking for fear of missing even a nanosecond of the other's pleasure. Her face is flushed and she's panting, her breath warming my face.

"I need you," I whisper. I'm not sure why that comes out of my mouth, but Venus seems to like hearing it—her hands slip down to my hips, and she rocks me back and forth. My clit caresses against hers and my brain short circuits.

The pleasure is building too quickly, too sharply. I want it to slow down, to savor it—but I also can't bear for it to stop.

"That's it," she murmurs.

I choke on my own breath as my release barrels into me, hitting me like a freight train. Throwing my head back, I cry out, letting the waves of pleasure lap at me until I'm nothing but water and the earth beneath. When I finally return to my corporeal self, I look up at Venus as she continues to grind her clit against mine. I'm twitching in her arms, the aftershocks coursing through me. Whatever she sees on my face sends her over the edge—she bites down hard on her bottom lip to stifle her cries as she meets her own release. I watch in amazement at her falling apart, feeling invincible.

I grab her neck, and our lips collide.

When we both have come down from our highs, we simply hold each other's gaze.

"This is the best visit to the lake I've ever had," I laugh breathlessly.

She chuckles with me, running her nose along my jaw-line, and I'm struck by the strangest revelation. Pressed against Venus, soaking in the comfort of her in one of my most sacred places that she had mostly destroyed, I realize this is a healing moment I wasn't aware I needed. I needed her here, to rewrite my memories of her. To take it back to the source and change it.

The forest around us may still be destroyed by her anger ten years ago, but it can be repaired—by me.

That revelation causes pride to swell in me and my magic does a little flip in my stomach.

As I look into Venus's midnight eyes, still bright from the orgasm afterglow, I open my mouth to share.

But then I stop myself.

"Come, let's swim out further," she says, squeezing me before letting me go.

I swim after her, puzzling over my hesitation. Perhaps a bit of secrecy between us isn't all bad.

Chapter Thirty-Two
Vivian

"Vivian, we have much to discuss."

I sigh and flop over onto my stomach. "I know, I know. My mother, the coven, Phanes, the High Priestesses training me, and remaking the wards. I get it, I do—we have a long to-do list."

Propping myself up on my arm, I look over at Venus. She's definitely made herself at home here. She's currently seated at my old desk, legs kicked up, her shadows swirling around and organizing the desk. They seem to be complete neat freaks, constantly straightening up the place. We've been at my mother's home for a few days and it's already looking a million times cleaner, thanks to them.

Venus met with the coven to explain where my mother went and that there's a new threat to witches prowling around. I stayed behind, hiding in the house like a coward. I know the coven would shit themselves if they saw me on Venus's arm, but I'm not ready to face them yet. Not while my mother is still in some dungeon.

And not while my aunt Judith's room needs tending to.

What my mother said has been nagging at me—that my aunt protected me with my amulet. When my aunt told me it would be used for protection, I hadn't thought much about it, but if what my mother claims is true, why would my aunt infuse her magic into a protection spell for me?

I hope some answers might be found in her room.

The door has been closed, and I haven't had the nerve to open it, so I'm not sure what I'll find in there. Although, I doubt my mother got rid of anything—she hated me and she left my room in pristine condition, so I figure the same will be true for my aunt's.

"I just want to tackle one thing at a time," I say to Venus finally. "Tackling my aunt's room will be the first thing, then we can do everything after. Promise."

"You also need to quit your job," she quips, examining her nails. "If you still even have it. It's been weeks and you haven't been in." A quirk of an eyebrow. "Worried that boy will move on if you finally quit?"

I eye her, wondering why she's bringing this up. "I don't care what he thinks. He was just a coworker."

She hums in a way that would seem noncommittal to most, but I know better.

"Are you jealous?" I chuckle incredulously.

She shoots me a look, her dark eyes unreadable. "I don't need to be jealous of mortal males."

"You certainly don't," I agree, lifting myself off the bed and prowling towards her. She lowers her feet to the ground, her boots making a loud thud on the hardwood. I position myself between her legs and lightly wrap my arms around her shoulders. Running my hands through her silky strands of onyx hair, I murmur, "No mortal has made me feel as much as you have."

She peers up at me, disbelief written across her face. "I'm sure you've never had a need to hate another mortal as much as you've hated me."

"True," I tease, wrapping her hair around my fist and jerking her chin back. Her eyes flash but she doesn't resist me.

Her throat is bared to me. If I was smart, I would wrap my hands around her beautiful neck and squeeze until she stopped breathing. She would let me, I think. She thinks she deserves it, after everything she's done to me.

But that's not what I want.

I lean down and press my lips to hers softly. "I don't know how to describe it. You just make me feel, period. It's like my emotions are heightened whenever I'm with you. Happy, sad, angry, aroused." I laugh softly against her lips. "It's like a fire has been started inside of me since you showed up."

Venus leans forward and smashes her lips against me, and we're a cluster of tongues and teeth, warring with each other. I tug on her hair harder, causing her to whimper into my mouth. I swallow the sound like it's the most expensive wine, getting drunk on it. Her hands grip my hips and I feel light touches all around my arms, my legs, my stomach—her shadows, not wasting time getting their fill of me. It makes me think of the first night they appeared to me, how they entered me. I groan at the memory, winding myself tighter. Venus's tongue swoops into my mouth as if she wants to taste the sounds coming out of me.

After a few breathless moments, we pull apart slowly. I let go of Venus's hair, running my nails along her scalp. She shivers in response. She looks beautiful—eyes glassy, mouth swollen, hair mussed. It makes me want to say 'fuck it' to our to-do list and just stay in bed together.

Reluctantly, I pull out of her grasp, my body instantly feeling cold. "I should get to it," I gasp out. I can't remember what I was supposed to do. "Get to, um, what I have to do. You know, the thing."

What am I supposed to be doing?

Venus's nostrils flare as she growls, "Right, the thing you have to do."

I nod furiously. "Later," I promise, running my eyes up and down her body. She goes still under my gaze.

It's been a few days since the lake, and we've barely been able to keep our hands off each other. I would have missed entire days to the sex if Venus hadn't stopped to feed us. Which is good, I suppose—a body's gotta have fuel to keep fucking.

Today is not a day for that, so I make my way to my aunt's room, counting my breaths as I go.

In for four beats, out for four. In for four, out for four.

I reach her door and halt with my hand on the doorknob. Dread has overtaken my body; I can't even seem to see clearly. "I can do this," I say to myself, but I can't. I can't, I can't...

My magic pops out, wrapping around my hand, acting like it's holding the knob with me. I stare down silently and watch my magic twist the knob for me—with me.

An overwhelming feeling that I can't place drowns out the dread. Tears spring to my eyes as I say, "Thank you."

I steel my spine and push the door open.

I've been in my aunt's room for what feels like an eternity and haven't accomplished anything but making a bigger mess than I was greeted with. My mother hadn't touched my aunt's room, much like how she hadn't touched mine. It still smells like her—jasmine and orange. I couldn't help myself when her signature scent lightly brushed past me—I jumped into her gigantic bed and burrowed into the sheets, face plastered into the pillows, inhaling deeply. I'm not sure how long I stayed like that, but after a while, I knew it was time to look around. I dragged myself out of the bed and moved towards her desk.

My aunt's room appears to be tidy, but upon closer inspection, it's just a cluttered mess. Small trinkets are piled on top of each other inside every drawer, books are shoved under her bed, and clothes are in disarray in her closet. While my mother's clutter screamed of her decline, my aunt's is organized chaos—she always seemed to know where everything was in here. One time, when I was eight, I had been looking for a spell book to teach me how to make frogs dance. I moved a few books around, looking for the right one. Hours later, my aunt had demanded she know who had dared to enter her room and take from her. I was so afraid of her reaction—I had never seen her angry before—but when I finally fessed up, her eyes had softened and she had cooed, "Oh, my dear, that's quite all right. I'm glad you're wanting to learn! Just ask me next time, will you?"

It feels wrong to be in here, touching her things without her knowing. My skin feels oily from violating her in this way, but I continue, searching through her various drawers for any information on the protection spells and my amulet.

Why this amulet? Why did I need protection? From Venus—or from something even more sinister?

My questions keep me going, flipping through some of her notebooks. Her chicken scratch fills almost every page. There's no rhyme or reason to her notes—some are recipes for meals, others are ingredient lists for potions, and there are even to-do lists in here. After the tenth notebook with nothing useful in it, I throw it across the room with a huff. It lands with a loud thud on the hardwood.

I close my eyes, trying to pull myself together, working through my breathing techniques, when a light emanates through my closed lids. I peek open to see something shimmering under the bed. It's glowing the same way the book that held the summoning stone in Venus's rooms did. Scrambling over, I push myself under the bed. Sure enough, a book is glowing under here.

After a few embarrassing moments of wriggling under the bed, I manage to get the damn thing. I lean my back against the bed frame as I examine the cover. It looks like any regular leather-bound notebook—no writing on the front or the spine. The book continues to glimmer softly. I flip it open to the first page and gasp.

My dearest niece,

You have finally found my secrets. I was waiting for the day that you would be nosy enough to come snooping. Please tread lightly. Magic is fickle.

You have always been the light of my life. I hope to see you in the next one.

Aunt Judith

Tears drip onto the page, staining the paper. I quickly wipe my tears to avoid smudging any of the words. I drink in her letter, reading it over and over until it feels like my eyes have dried out. She left this for me. She wanted me to find this, which means I must be getting closer.

These moments feel like different pieces of the same puzzle—and I might have just found the one piece I need to see the picture. The pages are full of various spells specific to altering the earth. How to create hills or craters, how to manipulate crops to either grow or wither away, even how to animate an entire landscape.

I gasp, realization dawning on me. I've done that before when I escaped from Venus. In my panic, my magic must have worked to protect me by animating the trees and allowing them to escort me out safely.

I'm furiously reading each page, absorbing the knowledge as best I can. This is a treasure trove of information and spell work I never knew I needed. The final page, scribbled in barely legible handwriting, reads:

Beware, my child of the earth, they have been searching for you.

My breath catches in my throat. I flip the page back and forth, looking for more—for anything else—but that's it.

No answer on what 'child of the earth' even means. A very large part of me is terrified, while a very small part of me is a bit peeved by the name itself. It's obviously a nod to my magic, but I'm not sure what else it could mean.

Chapter Thirty-Three
Vivian

"Should I get bangs?"

"Why are you asking me?"

"Because you're the one who would be looking at them."

"But wouldn't you be the one who would have to deal with them?" Venus asks.

"Excellent point," I respond. "Maybe not bangs-bangs, but like, long bangs."

"I don't understand any of the words you're saying," she admits, exasperated.

I'm standing in front of a boutique's floor-length mirror, considering the outfit I'm trying on. It's a navy mini-dress with a white collar. It goes great with my knee-high white boots. I pull my hair into a high pony and hold it, admiring the angles with my hair up, turning this way and that.

"I just think bangs would really work for me because I'm going through such a moment of change," I chirp, but then I consider for a moment. "Or a mental breakdown. Everyone gets bangs during a mental breakdown."

She throws me a bemused look. "Is that what this is—a mental breakdown?"

I give her an offended look in the mirror. "This is retail therapy. I think I deserve it."

And I do, dammit. Not only did I find my aunt's grimoire, but I also finally called my job and quit. I gave them some excuse that my fake dead uncle's estate needed managing. They hadn't seemed surprised.

The part of me that would usually be sad and angry about having to leave my new life behind hasn't been so loud this time around. I'm sure it's because I'm so busy, saving the entire world and all.

No other reason.

I needed something to feel like myself again. So I told Venus I needed new clothes—I couldn't try squeezing into my clothes from when I was a kid anymore. They didn't fit properly, with my ass and my boobs spilling out. She had told me she didn't mind that one bit but had flown us into town.

The town is about thirty minutes from the commune. It's changed a lot in the past ten years—what used to be a rundown gas station and local grocery store is now a thriving retail center with boutiques, a bookstore, coffee shops, and a few fancy-looking restaurants.

Venus shrugs, acting like she's unbothered by the conversation or standing in this girly shop. It's clear she's not usually around people who don't know how powerful she is. When we entered a shop down the street, she had the audacity to demand they close it down so I could have a private shopping experience. While the idea was a great one, it was definitely not appropriate—the workers were nearly scared shitless when she snarled at them after they told her no. I was super annoyed to have to drag her out of there; the clothes were so cute and now I can never show my face in there again.

Venus kept her mouth shut while I perused the racks in other shops, trailing behind me and wordlessly taking any articles of clothing I wanted to try on in her arms. This is currently outfit number seven I've tried, but it's just not hitting the spot in my brain my little treats usually hit. I let go of my hair with a huff and storm over to the dressing room, shoving the curtain closed with a bit more force than necessary.

"I thought that one was nice," Venus supplies from the other side of the curtain.

I snort. "It's nearly black—of course you think that."

Ripping the dress over my head, I throw it down on the floor...then quickly pick it up, straighten it out, and place it back on the hanger. My bad mood isn't the retail worker's fault.

"What's wrong?" she asks me.

"I don't know," I respond a bit sharply. "Shopping usually helps me when I'm in a mood, but it isn't today for some reason. I'm not sure what's up with me."

There is silence on the other side of the curtain. Then it's pushed back, and Venus is standing in the doorway.

"Venus!" I shriek, covering my naked body. "I'm *changing*!"

She simply rolls her eyes like I'm being dramatic and pushes her way in, shutting the curtain behind her. She crowds me, her warmth enveloping me, holding me.

"Tell me what's wrong," she demands, her fingers trailing across my cheek delicately. I nearly melt under the soft touch.

Looking into her midnight eyes, it all comes spilling out. "I'm afraid. I'm afraid of what your *father* really wants. Why does he want to get into Hell? Why is he attacking covens? Why would he speak to me, of all witches?"

"I assumed he was after the realm due to his own vendetta against me...but I don't understand how you play into it," she admits.

"I'm just afraid of what this all means for me. I feel like, yet again, I have no choice in any of this. I'm, like, destined to be embroiled because I'm a 'child of the earth'? Which, by the way, is a horrible nickname. Like, what does it even mean—that I'm literally born from dirt?" I scoff, picking up my own clothes and throwing them on.

Venus goes still at my words, observing me with an unreadable expression on her face.

"What?" I snap. "Why are you looking at me like that?"

"Maybe it doesn't mean *you*." I furrow my brows at her. "The High Priestesses told me your magic is unique, somehow. That it was created by the earth itself. I didn't get the specifics, but..." She trails off, her eyes wide as she takes me in. I can see a new sense of urgency thrumming through her body.

I reach into myself, poking at my magic. *Do you know anything about this?* I ask.

It seems to flicker with both anger—pure, undiluted anger—and fear.

Is Venus right? Are you...what Phanes is talking about?

It cowers further inside of me.

"My magic...something is up," I tell Venus.

"I can feel it—the shift," she informs me. "We need to get back to Hell. Right away. We need to see the High Priestesses."

An hour later, we're standing at the monolith in the clearing. Venus nearly carried me out of the boutique and flew us here, a near-feral look of panic on her face.

"Can't you just teleport us to Hell?" I ask, bouncing from one foot to the other. The air is chilly now—it seems the temperature has dropped significantly since this morning.

"I worry about being detected," she murmurs.

"Phanes can track us?" I squawk.

"I'm not sure," she admits. "But I'm not willing to chance it."

She steps to the monolith, power radiating from both her and the pillar. It makes my blood go cold. The last time I touched that monstrosity was during my ceremony. I don't know if I can relive it just yet. Venus touches her palm to the smooth stone and the sensation of magic surrounds me, near-suffocating. I gulp down air, forcing my lungs to keep working.

Her hair floats lightly upwards, her wings unfurling and stretching to their full power. Shadows dance around us, some skirting around my feet, my arms. My magic seems to shrink further into me, which concerns me—it's usually pushing at every chance to be free.

Venus turns her head to look at me, her eyes wild with magic. "Come," she says, her hand outstretched to me.

"I prefer the snake squeezing me to death than this," I mutter.

Her mouth lifts to one side. "I'll keep that in mind."

Swallowing down my fear and panic, I lift my hand and hers envelopes mine, her calluses brushing up against my skin in a familiar way. It relaxes me and I let out a little sigh as I step closer.

The power radiating from the monolith continues to stretch outwards, gripping me, trying to pull me into the monolith itself. I slam my eyes shut. I feel sick; I can't do this.

A squeeze from Venus's hand brings me back into my body. She becomes my anchor, my pillar to hold onto while we weather everything and anything. Tears fill my eyes, but not from the teleporting. I squeeze her hand back, hoping my face says everything to her I can't yet voice to myself.

Chapter Thirty-Four
The Dark Lady

Traveling to Hell was...rough. It's never pleasant, but bringing someone with is particularly nasty. Vivian is currently throwing up on the floor of my room, with me holding her hair out of her face. I stroke her back gently, murmuring sweet nothings as she continues to empty the contents of her stomach. It's safe to say we won't be using summoning places again.

"How did you manage to handle the summoning stone?" I muse.

In between her heaving, she responds, "I'm not"—heave—"really sure"—heave—"but I was a mess"—heave—"and passed out after."

I hum as I draw circles up and down her spine.

Eventually, the shudders stop, and she sits up. Her eyes are glassy, and her face is pale. Without another word, I vanish the sickness from the floor and scoop her into my arms. Once she's deposited gently onto the bed, I ease her out of her clothes. She doesn't fight me, but she also isn't much help—she lays there like a dead fish, not holding her own weight as I work her pants down her legs. I grunt as I get the damn things off her, exposing her undergarments.

A spot on her panties has me spreading her legs for a closer look.

"Vivian," I say, my voice guttural, "you're bleeding." A small spot of dark blood is in the center of her panties.

She groans a bit. "That explains why I feel so out of sorts. I can't believe you almost allowed me to get bangs."

I can't joke with her right now—I'm too fixated on the little spot. My heart is hammering in my chest. I try to tighten the leash on myself to no avail. Without thinking, I peel the panties down her legs, exposing her to me.

"Venus," she whines, "I'm gonna bleed all over the bed."

"Fuck," I groan. I'm not sure what's come over me. I've never had much of a thing for blood—it's never caused such a reaction from me.

I lean forward and hover my mouth over her center, blowing on her gently. "Vivian," I growl, "I need to taste you."

"I—what?" she asks, struggling to lift her head and look down at me.

Pressing a kiss to her, I groan again and squeeze her open thighs. "Please," I beg.

"Um, you're not worried...?"

I huff a laugh into her, causing a shiver to work through her body. "I know we have so much else to deal with right now, but I can't resist this."

"Okay, then," she replies, her voice small.

I dive into her, the leash I tried to hold myself back with snapping. I feast on her like I've been starved my whole life. Perhaps I have been—starved of what I truly needed until she came barreling into my world and threw everything upside down.

I lap at her, the mixture of her arousal and blood coating my tongue. Shivers wrack my body as I taste her and moan into her.

"Ooh," she cries out, hips straining to meet me. "Yes, yes, that's—" A little gasp escapes her lips, cutting off her words, as I suck gently on her clit. Her scent, her intoxicating, dangerously erotic scent, has flooded my system as I lick her. I can't get enough—can never get enough. I take her thighs and push them to her chest before I dive right back in, licking her from her ass to her slit to her adorable little clit.

She's writhing against me, but I hold firm, letting myself get my fill. Her center has blood and my saliva smeared all over her, and it's the most beautiful thing I've ever had the pleasure of seeing. Sticking my tongue into her channel, I pump in and out, unable to get enough of her. Her moans grow louder. She grips my hair in one hand roughly. Pain ripples across my scalp, spurring me on. Her blood and arousal leak down onto the sheets and it causes my brain to short circuit.

This is going to have to be a monthly occurrence from now on.

Her channel tightens around my tongue, her release causing her to cry out at the ceiling. I ride her through it, my tongue spearing her until she settles back onto the bed.

I lift myself a bit to admire my work.

Vivian is stretched out before me, panting lightly, a sheen of sweat on her beautiful skin. Her eyes are barely open, her hair a wild mane around her face. And she was right; she got blood all over the sheets.

I'll make sure they're never laundered.

I crawl up her body, pressing a kiss to her lips. She giggles when I pull back. "You look like a lion after it's caught a meal."

She can tell I'm confused because she clarifies, "You have blood all over your mouth."

I hum, an alien feeling working through my veins. Looking down at her, I never want to be without her. I've felt that way since finding out she exists, but it's morphed into something else—something softer.

Perhaps she is simply smoothing all my jagged edges.

I settle in next to her, wrapping her into my arms and cocooning her with my wings.

"You're in no state to see the High Priestesses now," I say to her.

She snorts in response. "Like you are either."

I rustle her hair gently and chuckle into her ear. "Perhaps not," I admit.

That evening, I'm sitting in one of my smaller meeting rooms across from the three High Priestesses, Vivian on my right. Her hand is gently cradled between both of mine as they rest in my lap. I mindlessly circle her skin with my thumb, causing Vivian to shoot me a gentle smile.

Aradia coughs awkwardly, causing Vivian and I to snap our attention to the three witches across from us.

I clear my throat and face the three witches across the table from me. "We suspect Phanes is hunting for Vivian. I fear having her in the realm of the living will allow him to take her."

"Our wards have been failing," Marie reminds me. "And she is not ready to remake them."

"I'm not," Vivian interjects, looking at Marie with an unflinching confidence. My blood heats at the strength she's exuding. "My magic and I aren't exactly buddies, but we've been working through our issues." She throws the witches—the three most powerful witches in existence—a lopsided grin.

"Your magic is too strong for you to wield," Aradia replies, her face contorting in a frown. "Even if we start teaching you today, it will take far too long to get you and your magic working as one. Phanes will have broken down our doors and stolen you away before then."

Panic strikes me like a lightning bolt. A growl works its way up my chest. "Phanes wouldn't dare step foot in this realm."

"If he's desperate for her, he will," Isobel argues.

"Why does Phanes want me, anyway?" Vivian asks, looking between me and the priestesses. "What's so special about little ol' me?"

"It's not about you—it's about your magic," Aradia replies. "Phanes must know what magic you possess, and he must want it. Badly."

"But *why*?" Vivian pushes. "Who cares where my magic came from? What does he want it for?"

"We aren't sure," Marie admits. "He has always been greedy. He might think you're the key to destroying his last child. Or he might simply want your magic as his new plaything."

I bare my teeth, anger rising to meet my initial panic. Vivian throws me a surprised glance as the witches flinch back. I can feel my shadows growing in the space around us as scenarios, both real and imagined, swirl in my mind. Lilith being captured. Her soul being destroyed—never to be at peace. Vivian being taken the same way. It's too much. I can't live through losing her. I don't think I'll survive this time.

"Venus," I hear Vivian murmur. I snap my eyes to her. She's looking at me with open concern, her other hand placed on my knee. She squeezes me gently, bringing me back into myself slowly. "I'm right here," she says, her hazel eyes shining in the candlelight emanating from the table. Her cherry blossom and pomegranate scent wraps itself around me, seeping into my muscles and bones, relaxing me. I loose a breath and squeeze her hand back. "I'm here," she says again, a soft smile on her mouth. "I'm here with you."

I nod, unable to articulate what those words mean to me. What they will always mean to me now. She's here. She chooses to be here with me. We might be bound by tradition and circumstance, but we continue to choose one another—even when we do not have to. Her eyes tell me all that as they gaze into mine. She chooses me. I feel myself relax, letting her touch be my guiding light back into myself.

"My apologies," I grit out, contrition a foreign thing on my tongue. The witches struggle to hide their surprise. "What can we do now? How do we make sure to protect the entire realm?"

"We can try a concealment spell. It would allow for Vivian to move about, hidden from other magical beings," Marie informs us.

"What does it entail?" Vivian asks.

"We will have to infuse the spell into an object—a necklace, a charm that you could keep on your person."

"Like the amulet from my aunt," Vivian says to me, hurt flashing through her eyes before clearing. "I've had one before, apparently. I was told it was for protection...but I guess it's not really that different, is it?" She removes her hands from me and holds the amulet up. "Can it be infused with this?"

"We will have to inspect it—see if there's any lingering magic left," Isobel replies, her eyes assessing the amulet from afar. "If there is, it might prove difficult, although not impossible."

"My mother told me the spell from my aunt ceased because she...died."

"A witch's magic changes once they die. As their soul departs one realm and enters the other, the magic will eventually dry out, but it does not happen immediately. The only time that hasn't happened was with Lilith's wards—although they are fading too." Aradia shrugs.

Vivian chews on her bottom lip, seeming to process this. I raise my hand to the back of her neck. "They will need to see the amulet up close."

She turns her head to look at me, a soft, vulnerable expression on her beautiful face. "I haven't taken it off since she gave it to me," she murmurs.

I nod and lightly squeeze her neck. There's no proper way to respond, no way to push her past her feelings. I stroke her soft skin. "You'll get it right back."

She searches my face for a moment—for what, I'm not sure, but whatever she finds seems to satisfy her. She reaches up to unclasp the gift from her beloved aunt, but I stop her. I quickly undo the clasp myself and take the necklace from around her neck.

I give her one more look to say, *you're sure?*

She nods.

I place the amulet on the table and slide it across to the awaiting priestesses.

Aradia nods to Vivian. "We will waste no time. For now, stay close."

Chapter Thirty-Five
Vivian

I've been in Hell for three days, and it's already vastly different from the first time I came here. Venus can tell I'm in a funk. It's just that so much has happened in such a short amount of time. My entire life has turned on its head and now I'm being hunted by my somewhat-girlfriend's crazy dad.

Girlfriend or partner is the entirely wrong word for what Venus is to me. Originally it was Dark Lady, then it was stalker, then it was colleague, and now...it's all just been a bit of a mind-fuck.

Venus has been the one part that I'm actually enjoying. We spend our days glued to each other. I know it's out of fear of me being taken, but there's more here. Just like there was more when we got here. Just like there was more during our meeting with the High Priestesses.

"We should do something today," I tell her as I stretch out, kicking her a bit. We've been in bed, awake, for the past few hours, simply holding each other. No words, no sex. It's more intimate than we've ever been.

"Like what?" she grunts, grabbing me by the ankle to stop me.

"I don't know," I say. "I didn't really get to see Hell when I was here last."

"I know. You were too busy being a thorn in my side."

"And you were too busy keeping things from me."

She hums noncommittally, causing me to kick her with my free foot. She grabs that one too.

"I want you in my bed where I can keep a close eye on you." Her tone is playful, but I know she's serious.

I groan. "What do spirits even do in Hell anyway? Just float around?"

"They live normal lives. They reside in homes, they walk around their city, enjoying all that the afterlife has to offer."

"Which is exactly what I want to see," I point out. "Just for a few hours."

"I unnerve the spirits when I visit their dwellings."

"That's fine, I'll go with someone else," I argue.

"Did you not just hear me say I want you close to keep an eye on you?"

I snort. "You've only been saying it constantly for the past three days. C'mon, just a few hours." I poke her in the ribs playfully.

"If you're hoping to run into your aunt, I'm afraid you'll be disappointed."

Her words feel like a stone dropping into an ocean of my grief. I still, fighting the feeling of sorrow that is trying to wash over me. "I wasn't planning that," I murmur quietly.

Venus releases my feet and shifts to hover over me, peering down at me with her onyx eyes. "I'm sorry," she replies, stroking my cheek gently. "New souls need some time adjusting before being thrust into the new realm. Sometimes, it can take a soul decades or even centuries before they are ready. She most likely won't be ready to see you. I don't want to make things worse for you or for her."

I nod. "I get it. I just...I just want to understand, you know? Like, why did she leave her grimoire for me to find? Why provide me with an amulet that carried a protection spell? There are so many unanswered questions."

"I understand you're frustrated. I'm frustrated too," she says, brushing some of my hair back from my face. "We will get our answers at some point. All I want is for you to be safe."

"I know," I sigh.

Venus studies me for a moment before sitting up. "Come on. Let's go."

I blink at her as she rises from the bed, shaking her wings out. "Go? Go where?"

"I want to show you my realm," she replies, her tone definitive.

"Really? I thought the spirits got spooked by you."

"They do. We'll be going in secret."

Before I can ask what that means, her shadows appear, dancing around her shoulders.

It takes me only a moment to realize.

"We're going to walk *inside* of your shadows?"

Venus grins. "They'll allow us to navigate around, hidden from sight."

"How do I know one isn't gonna try to grope me while we do this?"

"You don't. That's part of the fun."

I roll my eyes, but I can't deny the excitement building in me. Finally, a chance to do something somewhat normal—if you consider walking through downtown Hell with the Dark Lady normal.

"I gotta plan my outfit!" I squeal, jumping off the bed and running to the bathroom. Venus had transported my suitcases from our coven investigations straight to her room, giving me access to all of my favorite ensembles.

"No one's going to see it anyway!" she shouts after me, her voice full of laughter.

"Don't care! I'll know I'll look cute and that's all that matters!"

Hell looks like a city frozen in time.

Gothic buildings with large archways and stained-glass windows look over us as we move through the bustling city that is nestled within a sprawling forest. Venus had told me of the creatures lurking in the wilderness, and it was enough to make me never want to step foot past the tree line.

All manners of creatures walk the streets. Demons of all colors and sizes haggle with shop owners, spirits flit by as witches fly low on their brooms. A cacophony of noise rises as we move into what appears to be a town square.

We're firmly within Venus's shadows. Somehow, no one reacts to us—it's as if we're truly invisible. When I asked Venus how it works, she simply shrugged and said, *"Magic"*.

We've walked for hours, soaking in the vibrancy of this place, this realm full of the dead and haunted. A realm I've been dead set on never returning to. I don't want to blink for fear of missing out on something. My insides twist when I'm reminded what will happen to me if I don't hand my soul over to Venus.

"Come on, I can tell you're tired."

Her words snap me from my thoughts. I snort. "I am not."

"You're dragging your feet. You never do that."

"Okay fine, maybe I'm a bit tired," I admit.

In reality, I'm ready to get back into Venus's enormous bed and get naked. I'm never too tired to fool around.

Venus halts as soon as the castle comes into view, her back going ramrod straight. I pause too, confused. "What's up?"

Venus doesn't respond. She doesn't move a muscle. My magic seems to react similarly, going on high alert. I peer around, not seeing anything out of the ordinary. "Venus?"

She grips me and throws me over her shoulder so quickly, it knocks the breath from my lungs. She's sprinting through the streets, zigzagging, jostling me with each movement. Her shadows swirl around us, keeping us hidden.

"Venus!" I call to her, trying to keep my head from spinning.

"He's here," she rasps without stopping or slowing down. "He's here—I can feel it."

I know exactly who she's talking about. My blood goes cold, and my body goes limp.

How? I wonder to myself. How could he possibly get in?

The pieces start to put themselves together. The wards are failing. The concealment spell wasn't completed in time.

I led him right to us.

Then I feel it.

It feels like an earthquake. The ground beneath us rumbles. Buildings we dart past shake. Demons, witches, and other spirits all seem confused about what's happening, looking for the source of the sudden change.

Venus doesn't stop. She's somehow sprinting at full speed, darting down side streets.

"Get airborne," I choke out. "The buildings—"

"Can't," she responds, her voice tight. "He'll see, even with the shadows."

I watch as the cobblestones start to crack, the rumbles becoming stronger, until—

"Oh my god," I gasp out, not believing my eyes.

A giant serpent rushes down a street perpendicular to us, taking large chunks out of buildings too close together to accommodate it. Screams and shouts rise behind us.

"Venus," I whisper, or shriek, or don't even say out loud, I'm not even sure anymore.

I look over my shoulder, seeing the castle get larger and larger, when the ground shaking intensifies, a small building comes crumbling down. I scream, but Venus manages to dodge it just in time.

"Teleport us!" I'm yelling. I can't control the level of my voice—the world around us is so loud, I can't even hear my words.

"Too much magic!" she shouts back, taking another turn, the castle continuing to get closer but still just out of reach. "We just need—"

I'm flung sideways like a ragdoll, and I feel myself fly through the air, not sure which way is up or down. My magic lashes out, wrapping itself around me, as I land on the cobblestones. The air whooshes out of my lungs and my magic immediately gutters before going out, having taken all the impact. I'm on my back, staring up at the sky, my ears ringing. I sit up slowly, my head spinning, and look around.

It's like something out of a horror movie. Entire buildings collapse, leaving nothing but crumbled stone on the pavement. Bodies of demons and creatures litter the cobblestones as spirits fly back and forth, their mouths open in screams of terror and shrieking for help.

I look around, not seeing Venus anywhere. My heart seizes, snapping me out of my stupor. Scrambling up, I scan everywhere I can see, but there's no sign of her. No wings, no shadows.

"Venus!" I croak out, taking a few steps and stumbling, my vision blurry. The world around me spins. I put my hands on my knees and slam my eyes shut. "Come on," I mutter to myself. "Come on, get it together."

The ground begins to shake again. My eyes fly open and I run, unsure of where I'm even going. Shapes fly past me, but I can't make sense of anything I'm seeing. The shaking gets stronger and stronger, and buildings begin to crack under the pressure. I grit my teeth and will my eyes to see anything, just *fucking* anything—

And then I'm yanked so hard off my feet that it feels like my entire skeleton rearranges itself. I go to scream, but there's no air in my lungs.

"I've got you." Venus's voice caresses my ear, and I can't help it—a sob wracks my chest. She maneuvers me until I'm cradled in her arms, her powerful wings beating against the air.

My vision finally clears, her striking face finally coming into view. She's bleeding from her hairline and her skin is so pale. Her midnight eyes are wild as they scan over my face just as I'm doing to hers. Another sob slips out as I throw my arms around her neck.

"I've got you, I've got you," she continues to murmur softly to me. Her wings beat quickly as we gain altitude, taking us further and further from the destruction down below.

"What about the city?" I say between sobs.

"Forces are already on their way," she replies, gripping me tighter to her chest. "I'm making sure you're safe and hidden before I join them." Her tone is dark, wrapped in fury.

"I'm so sorry," I cry. "It's all my fault. He's here for me—"

She shushes me softly, the palace so close now. "It isn't your—"

I don't get to hear her voice again, as something slams into us, causing Venus to roar in pain as we separate. Then I'm free falling, the wind wrapping around me as I careen towards the earth below. My magic is spent. I can't see what happens to Venus. There's nothing to break my fall.

Just as the cracks in the cobblestones come into view, everything goes white.

Chapter Thirty-Six

Vivian

I must be dead. Why else would I feel like I'm sleeping on a cloud?

Stretching out like a cat, I can't even bring myself to be upset. I knew I'd die eventually. Guess it was just earlier than I originally planned.

I open my eyes and look around. I'm in a room of all white—white bed, white walls, white furniture. The only pop of color are some gold accents on the serpents depicted on the double doors. I blink a few times, my eyebrows furrowed in confusion. I hadn't given Venus my soul—I shouldn't be able to see anything if I'm dead, right?

My body, I realize with a start, is really sore. Another sign that I'm not actually dead.

Sitting up, I go to slide off the bed when a large hand presses down on my shoulder. I gasp and swing my head towards where the hand appeared from. The hand is attached to a man with golden skin, long white hair that's braided down his back, and black eyes, sitting in a chair next to my bedside. He's wearing white, flowing robes and a gold serpent armband around his bicep.

He removes his hand from me, smiling. "Hello, Vivian." His deep voice booms through the room, making my head pound. "Welcome to my home."

My brain takes a minute to piece everything together. The serpent depictions, the fact that I feel like I've been run over by a truck, and the man sitting next to me...he has the same eyes as Venus.

"Holy shit," I breathe, my body locking up. "Phanes." I shuffle to the opposite side of the bed.

He chuckles, his eyes—Venus's eyes—tracking over my face. "It is so exciting to finally have you here."

Death would have been a much better alternative than this. I'm currently in Phanes's bed, wrapped in some white toga that matches his. I shudder at the thought of someone removing my clothes while I was unconscious.

"I...where am I?" I dare to ask.

His smile widens. "You're in my home."

"And where exactly is that?"

His smile falters. "My palace is nestled amongst the clouds. Think of it as a separate pocket of the world that others cannot get to unless I will it."

Panic strikes through me at that.

"You were injured by my pet, unfortunately. I apologize for that."

His pet. The giant serpent that destroyed Hell's city.

"I wanted you retrieved without injury," he sighs, "but things happen."

I flare my nostrils. "You killed innocents. Destroyed a city."

Chuckling, he replies, "You believe those creatures are innocents? If only my daughter had handed you over once she became aware of your existence, we could have avoided any bloodshed."

I highly doubt that.

"I healed you to the best of my ability, but you might be sore for a little while," he informs me.

"What do you want with me?" I ask.

"Now is not the time for questions," he responds. He stands and sits on the edge of the bed. "You should rest some more—your mortal body will need more time to heal. I'll join you."

"What?" I blurt out. "Have you been…" I don't even want to picture it.

"I know it must be confusing to be here, Vivian. I'm sure there's so much my daughter and her minions have not told you." He seems to consider his words for a moment. "Or they've fed you lies about who I am and what I want."

"Is that so?" I grit out, my temper snapping at the leash I try to keep around its neck.

"We will spend a lot of time together," he responds. "It will give me the opportunity to educate you."

I bristle at the sheer possession in his tone. "I've had enough education, I'm afraid, and I spent most of my college years high out of my mind, so I don't think more schooling is really for me."

He chuckles, although I note an edge in it. "You were able to get away with so much," he sighs. "If only I had found you sooner. I would have made sure you were well taken care of. Cherished, even."

I snort. "I think I'm good, thanks."

His nostrils flare. A rumble of magic flows through the space. "And I would have made sure you had better manners." My magic cowers inside of me. I do something smart for once and snap my mouth shut. He seems to like that response, because the rumbling stops, and his face relaxes again. "I'd like for us to spend some time together, Vivian."

Alarm bells start ringing in my head.

I pivot and throw myself off the bed, scrambling to the door and gripping the handles, yanking them with all my might.

They don't budge.

"I won't harm you," he says to me, but I don't believe him. I'm throwing all my weight into getting these doors open, but they're sealed shut.

I spin around, my panic giving way to enraged hate. "Let me out," I snarl.

He simply pats the mattress next to him. "Don't be silly, Vivian. Come here."

"I said let me *out*."

The ground rumbles underneath us, the entire palace shaking beneath our feet, but this time, I realize in surprise, I caused this.

My magic caused it.

My magic is swirling within me, its indignation amplifying my own anger. I close my fists at my side, ready to punch through the doors. My magic presses against my skin, ready to break free, to wreak havoc and bring this entire castle down on itself. This fury feels...different. It feels ancient, otherworldly.

"My dear," Phanes says, seeming unperturbed by my outburst, "I will happily let you free within the confines of this palace tomorrow, and I will answer any questions you may have after we get some sleep, but only if you're good." He gestures to the enormous bed. "Please, come lay with me."

"You're absolutely deluded if you think I'd do that with you."

"Things will be so much easier for you if you simply behave," he responds. "I swear to not harm you."

I scoff out a laugh of disbelief. "I'm sure you *totally* mean that."

"You are welcome to get yourself together in the bathing chambers if you need to freshen up first," he offers, gesturing to the other door.

I race to the other room, ripping the door open, and slamming it behind me. Sliding down the door, I realize I'm in a nightmare. He's locked me in a room with him and expects me to sleep next to him?

He definitely expects me to sleep with him.

I'm going to be sick. I crawl on my hands and knees to the toilet, quickly emptying the contents of my stomach.

My magic is freaking out too, pressing against my skin, desperate to search for alternate exits, but we both know they don't exist. When I'm done puking, I flush the toilet and take in the bathroom. Just like the other room, everything is white. White countertops with two sinks, a white claw-foot tub, and a white shower. This place looks like it belongs in a catalog for millionaires to buy a mansion they'll never live in.

I crawl over to one of the sinks and pull myself up, looking at myself in the large mirror hanging in front of me. I'm not sure who the person looking back at me even is—her hair is frizzy and limp at the same time, her skin sickly pale, and her hazel eyes look sunken into her skull. She looks nothing like I did when I was spending my day with Venus.

Venus is probably panicking right now, I realize with a start.

Is she okay? I know she can't be dead, but she could still be gravely injured.

Does she know I've been taken? That our greatest fear has come true?

I shake my head. I can't think about the what-ifs right now. I need to figure out how to live to see tomorrow.

Looking around the room, I see a chair set against the wall next to the bathtub. Before my mind can panic at seeing a chair in the bathroom, I grab it and jam it under the doorknob, locking myself in—and locking him out. Some of my panic recedes once I feel there's more of a barrier between us. I inspect all the various bottles on the counter, and after sniffing a few, I determine they're safe to use. I grab a towel and turn the shower on, keeping one eye on the door—if he breaks it down, at least I'll have a bit of a warning.

I strip down and shower quickly, refusing to enjoy the warm water or the scents of the shampoos and body wash. The thought of being cloaked in his scent makes me want to vomit again, so I jump out of the shower and towel off quickly.

Putting my clothes back on, I eye the tub. It's the furthest thing from the door, and sleeping on the floor sounds horrible.

"Fuck it," I say to myself and begin throwing all the towels into the empty bath. Once I've made a little nest of towels, I hop in, covering myself with one.

I know I won't be able to sleep, so I curl up on my side and do my breathing techniques.

In for four, out for four. In for four, out for four.

Unfortunately, I don't think there are enough breathing techniques in the entire world to make me feel better about the situation I'm in. Before I know it, tears are spilling from my eyes and staining the towels underneath me.

I spend what felt like years curled up in the tub, on high alert for any noise on the other side of the door. The chair is still lodged under the doorknob with no signs of being messed with. Breathing a sigh of relief, I climb out of the tub and splash water on my face at the sink. I refuse to look at myself—I don't want to see the person who will be looking back at me.

I pat my face dry and consider my options.

Stay in here until Phanes either breaks the door down or until I die from starvation. At this point, I'd prefer starvation, but neither option sounds pleasant. I could go out there and raise Hell. This sounds nice in theory but maybe not in practice. He seems quick to anger and I don't want him obliterating my soul. Or...I could go out there and play nice. My stomach roils at this option—and so does my magic.

"Think about it," I say to myself and my magic. "He said I—we—will get answers if we're good. Maybe I can trick some important information out of him. Information that will tell us how to get out of here." My magic is thrashing inside of me, making it clear this is not what it wants. I shove back at it firmly. "It'll be fine," I say to us. "Just...we'll tread lightly. No outbursts, please. Unless it's absolutely necessary to save our asses. We work together now, okay?"

My magic kicks me in the kidney to show its displeasure, making me wince, but settles back down. Watching, waiting. Ready to strike if necessary.

I eye all the products on the counter again, considering if I should make myself presentable, but decide to ignore them. I can pretend to be cooperative, but I don't need to go the extra mile. Maybe my morning breath will keep Phanes at arm's length. Taking in a few deep breaths, I slowly remove the chair from the doorknob and open it into the bedroom.

Phanes sits on the bed, leaning against the headboard, reading a book. He looks relaxed, like he's on vacation and not keeping a woman hostage in his house.

I steel my spine and walk into the room, slapping my feet against the floor to make myself known. Although I doubt he needs the signal.

He looks over at me and smiles. "Good morning, Vivian. How did you sleep?"

"Like a baby," I say, trying to keep the biting sarcasm out of my tone.

His smile falters a bit and I cringe internally. Playing nice is apparently going to be harder than I thought.

"How did you sleep?" I ask quickly.

"I would have slept better if my guest had joined me," he replies, his fake smile still plastered on his face, but his eyes have darkened.

I swallow and try to give a believable smile back, tossing my hair over my shoulder. "I don't usually sleep with someone on the first date."

He chuckles, breaking the tension in the room. I breathe a sigh of relief.

"I know I promised you answers today, Vivian," he says as he stands from the bed, "but first, I think breakfast is in order. Let us share the meal together."

I want to reply that he's the reason I have no appetite, but I keep the smile on my face and say, "Of course," instead.

He either doesn't notice my disheveled appearance or he doesn't care. He walks over to the entrance and places his palm on the door, letting some of his magic flow from him and into the wood. After a few moments, it hisses and the lock clicks before the doors swing open, revealing a blindingly white hallway beyond.

When he gestures for me to follow, I fall into step behind him—just out of his reach in case he decides to swing around and grab me. There's no one in the halls but him and me. The sound of our feet against the marble is the only sound echoing through this building. This is such a departure from Hell, I think. I wouldn't even consider it a novel thought, but it strikes me all the same. The halls are bright, but they feel hollow. In Venus's home, there's art throughout the halls. But here? Nothing.

"Why is there no one around? Servants or court people or whatever?"

"Servants are not to be seen or heard," he responds arrogantly over his shoulder. "And, unfortunately, my daughter destroyed the rest of my court."

When she and Lilith killed the other gods.

Phanes approaches another set of doors and pushes them open, revealing a dining room with a long white table and matching chairs. I notice two plate settings, one at the head of the table and the other just to the right. I swallow my groan and make my way to what is clearly my seat as Phanes takes his own.

The spread of food is the only color in this place. Assortments of all fruit, biscuits, muffins, scones, and pitchers full of what looks like fresh juices.

I'd usually die to have a spread like this, but today...my stomach churns.

Phanes doesn't seem to notice my discomfort, grabbing the small plate in front of me and loading it up with food. "I expect you'll want to change into something else." His eyes dart over my outfit with a hint of disapproval. I look down at my rumpled robes.

"It's quite comfortable," I respond.

He hums with disdain, placing my full plate in front of me. "Eat," he commands.

I slowly pick up my fork and spear a piece of watermelon. I shove it into my mouth, forcing myself to chew, to swallow, to not immediately throw it back up.

He watches me expectantly, so I do it again. And again. And again. I've finished half my plate before he speaks.

"I promised you answers if you behaved. While I'm not thrilled about your stunt with the bathing chambers, I'm glad to see you are open to my suggestions." I nearly snort at that but rein it in. "There's a story I've made sure has been told, time after time. That I was the first God here, and I created all that you see before you. I created other gods, humans, all of it. What really happened has been erased from history. Now, it is only mere fairytales amongst the witches. I'm sure most of them don't even remember." He chuckles, like what he's saying is funny.

"What's the real story?" I ask.

He nods down at my untouched plate. I quickly scarf down a few bites to keep him talking.

Seeming pleased with me, he continues, "Your magic, as I'm sure you know, is different. Special. No other witch has ever had your form of magic, except, of course, Lilith. But did you know Lilith was not the first to have the magic, either?"

Shock ripples through me. I poke internally at my magic. *Did you know?* I ask.

It gives me a sheepish poke back, as if to say, *yeah, of course I knew.*

I rein in my annoyance at being the last to know things—especially things related to my own magic.

Phanes continues, "There were few before Lilith. All of them lost to time. And none were as foolish to cross me." My magic flares with anger at that. "You want the true story, Vivian? You are asking the wrong person." He points at me. "You should ask your magic."

I grit my teeth. "I've tried," I admit.

He smirks. "Magic is a fickle thing, it's true." He leans back in his seat. "That's partially why I want you here with me. To uncover the true depth of your magic. To control it, versus the other way around."

"I don't believe that," I respond. "I don't believe you have my best intentions in mind at all. This is all about what you can gain from me."

He shrugs. "We'll be helping each other. You learn about your magic; I'll learn more about you and how you may be of use to me."

Panic and anger rise in me, mirrored by my magic's, but I can't flip out here. Not now. I breathe in deeply and hold it, then let out a noisy exhale.

Phanes tilts his head, examining me. "I will admit, you're quite different from Lilith."

I blink at him. "How would you know that?"

He snickers. "Oh, we spent a lot of time together, she and I. Right before she died, of course."

Yeah, before you killed her, I think.

"Well, we're different people," I respond, picking up a strawberry and pushing it into my mouth, forcing it down, even as my stomach sours.

He tracks the movement, something predatory entering his gaze as I chew and swallow. I hate this look the most. I never want to see it ever again.

"You are," he concedes, still staring at my mouth, "but your magic is the same. Usually, magic is not passed from person to person. Magic is not sentient in the way yours is, and different abilities pop up due to a variety of factors. But yours...dare I say, your magic chose you."

I freeze. An intense wave of...sadness comes over me.

My magic *chose* me? I'm not even sure what that really means. Like it was walking down the street one day and was like, *hey I like that one, I'm gonna sit inside her body and make her have an unnatural green thumb?*

Phanes leans forward, wiping the side of my mouth with his thumb. I jump back, slamming my body into the back of my chair, freaked out that he felt entitled to just touch me.

He pulls his arm away, having the audacity to look sheepish. "Forgive me, I don't mean to frighten you. We'll get accustomed to each other, I'm sure."

I want to throw up the food roiling in my stomach. "Am I what you've been searching for? Why you attacked those covens?" I ask, my voice sounding small.

He leans back in his chair. "Yes. I've been keeping tabs on you—following you to wherever your magic was released, but I could never get a clear read on you. It was like you were partially hidden from me."

My amulet. I reach up to touch it, but then realize I handed it over. I drop my hand back down to my lap.

Phanes continues, "So I sent my pet to the covens closest to where I felt your magic. He didn't find you, of course, but he got a nice treat out of it." He chuckles.

My skin feels oily.

"But, finally, I found you—in my daughter's realm, of all places."

"How did you get into Hell?" I press. "They have wards around it."

"I'm well aware of the wards," he responds, his voice dangerous. "I've been testing them ever since they were erected and, finally, they were weak enough for me to break through."

I'm going to be sick.

The covens are dead because Phanes was searching for me. I led him right to them—and right to Hell.

All of these deaths are on my hands.

"I think I'd like to lie down now," I say quietly.

He looks down at my mostly full plate with a look of disdain but nods. "Of course. I'm sure you're exhausted from sleeping in the bathing chambers all night." His tone is clearly disapproving, his eyes narrowed.

I plaster a smile on my face and mutter a, "Mmmhmm."

He rises from the table, and I follow suit, trailing after him out into the empty halls and back to the bedroom. He opens the doors with his magic but doesn't enter himself—instead, he simply gestures to the barren room. "I have a few things to attend to, but please, make yourself comfortable. I'll be back later."

His words sound like a threat.

I throw my messy hair over a shoulder and say, "Thank you," before hustling into the room.

Peeking over my shoulder, I see him shut the doors behind me. Sealing me in.

I nearly double over from the fear. I've never been claustrophobic before, and this room is huge, but it feels like the walls are closing in on me. I'm gasping for air, trying to get my lungs to keep working, to get my heart to slow down. It's not working. My limbs tremble and my eyesight goes blurry. My chest feels tight, like my heart is being squeezed by a fist. I'm having a full-blown panic attack, I realize. I've only had a few in my life, but damn, they're brutal.

My magic nudges me gently, as if to show me it's there and to help me snap out of it.

"I can't," I sputter out. The tremors in my limbs become so intense I slump to the floor, shutting my eyes against the onslaught that is dragging me further and further into a spiral.

I'll never get out, I keep thinking—over and over on a loop, circling and twisting its way through me until I feel like I've finally reached the end.

It won't be Phanes who takes me out. It'll be myself.

The thought is both horrifying and comforting as I let the panic consume me whole.

Until I feel a nudge again. I fight to pay attention to it, to respond to my magic, but—

There—another nudge. A caress against the walls of my mind. Gentle, calming. Loving even. The push allows a stray thought to break through the spiral.

"Did he mean what he said—about you picking me?" I ask my magic, even though it can't speak to me.

Another caress, as if to say, *yes, yes, I chose you.*

Somehow, that reaction causes the panic to recede just for a moment.

"What are you?" I breathe.

I'm not sure how or why, but I feel like I already know the answer. *I am life itself. I am the earth and the sky and the wind and rain. I am the soil and the waves and the early blooms in spring.*

"Poetic," I say jokingly. My magic flips inside me, causing me to gasp out a laugh. Then I say with fear in my voice, "I don't want him to get to you. I don't want him to get to us."

Another nudge, as if to say, *do not worry—I will protect you, and you will protect me.*

"I don't know how I can protect either of us," I admit, tears pricking my eyes at the gravity of being trapped in this sterile tomb. It's like a doctor's office from Hell. Even Hell itself is better than this.

We will get out of this, I feel my magic express to me. *Venus will be here to rescue us.*

The tears in my eyes spill down my cheeks as I say, "I hope you're right."

My magic presses against my skin, kindly asking to be let out. I give in, letting it wrap around me like a security blanket. Warmth seeps into my skin as I'm shielded from this room, from Phanes, from this whole fucked up situation.

"I'm so sorry," I tell my magic. "I'm so sorry I pushed you away and ignored you and wished you never existed." I'm sobbing now. It's like the floodgates open and I can't stop. "I never—I just—" Sobs wrack my chest as my magic gently soothes me, wrapping tighter around me until it feels like a second skin.

As if to show me it's alright. I'm forgiven.

I'm not sure how much time passed after my little episode, but I feel drained. Drained but somehow...lighter. Like, yes, I'm in this fucked up situation in this creepy castle with this murderous psycho, but my magic and I are more in sync than we've ever been, and that counts for something.

I decide that continuing to play nice is still my best option. I just have to figure out how to do that until Venus can get here and bust me out.

Scoping out the room, I notice a hidden door on the opposite side of the room from the bathing chamber door. Surprisingly, it opens when I press on it...into a walk-in closet, full to the brim with extravagant dresses—all in white.

Like wedding dresses.

It gives me the creeps, so I back out slowly and shut the door. The other door behind me hisses, alerting me to Phanes's return. I quickly dart across the room, closing myself into the bathroom. Slamming the door shut, I press my ear to it. He's silent on the other side.

A beat passes, and another, and another.

Until the knob of the bathroom door begins to turn. Gasping, I jam the chair underneath the knob, halting its movement.

"Vivian, open this door." His tone is deadly, and the door trembles under the power.

"Sorry!" I sputter out. "Just...tending to a few things! I'll be out in a moment!"

"I expect you out of there shortly." He doesn't have to say what he means; he'll break down the door if I don't come out.

I try to calm myself by breathing in for four, out for four, but it does nothing to stop my clammy hands and hammering heart. Steeling my spine, I exit the bathroom. Phanes is pacing at the end of the bed, and his head snaps up at the sound of me entering the room.

"You will lose privileges to use the bathing chamber if you keep locking yourself in there," he growls.

I nod my head furiously. "Yes, of course. I'm sorry. I just got a bit overwhelmed."

His eyes soften, and it makes me want to throw something at him. "Of course. I'm sorry. I know this must be a lot for you." He moves to sit on the bed, gesturing to the space next to him.

I drag myself over to sit next to him, forcing my body not to recoil when he lightly lifts a lock of my hair with his fingers.

"I'd like for us to start over," he says, dropping my hair. His dark eyes burrow into mine. "We'll get to know each other...intimately. It will be good for us."

My breath stalls in my throat. "I'm not fully comfortable with that," I push out.

He nods. "We will take it slow. Get used to one another. You'll get used to your new home."

I'm trying very hard not to let the walls cave in on me. "I've never really had a home," I whisper, but I realize that's no longer true.

Venus became my home.

The thought has tears spilling from my eyes before I can stop them.

Phanes doesn't seem fazed by my tears. He slowly wipes them away with his fingers, which makes me cry even harder.

"Perhaps you need more time to...calm yourself," he murmurs.

I sniffle but don't say anything. He eases himself from the bed, crossing the room with preternatural grace, before locking me away in here. Again.

I curl up on the edge of the bed, a bone-deep tiredness taking over my body.

Thinking of Venus causes an ache in my chest that feels like it will never go away. Venus forced me to run from my childhood, from my destiny, but...I ended up running back into her arms. We were forced back together, but with her is where I want to be. Where I belong. She became my home.

And I will never have another without her.

Phanes must think I'm hysterical because he leaves me alone until the next morning when he unlocks the door and instructs me to get dressed for breakfast. I haven't eaten since yesterday, but I find I'm still uninterested in stomaching anything. I don't say that, though—instead, I throw on one of the many white dresses in the closet and trail behind him.

We don't speak until we're seated at the table, my plate filled with an assortment of pastries and fruits. He looks pointedly at my uneaten food, which I try to force down.

After what feels like an eternity, he finally clears his throat. "I think today would be a good day to see your magic."

I pause, a muffin halfway to my awaiting mouth. "What does that entail?"

"You will let your magic out so I can assess how powerful it is," he says matter-of-factly.

My magic roils inside me. I place the muffin down and face Phanes fully.

"I don't think my magic wants to do that."

He shrugs, leaning back in his chair. "If your magic will not come out on its own, I will have to force it."

The hairs on the back of my neck prickle. "Force it?" I ask in a small voice.

He nods. "I don't want to hurt you, Vivian, but we must do what is necessary."

I sit on my hands to stop them from trembling. My magic growls, wanting to strike him down where he sits.

I'm wrestling with my magic to keep it under control when Phanes says, "Let's begin."

Chapter Thirty-Seven
Vivian

Phanes guides me into another room, this one much larger than the two I've been in so far. Massive white pillars are erected throughout the space, leaving open air to waft across the room. There are no walls. If I were to walk off the edge, would I fall to my death?

There's a throne sitting atop a dais, golden arches with a serpent snaking around the back of the bright red cushions, its mouth open, ready to devour anyone who disagrees with him, but the ceiling is the real masterpiece. A mural telling the story of creation—Phanes being born from nothing, then creating his children, and once they grew and became restless, he created humans for them to rule over. Constellations spread throughout the mural, showering the entire thing in stars.

I'm craning my neck, circling slowly to capture it all. It's the first bit of color I've seen since I've been here.

"Yes, it's quite exquisite."

I stop spinning and look over to the voice that causes my nerves to jump. Phanes stands halfway across the room, his tanned arms pressed behind his back. A stance that is meant to show he's relaxed. Non-threatening.

My magic and I don't buy it.

"I had it painted when I created this palace," he says, his tone conversational. As if we're merely old friends, catching up. "I wanted everyone to know the correct story of the world."

I swallow down the hateful rage that burns in me at his words. I keep my face carefully blank. "It's beautiful," I agree, my voice coming out surprisingly even.

He walks slowly towards me, and I stand my ground, even though my instincts—and my magic—are telling me to *back the fuck up, bitch!*

He stops a few feet from me, tilting his head as he studies me. "Show me what I want to see, Vivian."

I gulp. My magic swirls within me, angry at the clear demand in his voice.

Just give him what he wants, I plead with it.

My magic growls.

Closing my eyes, I picture it as that ball of yarn, ready to spool out from my fingertips.

Nothing comes.

I take a deep breath and try again.

Nothing.

My magic is refusing to put on a show.

Gritting my teeth, I say to it, *Come on.*

Still nothing.

I open my eyes and say, "My magic is…struggling. It won't come forward."

Phanes sighs. "I wish it hadn't come to this, but I am not known to be very patient."

Before I understand what he's saying, I'm thrown backward, my body careening through the air. My back hits one of the massive pillars with a deafening crack.

Pain short circuits my brain. My body falls to the floor and I'm unable to move, to even breathe. My entire body is on fire. Something must be broken.

"Try harder, Vivian."

I hear the words, but I can't make sense of them. I just lay on the floor, gasping, trying to survive the pain. When I'm struck again, it feels like I'm being electrocuted. Every nerve ending lights up, screaming out in agony. I'm dying. There's no way I can survive this. The waves of electricity keep hitting me.

I'm going to die here.

When it finally stops, I'm convulsing on the floor, my body struggling to stay alive. Everything hurts—I hear him approach. It sounds like I'm underwater.

"Maybe your magic isn't as strong as I anticipated," he muses, like he didn't just fry me from the inside out. I blink repeatedly, trying to clear the blackness to look at him.

"That's a shame," he tsks, "but I can still work with that."

I hear his robes hiss on the marble floor as he turns and walks towards the door. "We will resume this another time."

I stay on the floor of the throne room for an eternity. I'm unable to move. My body screams in agony whenever I shift. I don't even have it in me to cry. I just lay here, broken and alone. Not even my magic tried to protect me. This is where I'll die, I realize. Maybe not right now or today or even tomorrow or the next day...but I will die here. In this tomb of a castle. At the hands of Phanes.

I am doomed to die here.

My magic gently caresses me, assessing me. "Go away," I croak out, my voice breaking. A wave of betrayal flows through me. My magic left me at Phanes's mercy, to deal with his cruelty all on my own. "Why?" I whisper. Why would my magic leave me behind like this?

It simply caresses me again.

That isn't enough, I decide. I can't rely on anyone or anything—I never have and I never will get to again. I can't even rely on my own magic to protect me. The loneliness I feel grows inside me, spreading through me like ink in water until it swallows me whole.

I sleep on the floor of the throne room, unable to get my feet underneath me to get to a bed. My body works to repair itself the best it can with only my mortal healing properties. If my magic assists in that, I have no idea—I'm too exhausted to dream. I wake to cool hands stroking my cheek and brushing my hair back. I sigh softly, nuzzling into the feeling.

Venus is here. She's finally found me.

I open my eyes and see her midnight eyes looking back at me, but it isn't Venus. Phanes brushes his thumb against my cheekbone, his face softened in what I'm assuming is sadness. I wasn't even aware he felt that emotion.

I'm too weak to pull out of his grasp.

"I'm so sorry, my Vivian," he murmurs. "Sometimes I forget how fragile your kind can be." He lets out a shuddering breath as if he feels any remorse. "It pains me to hurt you, it really does. If you had simply done what I asked, I wouldn't have had to take such drastic measures."

My hatred for him blooms in my stomach.

"I will take care of you," he says before swiftly scooping me into his arms and strutting out of the throne room. My body lays limp in his arms, like I'm nothing but a ragdoll being dragged by a child. Phanes takes us into the bedroom, bypassing the bed completely, and walks into the bathroom. He gently places me in the tub, my head leaning against the back. He undresses me slowly, peeling the now dark red dress from my skin.

I can't look at the damage he's inflicted upon me. I squeeze my eyes shut as my naked body is revealed to him. I hear him take a sharp breath before I feel his hands lightly press into my skin. Pain shoots up my spine and I gasp, my eyes flying open.

"Oh, Vivian," he groans, his voice sounding pained. "My apologies will never be enough."

That's for damn sure.

His fingers poke and prod for a few moments, causing me to grit my teeth in both pain and disgust at him touching me. Then a cooling sensation flows through me, soothing my jagged pain into dull aches.

"I will need time to heal you," he murmurs, his hands continuing to skate across me. "We will get you cleaned and back to health soon." His hands leave my body, giving me a moment of reprieve. He turns the tub's faucet on, and my body floats as the tub fills. Even with the pain receding, I'm too weak to stop Phanes as he brings the chair over, seating himself by my head. He's gathered various bottles, lathering his hands with a soap that smells so violently like him that I nearly gag.

His hands move over my body again, cleaning my bloody and broken skin.

I want to cry and thrash and break his skull open. Instead, I stay limp, letting him feel me everywhere, feeling him linger in some places more than others. His hands are gentle as he explores me, washing me with some sort of reverence. As if it erases how he nearly killed me with these same hands yesterday.

A broken sob works its way up my throat, but I swallow it down. There's no point anyway.

There's no reaction from my magic while he tends to me. Good. The connection between me and my magic is officially severed now.

I never want to wield my magic again.

I have lived many lifetimes by the time Phanes has finished cleaning me. He drains the tub and wraps me in a
towel, hefting me into his arms and carrying me out into
the bedroom. The bed swallows me as he gently places me
on the mattress, and he kneels so that our faces are   mere
centimeters away.

"My Vivian," he sighs, stroking my hair back, "I will
forever show you how remorseful I am." His eyes dip to
my lips and back up to my eyes. "This is good news, Vivian.
Your magic did not react to my attack. Do you know what
this means? It means your magic is much weaker than I
thought." He seems happy about this. I'm not sure why. I
don't want to know why. "I must leave you to rest," he says
regretfully. "Know that this is *good*, Vivian. This is very
good. Everything will be the way it is meant to be."

I lose track of time. Days blend together, turning into
weeks. I don't bother hoping Venus will show up anymore.
I've shunned my magic—I feel not even a whisper of it
inside of me.

Phanes seems ecstatic that my magic didn't react to him, though he never explains why, and I don't ask. He makes no move to touch me since he nearly killed me and doted on me afterward, although he insists on eating all meals together.

I become nearly silent, sometimes not speaking for days at a time. My voice sounds hoarse whenever I do. He's started to leave me free to roam the palace now, at least. I have this empty tomb to walk around in like a wraith, my white dress trailing behind me.

I'm walking through this empty corridor, trying to get lost in the maze of halls, when I stumble upon an open door. I puzzle over it for a moment. No door has been left open like this—I've tried every door I've passed. Throwing a cautious glance over my shoulder, I slip into the room.

I'm struck by the difference.

This room seems to be out of commission—furniture covered with large tarps and paint buckets across the floor. I step in, looking at what they're trying to cover up. It's the only color I've seen in this place, outside of the mural in the throne room.

It looks like another mural of some kind. I step closer to the wall. Large brushstrokes have buried some of the artwork, but not all. It looks like the earth was cut in half to reveal the core inside, but instead of hot magma, it's a white oval. From the white oval are lines like spider-webbing from the core up into the earth's surface, where trees and other foliage grow.

I touch the mural and my magic spools from me too quickly to react.

I'm no longer me—I'm seeing through my magic's eyes. The earth was created under our fingertips, anything we wanted created from nothing. An existence of peace and tranquility, just us and the earth.

Until he came along.

We don't know how he arrived. He appeared suddenly, with hopes of joining together. We were wary of him, of why he would appear to us out of nowhere, of what he truly wanted, but he gained our trust, and we eventually agreed.

He created, too, but he created violence. Madness. Destruction. His children were pain and suffering and destroyed everything we loved. We tried to destroy him, but he became too powerful. He struck us down, nearly killing us. With our remaining strength, we got away and dug deep into the heart of the earth to bide our time. To get stronger. To take back what is ours.

We rose a few times, once we were stronger, to carry out our mission, but he always won.

Not this time. We found the right witch. The one who will finally restore balance to the earth and return things to the way they were intended.

I fall backward onto my ass as I return to my body. I gasp at the mural, then down at my own hands. "You," I say to my magic quietly. "What *are* you?"

I am the earth itself.

Phanes wasn't the first being here. He didn't create the earth—even though he desperately wants to erase that fact.

No, he isn't the true God of Life.

My magic is.

"I knew it wouldn't be long before you discovered this."

I whirl at the sound of his voice. Phanes stands in the doorway, his face carefully blank. My magic pushes inside of me, ready to strike.

"This mural was painted so long ago—I used to come here and look at it, just to remind myself of how fragile the balance of life is. That things can be taken from anyone, even me." He saunters into the room. I back up. "Every time I encountered a witch with your magic, I destroyed them," he says conversationally. "I thought that was the only way to become the true ruler of this world, but the idea struck me once I realized your magic was still weak. What if we could become one? You would become mine—your magic would respond to me much like it responds to you. We would live the life we *should* live—as the true rulers over all."

My magic hisses.

"And then," he says, slowly advancing, "we would unite, and I would pump my seed into you, creating other beings that would replace the ones so brutally taken from me."

"You tried that already, and it didn't work," I snap at him, the ground underneath me beginning to rumble.

"It appears your magic finally spoke to you," he replies.

My magic causes the floor beneath our feet to shake in answer.

A sadistic smile warps his face. "It would be easier if you were willing, but I'm happy to take you any way I can."

"You're sick," I snarl. "And delusional. No one has even heard of you, you know. No one on earth knows who you are. You live in this empty palace, pretending like you're the ruler of everyone and everything, *when no one has even heard of you.*"

His own magic unfurls, causing static to rise in the air. "And that is an error that will be righted once we unite. We will wipe this earth clean and start over."

A hysterical laugh bubbles out of me. "So, you're going to destroy everything just because it isn't exactly how you pictured it?"

"I should be worshiped by all who live on this sad planet. I made them, after all."

"My magic was here first," I growl.

"And yet, it still isn't strong enough to defeat me." A smug smile twists his face.

I keep going. "Venus will be here soon for me."

He laughs. "You think she would bother? If she had to choose between saving you and keeping herself safe, which do you think she would pick?"

My breath stalls. Venus will come for me. She has to. She...

She has had so many chances to do the right thing, to be who I expect her to be, and she always says she will, but...what if she doesn't? What if she's happy to sacrifice me?

My thoughts must be evident on my face because Phanes grins. "You aren't strong enough to fight me, and my daughter clearly realized you weren't worth the trouble. I could always infiltrate your mind to make you do as I wish."

I immediately think back to when he spoke to me in my mind.

He's right. He could force me to do anything—whether by sheer force or by his magic controlling me.

As quickly as my fight rose up, it completely leaves me. I feel like a deflated balloon. Venus has given up on me. My magic isn't strong enough to save me.

I can't save myself.

"Come along, Vivian." Phanes holds out his hand to me. "It will be so much easier if you agree."

My magic thrashes inside of me, but I can't bring myself to even acknowledge it. There's nothing for me to do. I'm stuck here.

So I take his hand.

"It's time for bed. You've had such an exciting day."

We enter the prison of a bedroom, the bed taunting me, ridiculing me. I hate this bed. I hate this bed and this room and this sterile excuse of a castle. Phanes looks at me expectantly, and I swallow the bile in my throat as I make my way to the side of the bed. We both know fighting is useless. I don't even have it in me, anyway.

"Vivian." He stops me. I furrow my brows as I turn to look at him. "We can't get into bed wearing the clothes we wore throughout the day, now, can we?" He gestures down to his white robes.

I drag myself over to him.

"Go on," he coaxes, barely hiding his excitement.

My trembling fingers lift to undo the knot at his shoulder, the fabric falling away and pooling at his feet, leaving him naked in front of me. I pick a spot to look over his shoulder, trying to rein in my disgust as he slowly caresses my skin, taking extra time to undo the knots holding my dress to my body.

I feel the fabric drop.

His gaze feels oily against my skin, but he makes no move to touch me. Without a word, I show him my back and make my way onto the bed.

Shuffling under the covers, I wait for his large frame to do the same. I roll onto my side, my back to him, and when I feel the bed dip, his front presses against me. His arm snakes around my waist and his hot breath coats my ear as he says, "You do not know how long I have been waiting for you."

If the feeling of his cock against my back is any indication, he's been waiting a long time. I slam my eyes shut, trying to keep as still as possible. I don't know how long I can do this. How long will he be okay with this—just lying beside me? He'll want more, I know it. How can I keep him happy while keeping him at bay? Tears form behind my eyes as he slowly draws circles around my navel. He shudders as he whispers, "So soft."

He falls asleep shortly thereafter, his breathing evening out and his grip loosening, but I don't dare move. I had prayed that Venus would come to rescue me, but I've stopped hoping for that. It's clear she never saw me as anything more than a fun toy to play with.

So I lie here, silently crying into my pillow, wondering how I'll ever survive.

Chapter Thirty-Eight
The Dark Lady

The pain in my body is nothing compared to the splitting pain in my head. Any movement causes flashes of pain to radiate through me, and worse, the nightmares continue to plague me. I think that's what they are—flashes of memories mixed with my greatest fears. I can only hope they aren't reality. Lilith being ripped apart. Dropping Vivian and plummeting to our deaths. My father, laughing, as he takes Vivian from me.

I think I hear Vivian's name being spoken, but I can never make out who is saying it or what else is being said.

Finally, the light beyond my eyes is too much to avoid. I crack them open, blinking against the harshness. I look around and see that I'm in my bed with many hovering over me.

Luke is who I see first. His eyes widen as our eyes lock. "She's awake!"

Everyone is murmuring, witches are touching various parts of my body, Luke is trying to explain something to me, but it's all a blur. The pain doesn't cease, and I cry out, trying to get it to stop, to let it release from me. Then my eyelids flutter closed, and I'm being sucked back down, down, down.

Until I am no more.

All I dream of is Vivian.

Her laugh, her scent, her blonde hair flowing in the wind. The noises she makes when she's under me. The way she flips her hair over her shoulder. Her boldness, her curiosity, her bravery.

I'm in and out of sleep. When I awoke once, I was informed that Vivian had been taken. My magic exploded from me, in pain and despair and rage, causing my body's injuries to reopen.

The healers had to put me back under.

My body usually heals quickly, so these injuries must be extensive.

Now all I can do is dream of her. Sometimes it's of beautiful things. Sometimes it's of horrible things, but I can never escape her. And I never plan to. Once I wake up,

I will fight tooth and nail to find her. To crawl my way back to her and free her from Phanes's clutches.

I just hope I'm not too late.

The entire world will be nothing but ashes if I am.

When Death Blooms

That cliffhanger really did y'all in, huh? Don't worry, Vivian and Venus will be back in the sequel, *When Death Blooms,* out sometime in October(ish) 2024! *When Death Blooms* is the second and final book of their story, so be sure to check it out.

Acknowledgements

This book was a random thought I had one day that bloomed into what you hold in your hands today.

First, I have to thank my Beta readers, Mads and Kelsey, for understanding my vision so thoroughly.

Thank you to my editor, Kristen, for seeing where I wanted my story to go and for helping me get there.

To Gennifer, my proofreader—thank you for swooping in and saving the day.

And finally, a big thank you to you, dear reader. I hope you'll stick around for more.

About the Author

G.E. Masters is a writer of sapphic romance. Ever since she was a child, G was fascinated by imaginary worlds and created complex characters in her head.

Now, she's writing those stores to share. She lives in Chicago with her two cats.

When Flowers Wilt is her debut novel.

You can email her at gemasterswrites@gmail.com, or follow her on Instagram (@gemasterswrites) or Tiktok (@ge.masters.writer)